Hail Mary Full of Secrets

Nancy W Kaufman

Hail Mary Full of Secrets

This book is a work of fiction. Names, characters, locales, and incidents are either products of the author's imagination or are used fictitiously. Any resemblance to persons living or dead, business establishments, events, or places is completely coincidental.

ISBN: 1480250864
ISBN-13: 9781480250864

Dedication

To Jim, whose faith in me is no secret.

Prologue

The face is the mirror of the mind, and eyes without speaking confess the secrets of the heart.
St. Jerome

Dear Diary,

My name is Mary Ann. I have four daughters named Mary. My early delusions of raising virtuous daughters led me to name them after the Virgin Mary. In order of birth they are Mary Lynn (ML), Mary Margaret, Mary Susan (Suze), and Mary Patricia (Tricia). Usually they go by their nicknames, except when they do something god-awful like tell Sister Agnes that the dog ate their homework. At times like these I call them by their baptized names. "Mary Patricia Von Guten, what were you thinking? We don't even have a damn dog!"

Their names are only a problem when they're sick. The health insurance company can't keep them straight, no matter how many times I try to explain it to them. Over the years, I've sent the company dozens of official copies of their birth certificates. My sons Trip, Mark, and Patrick don't have that problem. It is implicit to those within our Catholic circle that Mark and Patrick were named after popular saints; however, Trip is another story. He was named after my husband, Joseph, Jr., so his baptized name is Joseph Christopher Von Guten, III. I would never put up with the blasphemous moniker JC the 3rd, typifying images of a longhaired fortuneteller and clairvoyant in a white robe and sandals, so I nicknamed him Trip, short for the triple Roman numeral I.

We live in a middle-class suburban neighborhood two blocks from St. Theresa's church and near most of our relatives, close friends, and many Chreasters – those who only go to church on Christmas and Easter. I am a homemaker, stay-at-home mom, housewife, or whatever you want to call me. Since Joseph often travels for business, commandeering the family car for his purposes, it is important that we live in a neighborhood where everyone and everything we need is only a watermelon seed spit away. Our friends are members of St. Theresa's parish, and all of our children were schooled there as well. The kids spend their free time playing sports, riding bikes, and setting off cherry bombs in the neighbors' mailboxes. The wives bowl in the church league, the husbands play cards and drink with the priests, and the kids play capture the flag, red rover, and kick the can.

Living in a parish makes us feel safe, as if God has thrown his protective cloak around us so nothing dreadful can happen. This immunity to the troubles of the outside world starts at Sunday Mass and continues daily with dinner and bedtime prayers. Religious artifacts, crosses, and statues decorate our home and make us impervious to Satan. The protective shroud is reinforced on school days when our children dress in plaid Catholic uniforms. To shore up our immunity against evil, we invite priests over for dinner. Having a brother as a priest is the Holy Grail in our community. God's custodial cloak couldn't become more unyielding. Paying for it is my job, and each Sunday I deposit an offering in the basket.

At least that's what I was led to believe. What I believed as a young bride is not what I believe today. I thought I knew everything about my family, but now I'm aware of the secrets that riddle our family tree like poison ivy. Is there a difference between secrecy and omission? A difference between feeling ashamed and being afraid to tell the truth?

I thought I knew the difference. What I didn't know was that the legacy I am bestowing upon my children is the art of keeping secrets.

Mary Ann

chapter

ONE

Cleveland Heights, Ohio
1969

"Far from being the basis of the good society, the family, with its narrow privacy and tawdry secrets, is the source of all our discontents."
Sir Edmund Leach

In the middle of her marriage, Mary Ann was at the end of her rope. Yet, like a magician performing the same act over and over again, she could turn the end of her rope into a long lariat—there was always more to hold onto. She couldn't blame her husband Joseph for her being at wit's end, although she wanted to. Deep down, Mary Ann felt she was living under Joseph's thumb. She knew he knew. For the past twenty-two years, her yielding ways had worked to some degree to keep their marriage intact, but now he was one-up on her. His years of drinking, gambling, and God only knows what else, were trivial compared to her mishap. He had nothing to gain by confronting her and everything to lose —her.

She and Joseph were good at putting up a façade in front of others. Today was a perfect example. They always hosted the Labor Day picnic, one of the many parties they held annually to celebrate family and holidays. This year's picnic had added significance for Mary Ann. She was celebrating her brother's appointment as archbishop of Philadelphia. From the time he was a young boy, Don was groomed to be a priest. His mother constantly reminded him that he was named after an Irish bishop from the first century. Don never liked the idea of becoming a priest, but over time he accepted his calling.

Mary Ann was slicing tomatoes in the kitchen when she noticed Jack through the window. She wasn't sure Jack would show up today. It would be his first time at their house since Carol had died.

Carol and Mary Ann were the epitome of girlfriends. The kind who could let it all hang out when they were together, like sisters that neither of them had. Carol wasn't able to have children but loved being around Mary Ann's kids and cherished the fact that they called her Aunt Carol. On days when Mary Ann thought she was going to lose her mind taking care of six kids, Carol would miraculously show up and give Mary Ann a hand. When things would settle down, they'd sit on the screened porch and talk and laugh for hours. They could be brutally honest with each other without hurt feelings. They could tell each other their deepest secrets and stay up all night talking nonsense. They had no barriers. No walls. No false pretenses. Just the purest kind of friendship. They were also partners in crime, like the time they smoked pot in the middle of the day.

In late February, Carol found out she had stage-four breast cancer. The doctors told her there was nothing they could do, and she only had a month to live.

For the last week of Carol's life, Mary Ann was at Carol's side every day and night, practically living at Carol's in order to take care of her best friend and comfort Jack. Joseph was furious Mary Ann wasn't home that week, but there was no way Mary Ann was going to leave Carol alone on her deathbed. Carol had no siblings and her parents were elderly and lived in Chicago. Mary Ann was the closest thing Carol had to family, and so she was there with Jack when Carol received the last rites from Don. It was the evening of March 16, a moment Mary Ann would never forget. The next day, Mary Ann was in no mood for a party, plus she needed to help Jack sort through Carol's things and plan the funeral. So, for the first time, Mary Ann and Carol missed the St. Patrick's Day parade and party at the church hall.

❧

Joseph wiped the sweat off his brow and took a prodigious swig of his Manhattan to calm his nerves. The infernal sound of the telephone ringing could be heard out on the patio where he was grilling and bullshitting with his brothers Peter and Richard, Father Don, and Father Burns. Twice, ML yelled that the phone was for him, but he pretended not to hear. She'd take a message.

"A little thirsty, Joseph?" Richard asked. "You better slow down or you won't make it through dinner. And if you keep drinking like that, I'll for sure take more of your money when I beat you at cards tonight. On second thought, let me get you another drink."

"The grill is so damn hot, it's making me thirsty," Joseph snapped.

Maybe this is what hell is like. The coals were hot and flickered with flames shooting up from grease drippings. Joseph was constantly looking over his shoulder, and he was a tangled mess of nerves. It was the price he paid for sleeping with the devil—for owing him money after a streak of bad luck with five-card draw. He was surrounded by priests and bishops and trying to dodge the devil.

Don nudged Burns. "Tell them the joke you told me in the car. Maybe that'll get a smile out of Joseph."

"I'm terrible at telling jokes, but I'll give it a try." Burns took a sip of his vodka gimlet, wiped the sweat from his forehead with his monogrammed handkerchief, and prepared himself for the delivery.

"Okay, here goes. There's this new priest, see, and he's nervous about hearing confessions. So he asks the old priest to sit in on his first session and give him some advice. After the confession is over, the old priest asks the new priest to step out of the confessional. Then he says, 'Listen, here's how you do it. Fold your arms over your chest and rub your chin with one hand.' The new priest tries this, and the old priest says, 'Good, now say things like, "I see. Ah, yes. Go on," and "I understand." Let's hear you give that a try. The new priest repeats what he's told. 'That's great,' the old priest says. 'Now, don't you think that's a little better than slapping your knee and saying, "No way! What happened next?"'"

Burns got Joseph to laugh, but Richard used it as an opportunity to get in another dig. "Was that priest listening to your confession, Joseph?"

Joseph did a slow burn, along with the burgers.

"I'm going inside to check on the Indians' score," Don said. "We were down by one a while ago. Burns, come with me and we'll see if Mary Ann is ready for us to bring out the food. My stomach's telling me it's just about time for us to feed the assembled."

"Good luck getting the kids to change the channel," Joseph shouted as the priests walked into the house. "I bet they're watching *Beverly Hillbillies* or *Petticoat Junction.* If *Batman* is on, you'll have to bribe them to change the channel," Joseph warned.

The three brothers were alone on the patio. "You pulled in late last night," Peter said. "Or should I say early this morning? When are you going to give up playing cards? You look like shit."

"I didn't know I had a curfew. And since when are you my father?" Joseph replied.

"Sorry if I hit a sore spot. What is it with you lately? Mary Ann not putting out? I wouldn't blame her. Who would want to sleep with a grump like you?"

"Screw you! What were you doing up at that hour anyway? Checking up on me? I never should have bought a house across the street from you."

"Calm down. I had to pee. I have better things to do at night than watch you weave your way up the driveway."

As the oldest of the Von Guten brothers, Peter set the stage for Joseph. When Peter moved to Devonshire Road, Joseph followed. Devonshire was one of the most beautiful streets on the east side of Cleveland, and was often featured in magazines and other publications to promote the city. It wasn't the wealthiest neighborhood on the east side, but it had the charm and character of a well-kept, middle-class, all-American neighborhood. It was where Peter wanted to live, so naturally Joseph moved in across the street.

When Joseph bought the house at 2822 Devonshire without showing it to Mary Ann, it had the bare minimum of landscaping. Mary Ann's mother gave them six deep-pink azalea bushes, which Mary Ann planted under the living and dining room windows. When ML and Trip were born, Joseph made his only contribution to the landscaping by planting two white dogwood trees, one on each side of the walkway that led from the sidewalk to the front door. Devonshire itself was lined with fifty-year-old oak trees that formed a natural arbor over the street. The emerald green lawns defined the street. Every year, there was an unofficial contest to see who had the best-looking yard. And every year, Peter and Judy won hands down. Joseph claimed that Peter cheated by hiring an Italian gardener to plant flowers that bloomed through summer.

Joseph couldn't be bothered with keeping up with Peter. This was mostly because he wasn't as wise as his brother when it came to managing money so he couldn't afford a gardener, and partly because he was often out of town on sales calls. His yard was as low maintenance as he could make it. Low maintenance meant never working in the yard when he had able-bodied sons available. He made it very clear to the boys that yard work was their job, and Mary Ann's job was to make sure they got the work done. Considering that the yard was taken care of by two teenagers and a mother of six, it didn't look too bad.

The phone rang again. "Trip, unplug the fucking phone!" Joseph yelled to his oldest son who was throwing the football around in the driveway with his brother Mark. Joseph rarely cussed in front of the kids, but today he was out of sorts.

"What did *I* do?" Trip threw the football into the bushes and stomped up the back porch steps, slamming the screen door and nearly running into ML who, instead of yelling from the house this time, came outside to tell her father the phone was for him.

"Take a message," Joseph said.

"Dad, why do you yell at us to answer the phone and then tell me to take a message? This man has called four times and says he really needs to talk to you. The next time he calls, please talk to him so I don't have to lie like you make me do to Betty."

Richard and Peter's eyes opened wide when ML let the cat out of the bag.

"He makes you lie to our secretary?" Richard asked ML.

"Don't ask me. Ask my dad," ML said over her shoulder as she walked back into the house.

"What the hell is that all about, little brother? Start talking."

The phone rang again. Joseph could feel his blood pressure rising. *Goddamn, this grill is hotter than hell, and the neighborhood troublemaker is setting off cherry bombs next door. Doesn't that asshole know the Fourth was two months ago? And those fucking fire truck sirens never stop in this town. This isn't a party; it's organized chaos and enough to give me a heart attack. With my luck, even if I had a heart attack I wouldn't die. And of course I have ML cover for me, because Mary Ann never would. She hates it when I'm out a little late playing cards. How pathetic am I for having my daughter lie to my secretary when, for God's sake, I'm the boss?*

Joseph was about to answer his brother's question when Jack Gallagher walked into the backyard carrying a box wrapped in pink, green, yellow, and blue floral paper and tied with a large white bow. By the wrapping alone, Joseph could tell it was from Shaker Gifts, Mary Ann's favorite store.

Joseph picked up the football that Trip had thrown into the bushes and wound up to throw a pass to his old friend. "Quick, catch!" he yelled. With the gift in his hand, Jack couldn't react quickly enough and failed to catch the ball. It whizzed by his head with only inches to spare. "You always were better at defense. How are you, Jackson?"

Joseph was happy to see him—maybe Jack would take some of the attention away from him. Jack and Carol were Mary Ann and Joseph's closest friends. They did everything together—bowling on Thursday nights, bridge games on a regular basis, and dinner together almost every Saturday. Because Mary Ann and Carol wanted to do things together as couples, Joseph and Jack became friends by default. Joseph liked Jack, but they were different enough that they wouldn't have become friends if it hadn't been for their wives.

"Ah, you shouldn't have," Joseph said.

"Actually, it's for Mary Ann. I want to thank her for everything she did when Carol was sick. It's a little late, but I thought she could use a little 'pick me up' in her condition. How's she feeling?" Jack asked.

"She's fine but as big as a house and only five months along. I don't know if she'll make it to December, let alone Christmas. It's a lot different being pregnant at forty than it was at thirty. She's in the kitchen with her mother. Go say hello and I'll make you a drink. But watch out, Mary Ann cries for no reason so don't be surprised if she tears up when she sees you. The doctor says it's her hormones, so don't take it personally. God knows I don't. What are you drinking?"

"What I need is one of your generous pours. Just the usual—an old-fashioned, but with saccharin, not sugar. I'm trying to watch my weight."

❧

"If you don't want me to tell on you, you're gonna have to share that with me," Trip said as he caught them in the act. Suze and Mary Margaret were pouring something out of a Vick's Cough Syrup bottle, which they had filled at the makeshift bar on the screened porch, into their ginger ale.

"Jesus, Trip, you scared the crap out of me. Get out of my room," Suze said.

"Naughty, naughty! Whisky and ginger ale, washed down with the Lord's name in vain while there are priests in the house. I think what we're looking at here is a visit to early morning confession," Trip said.

"Yeah, well, you tell and I'll tell," Mary Margaret said.

"Tell what?"

"Oh, I don't know. Maybe a story about a little pot."

Mary Ann found Trip's pot last January while cleaning out his gym bag. He told her not to touch his bag, that he'd put his dirty gym clothes in the hamper. Trip, being the teenage boy he was, of course forgot. At first, Mary Ann thought it was chewing tobacco. Then, in a mother's blinding flash of insight, she put it all together. Trip was spending a lot of time in his attic bedroom, his grades had dropped, and he was burning incense in his room.

He'd told her he liked the smell, but clearly he was burning it to cover up the pot.

Joseph was out of town the day of Mary Ann's discovery, so she called Carol and asked her for advice. "Let's smoke it!" Carol said. "They're all doing it. Let's see what's so great about it." They pinky swore like they did when they were kids and lit up the one joint that was already rolled. They sat on the screened-in porch passing it back and forth, praying that the smell wouldn't drift next door. What did drift was the sound of their raucous laughter as they howled uncontrollably about the slightest things, so much that their stomachs hurt. High, more from the thrill of the childish risk they were taking than the marijuana, they finished the joint and decided to go to the Cedar Lee Theater to see *The Exorcist.* Under normal circumstances, they never would have seen it. As devout Catholics, they believed it was possible to be possessed by the devil, and the thought frightened them. Not so much for them, but for Mary Ann's children. However, the pot made them feel they could handle it. Mary Ann's mother was already on her way over to watch the little ones so Mary Ann could go to the hairdresser, so she and Carol grabbed their purses and were ready to take on the devil.

Mary Ann was the kind of mom who came across as naïve to her children. Her children believed their father had the brains in the family, but in reality Mary Ann was the one with the college degree. She was valedictorian of Ursuline College's graduating class of 1946. Before she graduated, she had an offer from Procter and Gamble to work in the New Product Development Division. An offer she turned down to get married and raise a family. While she loved being a mother and raising her children, she often thought about what it would be like to get dressed up every day, go to an office in the far-away exotic city of Cincinnati, and bring home a large paycheck.

"No one's gonna believe you, Suze. You must have a pretty serious cough, there."

Suze's bottle of Vicks Cough Syrup had been emptied and filled with whisky, not unusual since she'd been drinking for several months with her older hippie friends. Unlike Mary Margaret, Suze didn't have many friends her age, nor did she care. She preferred to hang out with an older group of high school dropouts—kids she thought were cool. She constantly lied to her parents about where she was going. She would tell them she was going to Cumberland, the city swimming pool with her friends, but the truth was that she wasted her days drinking, smoking, listening to music, and hanging out in the cemetery where the hippies of the Heights spent their days. One afternoon last week, she came home drunk and threw up. Mary Ann believed Suze when she said was sick from the hot sun and from eating a hot dog from the pool snack bar. Mary Ann held her head and wiped her mouth as she puked into the toilet. Then she gave Suze ginger ale to settle her stomach and tucked her into bed for the night.

Suze chugged the end of the Vicks bottle and chased it with ginger ale. If the 'rents downstairs could party and drink to relieve their pain, why couldn't she? Mary Margaret moved the arm of the record player to the sixth track of the Beatles' new album, *Help*. "You're Going to Lose That Girl" was Suze's favorite song of the summer that was soon coming to an end.

Mary Ann jumped when she heard the screened door bang. She had asked Joseph to fix the spring on the door numerous times, but he always had an excuse for not getting it done. She and her mother, Catherine, were in the kitchen when Jack walked in. The scent of his Old Spice arrived before he did. When she saw him, tears welled in her eyes. She knew this day would come, but tried not to think about it. There was no way to prepare for this, the day he would walk into her house without Carol. Less than a year ago, Carol would have been in the kitchen with her making her laugh, spraying her with the kitchen sink nozzle, and drinking red wine while they prepared dinner. But today, everything was wrong: she was pregnant with her seventh child, her best friend wasn't there to help with the kids or the party, Trip and ML hated their father, Suze and Mary Margaret were constantly fighting, Joseph rarely spoke to her, and he stayed out until the early hours of the morning.

"Carol should be here." Mary Ann's voice was barely audible through her tears. Jack put his arms around her and she trembled as she cried on his shoulder. "She's here in spirit," he said. "She'd never miss a party. She'd feel terrible if she knew we weren't having fun at one of your famous cookouts. I'm going to pour a glass of wine and leave it for her on the counter. And don't even think about drinking it. You've got a baby to take care of."

"Is this for me?" Mary Ann smiled through her tears, looking at the package.

"I want to thank you for your help when Carol was sick."

"It's my favorite wrapping paper from my favorite store. You shouldn't have. Your friendship is the greatest gift I could ever ask for."

Mary Ann opened the box to reveal a Belleek porcelain vase with painted shamrocks.

"It's for your collection."

"I love the shamrocks," Mary Ann said.

"Me too. St. Patrick's Day will never be the same for any of us."

"Look, it has a Claddagh on the other side," Catherine said. "The heart, crown, and hands mean love, loyalty, and friendship. I'll put some flowers from the garden in it."

"Thanks, Mom." Mary Ann wiped away the tears on her cheek. "It's beautiful. Thank you," she whispered as she hugged Jack.

ML walked into the kitchen, the screen door slamming behind her like a clap of thunder. "Mom, what did you get?" ML waved the wrapping paper at her mother.

"Oh, Uncle Jack gave me this beautiful vase..."

Another screened door slam announced Joseph's boisterous entry. "Here's your old-fashioned, cheers!"

Jack took a polite sip of his drink.

Joseph continued, full of over-the-top enthusiasm. "Well, was I right, did she cry?"

"Joseph, leave me alone," Mary Ann said.

"The cheese is melting on the burgers so dinner is just about ready," Joseph said.

"Tricia and Mark went upstairs to tell the other kids to come down," Mary Ann said.

"What can I do to help?" Jack asked.

"Carry the bowl of potato salad to the picnic table, and ML and I will bring the rest," Mary Ann replied.

Jack opened the drawer to the left of the dishwasher to get a spoon. Mary Ann wasn't surprised he knew where the serving spoons were. Over the years, he had seen her and Carol open the drawer dozens of times while preparing dinner for the four of them after the kids had been fed.

She and Jack were the only ones who knew the story behind the bowl that held the potato salad. It was a story that had a life beyond itself. As the screen door clanged behind him, she chuckled to herself while thinking about the bowl's history, a comfort to her jumbled emotions.

After a brief stay outside to eat dinner with her family and guests, Mary Ann was back in the kitchen. Don followed her into the house for some time alone with his sister.

"Is something bothering Joseph?" Don asked.

"Who knows? If something's wrong, he won't talk to me about it. He says I'm too emotional these days."

"You're missing Carol, aren't you?"

"That's an understatement—I feel like I'm missing my right arm. Carol would have enjoyed today, both the party and the celebration for you. She and I used to talk about how great it would be if you became a bishop and then someday a cardinal. She had our trip to Rome for your ordination planned out in her head."

"Cardinal? That's a stretch. I think this is as far as I'm going in the Church. Anyway it's called an elevation not ordination."

"Ordination, elevation, what's the difference? It's all the same to me. Now that you're a bishop, you're all powerful, right? You can see to it that nothing will happen to my baby?"

"You have me confused with a magician. And where did that come from? Are you worried about the baby? Is there something you haven't told me?"

"No, no, nothing that I know of. It's just that I'm forty, and having a baby at my age puts me at risk."

"Mary Ann, this baby was conceived out of the love. Even if Joseph is a rascal and sometimes drinks too much, he loves you. I'm confident that your baby will be healthy, and you too. But if you're worried, isn't there a test you can take to see if it's normal?"

"Don, even if there were, I wouldn't take it. Those tests are for folks who wouldn't keep the baby if something were wrong.

You know I wouldn't do anything like that. I live by God's will. Remember? We're Catholic."

"Yes, I remember, it's not easy for me to forget. But I think God isn't opposed to gathering knowledge and understanding about what might lie ahead. At least you could prepare yourself if something is wrong."

"Well, I'm not taking any tests, so let's change the subject," Mary Ann insisted.

"Okay, why do you think Joseph's drinking so much? I have to admit, I'm a little worried, aren't you?" Don asked.

"Of course I'm worried. But a few months ago we talked and agreed on some ways to keep his drinking under control. He calls them guidelines, but you know me, I call them rules. I told him that if he doesn't stick to them, I'd ask him to leave. They're simple: He can't drink on weeknights; no more than one drink while he's grilling for a party; and he can't have a drink until after four in the afternoon on the weekends. The exceptions are his monthly card games with the neighbors, holidays, and family birthdays. But under no circumstances can he lose control."

"What about when he's out late playing cards with his so-called friends? How do you know he's not drinking?"

"I just have to trust him. Now, enough of that. I want to have fun. Let's get everyone to come inside and ask Jack to play the piano. Did you know he was a concert pianist before he went into business?"

"Of course I know, and since he plays as well as Burt Bacharach I'm going to ask him to play "Say a Little Prayer for You." It's a great song and so appropriate for tonight, don't you think?"

Dear Diary,

Everyone thinks I'm a real trooper, pregnant again with my seventh child at the age of forty, raising another Catholic baby for the Army of The Lord. I wonder—do they have a division for bastards? Speaking of bastards, why hasn't Joseph raised holy hell? He must know it isn't his. Does he think I don't know about the vasectomy? That he slept on the couch for a week, simply because he 'pulled a muscle' in his groin? That we didn't have sex for a month or more after Carol died? I feel so guilty, but if I didn't feel guilty about something I'd think something was wrong with me. I think there's liquid guilt in the water they use to baptize Catholics. Everyone knows it—everyone knows about Catholic guilt. Jews have chutzpah, and we have guilt.

I could barely make it through Mass this morning. I was afraid I was going to stand up and start screaming. Have mercy on me, Lord, for I am a sinner who hasn't confessed, and I hide my sins from my spouse and family. Worse yet, I hide them behind the consumption of The Body of Christ, which is another sin. As if one more in a marriage oozing sin really matters anyway. I'll have to ask Don about that sometime, maybe after my family is complete. God knows I thought that was going to be after Tricia was born.

We all have our crosses to bear, and right now mine is Joseph. I feel like I'm carrying him on my back, making sure he stays on the straight and narrow away from alcohol. But I'm afraid I'm losing that battle, along with the battle against his gambling. But I don't have the energy or the desire to watch over him. I have enough to worry about, and I need to take care of myself.

Mary Ann

chapter

TWO

"Guilt is the gift that keeps on giving."
Erma Bombeck

"Don't forget my bag," Mary Ann said. "It's in the back seat."

A nurse walked out of the emergency room pushing a wheelchair. "Mrs. Von Guten?"

"Unfortunately, that's me."

Joseph rolled his eyes.

"I didn't mean it *that* way. *You* try having a baby at my age and you'll know how I feel."

"Honey, don't apologize. He'll be fine. Let's get you up to maternity before I need another wheelchair for this baby. I'm Lori, and I'll be your nurse tonight, or should I say this morning? When you called earlier, I thought you'd be right in. Why did you wait so long to come to the hospital?"

"I had to wait for my mother to arrive," Mary Ann lied. She was covering for Joseph. When she went into labor at two in the morning, Joseph was nowhere to be found; he was most likely playing cards. But that was her problem, and she believed her problems were just that—hers. No one else needed to know what was going on in her life, especially Nurse Lori.

In the elevator, it was clear Joseph didn't want to be there. His arms were folded over his chest, he was chewing his nails, and his eyes were affixed to the changing floor numbers.

"Is this your first?" Lori asked.

"Seventh," Joseph answered without looking at her.

"And last," Mary Ann added as she looked at Joseph. He kept studying the floor numbers flashing on and off like fireflies.

"You two are very blessed. Mr. Von Guten, have we met?"

"I can't imagine we have. I've never given birth. Never been sick, either."

"Oh, I'm sorry. I rotate between maternity and surgery and I thought you looked familiar."

The elevator door opened.

"Finally," Mary Ann said. "Either I wet my pants or my water just broke."

"Mr. Von Guten, with six children you must know the drill. Wait in the lounge, and we'll take care of your wife."

"If you went into labor at two this morning, your water should have broken before or soon after labor began," Dr. Shapiro said. "But don't worry. We'll have this baby in your arms in no time."

"Does it mean something's wrong? Maybe I should have come in earlier. Did I do something wrong?" Mary Ann was scared.

"Everything's fine. Am I detecting a little Catholic guilt in your voice, Mary Ann?"

"What would a nice Jewish doctor like you know about Catholic guilt?" Mary Ann smiled, the residue of pain still on her face.

"I've been working here long enough to know more about Catholic guilt than I thought possible. They didn't teach us about it at med school. At first, I thought it was just a saying, but after more years of delivering babies than I'd care to admit, I've come to believe that many of you feel personally responsible whenever something bad happens.

"Slide closer to the end of the table. There, perfect. What I really don't understand, is that you all complain about what a drag Catholic guilt is, yet you continue to perpetuate it by passing it on to the next generation, your own children."

"Well, Doctor, if I were Jewish, could I blame my mother? AAAHHH!"

"Your contractions are getting stronger, hmm?"

"Nothing gets by you, does it? Enough psychology, I want this baby born. Do your thing, doc. Is everything down there okay?" Mary Ann asked.

"I'd like to get the baby hooked up to a monitor so I can keep an eye on its heart rate."

"Is it because of my age?"

"Ah, Catholic guilt again. I'm surprised this hospital doesn't have a busier psych ward. No, it's new technology, and the more I know about what's going on with this little guy or gal, the better off we are. Relax, you're doing fine. You're at six centimeters and progressing nicely. I'll be back in a little while to see how you're doing. In the meantime, here's the call button if you need anything."

Mary Ann lay in bed with her eyes closed, thinking about what her wise Jewish doctor had said. Did she dish out Catholic guilt to her children? No, she wouldn't do such a thing. Well . . . maybe she *was* guilty of passing down feelings of guilt. Just last week, she put the guilt machine to work with Mark. At the end of dinner, he asked if he could have some chocolate pudding. She said he could after he prepared for his phonics test. He told her he studied after school, but she didn't believe him and found herself sounding like her mother.

"Have you studied for school tomorrow?"

"I have a phonics test, and I went over it during study hall," Mark answered.

"Phonics? When I was in school it is was reading and spelling."

"Yeah, Mom, I know 'in the old days.' You're not going to tell me about walking a mile to school in the snow, are you?"

"Mark Anthony, watch your tone of voice. I'm trying to make sure you're doing your best, because it costs a lot of money to send you to St. Theresa's. If you're not doing your best, we'll send you to public school."

"Sorry, Mom."

"So, did you study?"

"Yes, Mother, I studied."

"Mark, look at me. God knows if you're telling the truth."

Mark got his phonics book out of his book bag and began to review his words.

At times, Catholic guilt is useful for a parent. But the doc was right, it was a drag. It was the reason she was scared her baby would be mentally handicapped. She hadn't known she was pregnant when she drank too much wine one Saturday night. To make matters worse, she'd overslept the next morning and missed church. Plus, her age put her in the high-risk category. Her thoughts were making her crazy, and she couldn't get herself to think positively. How could she? Nothing was right; Joseph was drinking during the week, the kids were constantly fighting, she didn't have room in the house for another child, and for the first time she was scared to have a baby.

"Fuuuuuuuuuuuuudge!" The pain interrupted her thoughts, and she let out a scream. She wanted to scream was the *real* f-word. Carol would have. The contractions were becoming more intense and closer together.

"Was that you I heard down the hall?" Don entered her room.

"What the heck are *you* doing here? I didn't think you were allowed in my room. They told Joseph to wait in the lounge."

"This white collar, sister, is a hall pass to any room in any hospital. Want me to get one for Joseph?"

"Wouldn't that be a sight? Joseph trying to pass as a priest. Ha! Like always, I'm doing fine without him around, thank you very much."

"I don't think he's doing well. I just saw him, and he's pacing up and down the hall looking very worried," Don said as he raked his thick hair off his forehead.

"*He's* worried? That makes me worry more. I have a bad feeling that something's not right with this baby. Something that everyone knows but they're not telling me. I never felt this way with the others."

"You're getting yourself worked up over nothing. I'm going to find Joseph. Maybe seeing each other will calm both of your nerves."

"Fine, but tell him he can't stay long," Mary Ann insisted. "Don, wait. Before you go, there's something I want, no, something I *need* to talk to you about."

"What is it?"

"Don, I can't do this anymore. I'm too old to be having babies. We're running out of space at home, not to mention the expense of raising another child. Obviously, the rhythm method isn't working for us, and I'm so fertile that I get pregnant just *looking* at an erection. Sorry to embarrass you."

"What are you trying to say? You don't want this baby?"

"No, I *do* want this baby. I want this baby very much, but no more. I was thinking maybe I should get my tubes tied. Please tell me it's okay with the church. Aren't there exceptions for health reasons?"

"Mary Ann, I can't tell you to use birth control. You have to decide what's best for you and your family. They won't tie your tubes here at St. Ann's. You'd have to go to Mt. Sinai for that. Have you considered using condoms?"

"I don't understand you, Don. Condoms *are* birth control, that's just as bad. With my luck they'll rip, and I'll get pregnant anyway. Forget it. Please don't tell anyone I talked to you about this."

"I won't, and don't *you* tell anyone I suggested condoms. I might lose my new job. You know I'll support you no matter what you decide." Don kissed his sister on the forehead. "I'll be right back with Joseph."

Nurse Lori entered Mary Ann's room, a surprised and approving look on her face. "That priest looks like Robert Redford's twin…he's *so handsome.* What a waste."

"That's my brother, Bishop Maloney," Mary Ann laughed.

"Oh, I'm sorry. I shouldn't have said that."

"Don't apologize. I hear it all the time. He is good-looking, and he'd blush if he knew you'd said thaaaaaaaaaaaaaaaat." Another contraction took her breath away.

"I've asked Dr. Shapiro to give you an epidural to ease the pain. You've probably never had one before. It's different than the old spinal blocks, but it works just as well without putting you to sleep. We need you awake and active during this delivery."

"That would be great. This is the worst pain I can ever remember. Why is everything so different this time? Is it my age?"

"No, the difference in pain has nothing to do with your age. Every birth is different, some more painful than others. I'm not suggesting the epidural for any reason except that you have pain. There have been great advances in childbirth since you had your last baby, and you shouldn't suffer if you don't have to."

Joseph and Don walked into the room. "Is it okay if we stay with my sister for a while?" Don asked.

Lori didn't hesitate when she saw the handsome priest. "Sure, we can use your help keeping her steady while we give her an epidural."

Dr. Shapiro entered the room discreetly holding a large needle. "Mary Ann, there's no need for a priest to be here. You're going to be just fine."

"Dr. Shapiro, this is my brother, Bishop Maloney, and my husband Jooooooo...." A contraction cut her off.

"Lie on your side, and stay very still while we prep you. Gentlemen, I could use your help. Mr. Von Guten, hold your wife's hand. Both of you talk to her, take her mind off of what I'm doing."

Before he had a chance to distract Mary Ann, Joseph saw the needle, turned as white as a marshmallow and broke out into a cold sweat. "I...I... don't feel so good," he stuttered.

"Don, Joseph's going to faint. Get him out of here!" Mary Ann yelled.

"He's beautiful! Did you see how much hair he has?" Joseph bent over to kiss Mary Ann. "But most importantly, he's healthy. So no more worries."

"The nurses told me his APGAR score was nine, and he has all of his fingers and toes," Mary Ann said in relief

"How are you feeling?"

"A little sleepy, and I can't move my legs much. Maybe the epidural was too strong. They said it would wear off in a few hours and I shouldn't worry."

"I'm sorry I wasn't there for you. When I saw the needle, I knew I had to get out of there. I was here a while ago, but you were sleeping. They said you needed to rest."

"I'm going to take advantage of resting as much as I can while I'm here, because I know I won't get much rest when I get home."

"ML's old enough to help you. At sixteen she could be a mother."

"Joseph, don't talk like that. She's still a child."

"I know, I know. I'm just saying. Still, she can be your helper. And now that she has her license, she can help you with errands. She'll drive anywhere just to get out of the house and into the car."

"Sometimes, I think she's with that boy when she says she's going to the library," Mary Ann said.

"I remember those days well. You and I were up to the same tricks when we were her age. And the boy's name is Stan."

"Speaking of which, I know what I want to name the baby," Mary Ann said.

"You want to name him Stan?"

"No, not Stan." Mary Ann, sure of the name she wanted, was unsure of discussing her choice with him. She didn't want him to think he didn't have a say in the matter, but the truth was that he didn't. She was certain of her baby's name and it didn't matter whether Joseph liked it or not.

"Well, this is a first. We had the others' names chosen months before they were born. This time, you never talked about baby names. Let me guess. You want to name him Robin, as Mark suggested."

"Very funny. Then Mark would want to change his name to Batman." Mary Ann paused, her eyes closed. "What do you think about Patrick?"

"Perfect. My youngest named after the patron saint of the Irish. You know how much I love the Irish and St. Patrick's Day," Joseph said, the sarcasm obvious as he shoved his hands into his back pockets.

"Come on, Joseph. It's a beautiful name. I'm Irish and you love me, don't you?"

"Of course I love you. We're still married, aren't we? And now we have our seventh child, named after a skirt-wearing snake basher. But, if that's the name you want, I'm not going to try to change your mind. Patrick, it is. What's one more saint?" He held his hands up in the air surrendering.

Tears gathered in Mary Ann's chestnut eyes. "Thank you. You're certainly becoming more agreeable with age. I thought I'd have to work harder to convince you. I'll tell the nurse so she can fill out his birth certificate. Patrick James Von Guten.

"James is a fine middle name. You have my blessing."

My blessing? You old fart. I didn't ask for your blessing. I asked you to agree to the name I'd chosen. Maybe even like it. I thought I'd have a battle with you, but you gave in, just like that. You were actually cooperative. Nothing's ever easy with you, Joseph, especially this past year or so. So what was all that about? Catholic Guilt? Guilt for not being a good husband? Guilt for not being a nice father? Guilt for drinking and gambling? Guilt for being a pain in the ass to live with? Or were you embarrassed for fainting and just trying to make amends for your weakness?

"Mrs. Von Guten? Sorry to interrupt you, but you have a visitor," Lori announced. "Shall I let him in?"

"It's probably Don or Burns. I'm going to go home and check on the kids while you visit. Don't let them stay too long, you need your rest." Joseph bent to kiss her goodbye.

"Yes, thank you." Mary Ann answered Lori, turned to kiss Joseph goodbye, and reached for her lipstick on the table next to the bed.

Five minutes passed and no visitor. She would have liked to go to the bathroom and freshen up, but her legs were still a little numb. Besides, if she went, she'd for sure miss her visitor.

As she lay there, she could feel her breasts beginning to fill with milk. She didn't breast-feed her other children, but she'd been thinking that maybe this time she'd try. Both her pediatrician and OB/GYN had said it was best for the baby. The only downside would be that ML and Joseph wouldn't be able to help her with feedings. As long as they helped take care of the other kids, maybe breast-feeding wouldn't be so bad after all.

"Mrs. Von Guten, I went back to the desk to tell your visitor he could come in, but he was gone. I looked in every waiting room and lounge on the floor, but I can't find him. The charge nurse said he left this at the desk for you." Lori handed her a caramel colored teddy bear.

There was a note attached. Mary Ann unpinned it and read, "Welcome to our world. Saints and angels rejoice at your birth." She rubbed her fingers over the silky shamrock embroidered over the bear's heart. There was a tag on the bear's bottom that said 'Made in China' along with the name and birth date of the stuffed animal, 'Patrick, March 17.'

"Was it a priest?" Mary Ann asked.

"He had a scarf around his neck, so I'm not sure." Lori said. "But believe me, it wasn't your brother. When I worked on the surgical floor, I used to know the priests who visited the hospital regularly, but on this floor we don't see many priests. Besides, I wouldn't forget your brother."

"Can you get the baby so I can breast-feed him? And if you don't mind, I'll need some coaching." Mary Ann could feel her face turn red with embarrassment, and she began to cry. *Why do I feel uncomfortable about something that's so natural?*

"Of course, and don't worry about a thing. Breast feeding is as easy as changing a diaper, but without the mess."

After twenty-four hours of unsuccessful attempts at breast-feeding, Mary Ann was so engorged with milk that her breasts looked like small cantaloupes. Joseph, who never knew the right thing to say, told her it looked like the "titty fairy" visited her. Then, he told her she was being stubborn. "Just give the kid a bottle. It worked for the rest of them, and they turned out fine."

But Mary Ann was determined. Lori spent hours working with her. They tried everything, including warm washcloths on her breasts. But no matter what they did, Patrick wasn't latching on. Lori thought that maybe Patrick was the one having the problem, not Mary Ann.

As a last resort, Lori brought in a radio and turned it to the classical music station. Within seconds, Patrick relaxed and his soft lips began to suckle at Mary Ann's breast. As the milk finally flowed out of her and into the tiny mouth of her new baby, tears of love and relief streamed down her porcelain cheeks.

1972

Dear Diary,

I should be happy and count my blessings. My youngest daughter, Tricia, will be ten tomorrow. I should be sharing her joy, but instead my heart is heavy for Suze. I know she's been drinking, and I'm deathly afraid she's taking drugs too. When I try to talk to her about it, she denies it, and I want to believe her but I'm afraid she's not being honest with me. The Lord knows I have tried to help her along the right path. Those friends of hers are no help at all. It seems they enjoy dragging others down with them.

I pray that Suze will have the inner strength of my mother. I hope I have filled her with enough sense that she will grow out of this, graduate with honors, and live a life full of hope and promise.

Mary Ann

chapter

THREE

We know we're getting old when the only thing we want for our birthday is not to be reminded of it.
Author Unknown

Tricia was sure she'd get new skates for her birthday. Her mother knew her old ones were too small and caused blisters. Tricia wanted nothing more than skates and a pair of bell-bottoms to wear to the ice rink. She wasn't a great skater, but she could skim backyards, pivot on one foot, and perform a figure eight—something she had been working on since Christmas. Ever since she saw Dorothy Hamill give a demonstration at the Cleveland Heights Ice Pavilion, Tricia had wanted to be a professional ice skater. She was one of the first girls at school to get her silky blonde hair cut like Hamill, a hairstyle that would soon become outrageously famous. At the age of ten, Tricia Von Guten was a trendsetter.

When Tricia came home from school that day, she knew she would find her mother sitting in her usual spot—the kitchen table.

And that is exactly where Tricia found her on her tenth birthday. She was talking on the kitchen phone, the mustard-yellow cord tangled, twisted, and hanging in a lump from the middle like an old sock on a clothes line. Patrick sat on the linoleum floor playing with Tupperware bowls he had pulled from the bottom drawers.

Tricia hung her coat on the handle of the Hoover vacuum in the back hall closet, straining to hear her mother whisper on the phone. That was usually a sign that one of her brothers or sisters was in trouble, again.

"Mom, is Nana coming over for dinner tonight?" Tricia said quietly to her mother.

"Call me if you hear anything. Bye-bye." Mary Ann hung up the phone. "It's a school night, why would Nana come over?"

"Mom, it's my birthday. Nana always comes for birthdays."

Mary Ann sighed and rubbed her temples. "Oh, right. Of course Nana is coming over tonight. I'm sorry. I wasn't thinking. Let's go pick up your cake at the bakery and get Nana on our way home. Get Patrick's coat while I look for my purse."

Did she forget it was my birthday? Maybe I won't get new skates. No, she knows it's my birthday. She sent me to school this morning with a bag of Tootsie Rolls to share with the class. She couldn't have forgotten since then. Could she?

Birthdays at the Von Guten household weren't any more hectic that the usual weeknight family dinners, just add cake and gifts to the domestic disorder. With eight people living at the house, chaos always lurked between the hours after school and bedtime.

"ML, you're back!" Tricia cheered. She ran toward her big sister and gave her a hug.

ML was carrying a large box wrapped in Barbie paper and a photo album under her arm. She and Stan had returned from their honeymoon in Florida. Tricia missed ML so much that she cried herself to sleep for a week after she married.

"I wouldn't miss your birthday. Give me a kiss, Tricia."

"Emma!" Patrick called ML. Only three years old, it was as close as he could get to pronouncing ML.

"How's my little guy? I've missed you, buddy!" ML scooped up Patrick and kissed him all over his neck, making him belly laugh.

"Emma, watch me!" Patrick showed off by jumping from the third step of the stairs onto the Oriental rug and rolling into a somersault.

"ML, do you like my new haircut?" Tricia tried to draw her attention away from Patrick.

"Oh, yeah, it's really cute. I can't believe how much Patrick has grown since I left. And his hair has gotten so long and curly. Mom, did he get more teeth?

Patrick, Patrick, Patrick. It's my birthday, not his. But he gets all the attention. ML probably brought him something from Florida and not me. I wish he were never born. Why does everyone like him so much? All he does is poop and pee in his pants. But, no, Patrick is soooooo cute. So funny. So kissable. So, so, so what? He's a pain in the butt.

"ML, come in the living room. I can do a back bend all by myself!"

"In a minute, Trish. I'm talking with Mom."

"Forget it," Tricia mumbled and left the kitchen.

While Mary Ann and ML were talking and cooing over Patrick, Tricia could hear her father and godfather, Uncle Don, on the screened porch. Don had made a special trip from Philadelphia to celebrate his goddaughter's birthday.

She stood alone in the living room, staring at her father's sport coat draped over the back of the faded wing chair. *Since I'm so invisible to everyone, they won't know if I take some money.* Tricia reached in the pocket, removed her father's wallet, snared a five-dollar bill, slid it in her pocket, returned the wallet, and bounded toward the stairs on her way to her room.

"Tricia, what's up?" Don said.

Tricia quickly turned around. *How long has he been there?* "Nothing. I have to get something from my room. I'll be right back."

Tricia turned and continued bounding upstairs. *It's not like I stole anything. I need milk money for school. I'll tell Dad I took it because I didn't want to bother him when he was talking to Uncle Don. He'll understand.*

Tricia's room was above the den where her mother, ML, Patrick, and Nana were now sitting. She could hear everything they were saying through the register in the floor. ML was showing her mother and grandmother photos from her honeymoon. *I thought she came over to celebrate my birthday, not to brag about her stupid trip to Florida. Too bad Stan didn't get eaten by an alligator while they were there. Who cares about seeing her dumb pictures of them sitting on the beach half-naked? Gross!*

"ML, is Stan coming tonight?" Nana asked.

"No, he…umm …has to work," ML said.

Tricia heard Nana singing the song she called "Tricia's Lullaby", a song she only sang to Tricia in the rocking chair at her apartment on Shaker Square. But now she was singing it to Patrick. How dare she. That was *her* song, not Patrick's.

"I love you, a bushel and peck,
A bushel and peck and a hug around the neck
A hug around the neck and a barrel and a heap
A barrel and a heap and I'm talking in my sleep
About you, about you."

That's it. I'm going downstairs to put a stop to all of this. This is my day, my birthday.

"Happy birthday to you, happy birthday to you, happy birthday, dear Tricia, happy birthday to you." Tricia's parents, siblings, Nana, and Uncle Don all applauded.

Mary Margaret continued to sing. "You look like a monkey, and you act like one, too."

"Hoch soll sie leben. Hoch soll sie leben. Dreimal hoch," Joseph added, raising his wine glass to toast his youngest daughter with a traditional German birthday greeting.

"Blow out the candles before they melt all over the cake." Mary Ann tried to rush Tricia.

"But first, make a wish," Nana added.

Tricia closed her eyes, inhaled, and held her breath while she thought of a wish… *my own room...ice skates…to be an only child.*

She couldn't decide which she wanted more, so she blew out the candles with hopes that at least one would come true.

"What did you wish for?" Mark asked. "Boobs?"

"Mark, stop that or I'll send you to your room. Apologize to Tricia right now," Mary Ann snapped.

"Sorry, Mom. Sorry, Trish."

Tricia thought his apology was shallow, but she dismissed it instead of getting caught up in a battle that would ruin the moment.

To be an only child...if only birthday wishes came true.

"Mom, where's Suze?" ML asked as she helped pass out forks for cake. Joseph looked up from his plate and glanced around the table, looking for his third daughter.

"I think she's studying for a test with friends tonight. She asked me earlier this week, and I said she could, but I'd forgotten it was Tricia's birthday. I thought for sure she'd come home when she remembered." Mary Ann began to cut Tricia's cake.

"Can I go first?" Mark asked. "I want to be the first one to tell a Tricia story."

It was a Von Guten family tradition to go around the table and razz the birthday boy or girl while everyone ate cake and got a sugar high.

ML tapped her fork against her wine glass. "No, I get to go first since I'm the oldest. One time, when I was babysitting," ML began. "But, when *wasn't* I babysitting?"

"Very funny," Mary Ann said, smiling sarcastically.

"It was about four years ago. Tricia was in the bathroom for a long time, and being very quiet. I knocked on the door to see if she was all right and she said 'Go away.' I asked her what she was doing in there, and she said, 'Nothing.' When I opened the door, our little Tricia had opened a brand new box of Kotex, peeled off the backings, and stuck pads all over the walls like they were stickers."

Everyone laughed, except Tricia.

"ML, I hate you, and I'm glad you moved out!"

Tricia stomped up the stairs and slammed her bedroom door shut in typical Von Guten fashion.

When ML walked into Tricia's room, she was on her bed crying, holding onto her Mrs. Beasley doll.

"Tricia, I'm so sorry. I didn't mean to upset you."

"Go away! You don't live here anymore."

"But I'm still your sister, and I still love you. Are you mad at me because I moved out, or because of the story I told?"

"You promised you'd never, ever tell anyone about that. That it would be our secret."

"I'm sorry, I did say that. I just . . . I just forgot. Please don't let this spoil your birthday. You have a lot of presents to open. Please come downstairs. I saw Dad come into the house with a gift for you. You know he always buys you a Madame Alexander doll. Please? Uncle Don drove all the way from Philadelphia for your birthday."

"Ok, fine, but no more stories. Tell them I'll only come down if no one tells more stories."

As they got up to go downstairs, ML saw a folded piece of notebook paper on the nightstand between Tricia and Suze's beds. 'Mom and Dad' was written on it in Suze's handwriting.

"What's this?"

"I don't know. It wasn't there this morning before school."

ML unfolded the note and read it. "Oh, shit!"

"What is it? What's wrong?" Tricia asked.

"Nothing, nothing that concerns you, anyway. Let's go downstairs."

Uncle Don and Joseph sat in the living room shuffling cards at the game table and drinking German wine. Mary Margaret and Trip were sitting on the couch with their arms folded across their chests, expressions of boredom written all over their teenage faces. Mark and Patrick were on the floor with a deck of old playing cards. Patrick thought it was fun to throw a handful of cards up in the air just to watch them fall all over the floor. Mark, with the patience of a saint, was demonstrating how to dig the edge of the cards into the cut-pile carpeting and lean them against each other to form a triangle, the foundation of a house of cards.

Tricia stood unnoticed, as usual, in the doorway to the living room. *Where are my gifts? And they put the cake away before I even had a piece. No presents. No cake. This is the worst birthday ever.*

"There's the birthday girl. Open your gifts, Tricia." Mary Ann entered the living room caring an armful of presents, ML and Nana right behind her. Mary Ann's eyes were bloodshot and swollen, a sure sign she'd been crying. She put the gifts on the coffee table, then discreetly slid Suze's note in front of Joseph. When Joseph read it and made eye contact, Mary Ann put her finger over her lips.

"Mom, I'm sorry," Tricia hugged her mother's waist. "Please don't be mad at me."

"I'm not, sweetie."

"But you look like you were crying."

"I had something in my eye. Open this one first," Mary Ann handed Tricia a gift.

"Mom, I didn't have any cake."

"There was a problem with the cake. I think the bakery used salt instead of sugar."

"Tricia, it was disgusting," Mary Margaret said. "Trust me, you don't want any."

This birthday can't get much worse.

Patrick decided to start opening Tricia's gifts and ripped off the bow.

"Patrick stop, that's for me!" Tricia said. As she unwrapped the gift, her blue eyes brightened, a smile beamed across her face, and she shrieked with joy.

"CCM! These are what Dorothy Hamill wears." The white champion deluxe girls' figure skates were the perfect size and the ideal remedy for what she thought was going to be a lousy birthday. "Thank you, Mom. I love them!"

"And to go with them, I signed you up for lessons on Saturday mornings," Mary Ann added in her counterfeit cheerful-mom voice.

Out of the corner of her eye, Tricia saw her father pass the note across the game table to Don, also motioning to him to keep quiet.

"Open my gift next, Tricia. I have to go soon because I have to work in the morning. Plus it's a school night, and you need to get to bed." ML handed Tricia the box wrapped in Barbie paper.

"How did you know I wanted these?" The denim bell-bottoms had a strawberry appliqué on the back pocket. Tricia had wanted them ever since she saw them in the window at Best & Co.

"A little birdie told me. They'll be perfect with your new skates for Friday night open skate. Maybe Stan and I can take you and some friends there this week. I love you, Tricia." ML gave her sister a hug and a kiss and said good-bye to everyone.

After Tricia finished opening her gifts, the room was as quiet as an empty church. All conversation came to a halt as Tricia looked over her gifts. While all eyes were on her, it was clear that everyone's minds were elsewhere—except for Nana, who was asleep in the rocking chair, gently snoring.

Trip picked up Patrick and swung him around while he sang, "...Because something is happening here, but you don't know what it is. Do you Mr. Jones?"

"I heard that on the radio in the car on the way from Philadelphia," Don said. "Who sings that?"

"Bob Dylan," Mary Margaret and Trip said simultaneously. Tricia also knew it was Dylan from sharing a room with Suze, a big Dylan fan. And she knew what was happening, as she had read the note hours before.

They think they're keeping a secret from me, but I'm not as dumb as they think I am.

❧

Suze's face was a muddy image . . . a blur. Mary Ann couldn't focus, beads of sweat covered her face, and she could taste the acid in her stomach creeping up. She tried over and over again, but she couldn't remember what Suze looked like. Were her eyes brown or blue? Her hair blonde or brown, straight or curly? Maybe this was just a bad dream and not every parent's nightmare. It was the first of the many sleepless nights she would have. She stared at the ceiling and wished she were dreaming. Since reading the note, she had become afraid that she'd never see her sixteen-year-old daughter again. How could she forget what one of her children looked like?

She turned around and looked at the portraits of her daughters hanging above her four-poster bed. There she was, third from the left, the third born of her four daughters. She had pixie-cut brown hair, sun-kissed freckled cheeks, mysterious eyes—one brown and one blue—and was the only one without a smile on her face. Suze never smiled for the camera or for the artist who drew the pastel portraits of the girls. Then she spotted Suze's school picture on her dresser. She held the frame in her shaking hands, closed her eyes, and touched it. There was no life under her fingertips. All she felt was the cold, smooth glass that separated her from her daughter. Reality sank in when she opened her eyes and saw the note, crumpled up in a ball from Joseph's fury. Mary Ann flattened the paper. The words jumped off the paper, as if they were taunting her and saying, *Na, na, na, na, na. Look . . . at . . . us.*

Dear Mom and Dad,

Please don't be mad at me, and please don't try to find me, because you won't. If I hear that you're looking for me, I'll make sure you never see my face again. I've taken a trip with some friends, and you don't know any of them or their parents. I'll be okay, so don't worry. I probably won't call, so don't freak out. Mom, I know you always worry, but don't. You have enough children to take care of, and I can take care of myself. I'm sure you didn't even notice I was gone until you found this note.

Tell Tricia I'm sorry I missed her birthday. She'll be happy she won't have to share a room with me anymore. That can be my birthday gift to her.

Suze

chapter

FOUR

Somewhere in South Dakota

"The Angels were all singing out of tune, and hoarse with having little else to do, excepting to wind up the sun and moon or curb a runaway young star or two."
Lord Byron

Suze crossed her legs and squeezed them tight to hold it in. She had to go, but she didn't want to be the one to ask. They had already stopped too many times because of her pea-size bladder. She tried to keep her mind off peeing by counting cows. The states were all beginning to look the same—pastures, cornfields, cows, cows, and more cows. They were in the middle of nowhere, also known as South Dakota. For more than an hour, they had passed umpteen signs on I-90 advertising free water at Wall Drug. Water was the last thing she wanted to think about.

Something reeked deadly. *That's a combination of hydrogen sulfide, methane, and carbon dioxide.* She knew the warm quiet ones were the smelliest because they contained bacteria. For a 'types of gases' assignment in science class she had researched flatulence, purely to piss off Sister Petra. Petra called her parents to say that even though Suze was the brightest student in the class and should have moved up a grade, she was insidious.

"Jesus, Doug." Suze cranked the window open as fast as she could. "Next time open a window."

"Don't be so quick to blame me," Doug replied.

"Yeah, right. Who had a burrito at the Dairy-Mart last night? Not I."

"We'll stop at Wall Drug in about ten miles. I feel more erupting."

"Thank God! I'm about to wet my pants, and I'm starving," Suze said.

"What's going on?" Eileen woke to the thunderous sound of an open window at sixty-five miles per hour on the highway.

Doug floored it and blasted the radio on the only station that came in clearly.

"Water's free. You have to pay for food," the waitress said as she plopped down four menus.

"Are you implying that we won't pay?" Doug asked, raking his bedraggled pubic-like beard with his nicotine-stained fingers.

"I've seen your type come and go here, and I've been stiffed too many times."

"I'm buying," Eileen said. "It's my turn."

Suze left her money in her pillowcase in the backseat of the car. She didn't want them to know she had $325—her First Communion money that she'd been saving for eight years. When Doug asked her to drive to California with them, she said yes but lied about not having money. "I'll take care of you," Doug promised. In an obscure way, he was her knight in shining armor, rescuing her from her parent's prison where she suffered from teenage-hood.

The waitress smirked and walked away, mumbling something about hairy hippies. Suze thought it was cool to be called a hippie. Now she was one of them. No more school, homework, dishes, babysitting, sharing a room with a little sister, curfews, and groundings. This was freedom. No parents, no responsibilities, just peace, love, sex, drugs, and rock 'n roll.

"I'm stuffed. I should have stopped after the cheeseburger and fries. That sundae made me feel sick," Doug said.

"I hope that doesn't mean we're in for another smelly car ride," Stu said.

"Miss 'I have no bladder,' why don't you go to the bathroom before we go. I don't want to stop for a while. You've slowed us down enough," Doug said to Suze.

"Eileen, do you need to go?" Suze asked.

"No, we'll meet you at the car after I pay the bill."

There was a line for the women's room. She thought about using the men's but chickened out at the last minute. Finally, there was a free stall. She had gone before they ate and didn't have to go. She flushed the toilet, hoping the sound of rushing water would percolate her pipes. Suddenly, she felt a warm trickle. Suze wiped herself and was elated to see blood. She didn't tell Doug she was late. He would think her running away with him was precipitous and based only on the fact that she couldn't tell her parents she was pregnant. *Thank you, God!* Tampon-less, she folded up several sheets of toilet paper into a makeshift pad and hoped it would last until the next stop—whenever and wherever that would be.

When Suze stepped out of the famed Wall Drug into the dirt parking lot, the sunlight was blinding and the wind kicked up dust. She squinted and shielded her eyes, but the car wasn't where they parked it. She scanned the lot thinking maybe they went to the gas station next door. *Shit. They've left without me. My money!* Her heart was pounding, and she was about to lose her lunch.

"Hey, hippie!" the waitress called. Suze looked over her shoulder and saw she was coming after her. Out of nowhere, the Pontiac—her knight's white horse—screeched to a stop thirty yards in front of her.

"Hurry up, run . . . quick, get in the car!" Stu yelled from the front passenger window. Eileen threw open the back door, and Suze jumped in. They sped away before she was all the way into the car.

"Sucker!" Doug shouted as they pulled out of the lot and barreled back to I-90 west.

Suze reluctantly joined in their laughter, not quite sure what had just happened. She couldn't believe they would leave without paying, but then again she wasn't surprised. They seemed indifferent to not having money. They had planned to pull a fast one on the waitress all along. None of them had much money, yet they ordered an abundance of food as if they could afford to buy the restaurant.

The landscape whirled past the car window fantastically fast, like cinematography for a documentary on rural America. The green pastures and cows turned into sand dunes and barren prairies, interrupted by red clay spires that shot up through the ground into rugged peaks towering over canyons. Suze couldn't help but think about how much her mother would love this part of the country. Mary Ann talked about traveling so much that you would think she was a travel agent. She dreamed of renting a mobile home and taking all of the kids on a trip west. She had piles of AAA trip tickets and guidebooks to almost every state in the country, hoping to take a road trip one day. Suze stared at the caramel colored car seats full of cigarette burns and the clutter on the floor—the landscape of her new life as a runaway—and wondered how the hell she had the nerve to flee and hurt her mother again.

The joint Doug and Stu were smoking was the answer. She had been tripping on LSD or high on pot almost every day for the past two weeks, which made her want to get as far away from her parents as possible. When she used, she wouldn't come home for hours because she didn't want her parents to see her like that. They always sent Trip to find her. But she would do it all over again the next day. Mary Ann and Joseph confronted her about drugs, but she denied ever using. And they believed her. Mary Ann and Joseph's gullibility was irksome to Suze. She had made a habit of mocking her parents' hypocrisy and naïveté and was determined to show them once and for all by running—and this time staying—away.

She needed to get her mother out of her mind. She closed her eyes and quickly fell asleep and began to dream. She was sitting in church next to her mother, the scent of Estee Lauder looming in the air as she was mesmerized by the numbing sweetness of Mary Ann's singing. Her mother's beauty was palpable. Suze reached over to touch her, but felt emptiness. She felt nothing. Her fingers flowed through the apparition of her mother. She was visible, yet intangible. She attempted to stroke Mary Ann's ash-blonde hair that always felt like silk. Again, she felt nothing. She inspected her hands to see if something was wrong, but her long fingers, soft skin, and perfectly filed nails showed nothing out of the ordinary. She gave herself a paper cut with one of the Mass missile pages and watched the blood flow. *Why can't I feel her? Mom! Look at me!*

Mary Ann didn't respond and continued her prayers, "…and lead us not into temptation but deliver us from evil. Amen." Suze desperately tried to make contact with her. Again, she reached for her arm, her face, her hair, hungry to touch her, anxious to feel the tenderness of her mother. Nothing. Two angels surrounded her mother: one with the face of Mary Margaret and the other ML. Her mother was vanishing before her eyes, floating to the ceiling of the church and through the roof as if she were the Virgin Mary ascending to heaven. *Mom, don't leave me! Come back, please!* Only the angels looked back at Suze as they escorted her mother above and out of sight.

It smelled like church incense, but Suze knew better as she woke from her dream.

"Shit, that stuff is good," Doug said as he passed the joint to Stu. "I'm going to make a fortune selling this hooch in California."

"No doubt," Stu said.

"It's really messing me up. Suze, you drive," Doug said.

Suze thought about taking a few hits of the joint before jumping into the driver's seat. She needed something to keep her from thinking about her mother. She'd have to wait until she was done with her turn at the wheel.

The air turned cool as the sun began to set, so she couldn't open her window. The car was a smoke chamber from the other three sharing joints. Suze began to feel the effects of the secondhand smoke but managed to stay focused on the road ahead. She had no idea where she was going except west. Stu was passed out, leaning against the front passenger window and drooling. In the rearview mirror, she saw Doug with his eyes closed and his head tilted back. Eileen must have fallen asleep on Doug's lap.

Suze thought Doug was extremely high from a combination of Jack Daniels and pot. His moans were getting louder and more intense. She turned up the radio to drown him out with the static sound of Crosby, Stills, Nash, and Young. With a coat hanger as a makeshift antenna, the reception was anemic, but it was preferable to listening to Doug.

"Does anyone have a Kleenex, napkin, or something?" Eileen sat up.

There was nothing but the sound of silence. The radio cut out. Suze's chest tightened and her heart rate spiked to that of a sprinter. She tensed up terribly and revved the horse up to seventy-five miles per hour.

"How was it? Sweet? I heard that the more candy you eat, the sweeter your cum."

"Doug, you're sick," Eileen said.

Eileen was Suze's best friend and the one who fixed her up with Doug. *How could she? This can't be happening. Oh God, what should I do? Let it go? If I did that to Stu, she would never talk to me again.*

"Suze, you could learn a few things from your friend. She knows exactly how to please a man," Doug flaunted as he made eye contact with Suze in the rearview mirror. Stu continued to sleep and drool, oblivious to the back seat philandering.

As though he could read Suze's mind, Doug said. "Stu won't mind, and neither should you. We're all in this together."

They camped under the stars that night. Afraid of the dark and fearing wild animals, Suze numbed her nerves by smoking a joint and drinking with Eileen. At dawn, she woke to the distant howls of coyotes and cawing crows. The black birds' cries were haunting her as she watched them swoop through the air, incessantly circling the campsite. The morning-after effects of drugs and cheap wine, combined with an eerie feeling that the crows were her father's messengers chastising her for putting her mother through such angst, made her head pound, her vision blur, and her stomach queasy.

She felt something move by her feet and whipped back the blanket to reveal Stu beginning to open his eyes. She didn't remember much about last night and hoped he didn't either. But she would make sure Doug noticed that Stu slept next to her. He and Eileen were still asleep in the same sleeping bag on the other side of the burnt-out campfire.

chapter

FIVE

1974
Cleveland Heights, Ohio

"If death meant just leaving the stage long enough to change costume and come back as a new character...Would you slow down? Or speed up?"
Chuck Palahniuk

Mary Margaret was in no mood to talk tonight, so she hoped Mary Ann made their favorite meal. When she served beef burgundy for dinner, no one talked. But it turned out that tonight was turkey tetrazzini, the family's least favorite. Everyone was eating, except for Mary Margaret who had other things on her mind. Even though turkey tetrazzini was no beef burgundy, no one was talking.

"One time, at band camp..." Trip said, and the silence was broken. It was a family joke to begin a story with the band camp line. No one went to band camp. In fact, they would never even *consider* being in a marching band. When Tricia told Mary Margaret she wanted to join band, Mary Margaret explained that band was for nerds and geeks. And no Von Guten was either.

"Mary Margaret said she'd never get married," Trip continued. He looked up from his plate and glared at her across the table. The look turned into a smirk.

"Trip, you're such an ass," Mary Margaret said. The anger inside her was churning, and her face reddened. Trip had a way of getting under her skin, and tonight he was using a knife to peel it back.

"Then why *did* you, Mrs. Malone?" Mark quipped.

"Enough! What's this all about?" Mary Ann asked.

Joseph put down his fork, folded his arms across his chest, and leaned back in his chair. He stared down the table and glared over his glasses at Mary Ann sitting at the other end. The hair on Mary Margaret's neck stood up. Her father was about to blow his top at Mary Ann's expense. Whenever there was a problem, he blamed her. Or at least he did his best to make her feel like it was her fault.

"I was going to tell you later, but thanks to Trip, I'll tell you now," Mary Margaret said. "Billy and I got married when I went to see him." She had recently returned from visiting Billy who enlisted in the Army the day after graduation. "I'm nineteen. It's not a big deal."

"I told you we shouldn't let her go," Joseph gloated. "He's in the Army for God's sake. Mary Margaret, what were you thinking? He can't just leave and come back to be your husband."

"Did you get married in a church?" Mary Ann asked.

"No, we got married on the base by an officer."

"Well, it might be legal, but the Church doesn't recognize it. You have to get married in the Church. Mary Margaret, I don't understand why you did this to us. Why didn't you talk to me about this before?"

That's a good question. Why hadn't I talked to them?

Mary Margaret pushed the turkey mush around her plate. She was scared of her parents. Scared of what they would do to her. Scared they would take her away or make sure Billy never came home. But she was also angry and resentful. Resentful that they thought this was about *them.*

"Mom, I didn't do anything to you. We got married for us. This has nothing to do with you and Dad."

Mary Margaret rarely called her 'Mom.' She usually called her Mary Ann. There were millions of moms in the world, but only one Mary Ann who mattered to her—Mary Margaret's Mary Ann—*her* mother. And Mary Margaret thought she deserved the respect of being called by her name, not a label. At first, Mary Ann told Mary Margaret it was disrespectful *not* to call her 'Mom.' Once Mary Margaret explained her reasoning, Mary Ann gave her permission to call her by her name.

"Bullshit," Joseph snapped. "This has everything to do with us. You're our daughter, living in our house, and you should have had the courtesy and respect to tell us—and Billy should have asked for my permission—before you did such a stupid thing. Do you know how this will look? Do you know what people are going to say? It's humiliating that you eloped. It's a slap in my face." Joseph slammed his fist on the table. "I'm getting a drink."

Yeah, get a drink. You're not the same dad I had growing up. Back then, a hundred years ago, you were fun, kind, easy-going, and you loved me. When I was little, I used to dance with you in the kitchen. I'd stand on top of your cordovan Johnston & Murphy's and hold onto your belt loops while you whisked me around the yellowed linoleum floor to the music of Johnny Mathis and Frank Sinatra.

When I told you about my friend Sally whose dad died when she was three, and that I felt bad that she didn't have a dad to dance with, you said, "Bring her over for dinner, and I'll dance with her." For selfish reasons, I never did. I didn't want to share you with anyone. I already had to compete for your attention. But Sally never got to dance because she died when she was twelve from Cystic Fibrosis. If I could do it again, I'd let Sally borrow you for as long as she'd like. If Sally were still alive, I'd let her have you for her dad.

"Clear the table and start the dishes while I talk with Mary Margaret," Mary Ann said to Trip, Mark, and Tricia. "And take Patrick in the kitchen with you."

"I'll call Uncle Don," Mary Ann said when they were alone. "You'll have to get married in the Church when Billy comes home on leave. I hope St. Theresa's will let us have it there on such short notice. Until then, don't tell anyone you're already married. I don't want to be the talk of the town."

"He'll be home in three weeks."

"Did he give you a ring?"

"Not yet."

"What do you mean 'not yet'? Is he planning to give you one? It's the respectable thing to do, you know."

"He's going to ask his grandmother for one of her rings. She said she would give him one when he got married. And since she lives alone, we're going to live with her in Chesterland."

"That's forty-five minutes from here!" Mary Ann rubbed her forehead and held her face in her hands. "You need to stay in dental hygiene school. If you don't go to college, you will need a skill to make you employable," Mary Ann said.

"Mom, just because I'm married doesn't mean I'm not going to work." She was lying. She didn't let on that Billy didn't want her to work, that he wanted her to stay home and take care of his grandmother.

"I'll call Billy's mother after I talk with Uncle Don. We'll have the reception here. It's not how I would like your wedding to be, but it will have to do."

"Can I wear your dress?" Mary Margaret asked her mother.

Mary Ann sighed. She had told her daughters she wanted them to wear her dress when they married. Mary Margaret knew Mary Ann was sentimental about her dress. Not because she had a perfect marriage. Hardly. Because it was a piece of art made by the woman she admired most. Her grandmother had sewn every stitch, every pearl button (thirty running up the back), every piece of lace, and hundreds of sequins all by hand.

Mary Margaret was well aware that her parents hated Billy. She heard her mother tell ML that he drank too much and that he wasn't the kind of boy she wanted her daughter to date. The only thing she liked about him was that he was Catholic. Mary Ann hated the fact that he never came to the door when he picked her up. He would beep the horn and wait in the driveway. The first time he did this, Mary Ann made Mary Margaret sit in the den and wait and wait and wait while he beeped over and over again. She wouldn't let her leave with him until he rang the doorbell.

Mary Ann liked everything to be perfect. And this wasn't a perfect wedding. Mary Margaret was sure her mother didn't want her to wear the dress for many reasons, including the fact that she believed only virgins should wear white wedding dresses.

"Are you sure you want to? It has long sleeves, and it's been so hot."

"That's okay. I love that dress. Please, Mary Ann, let me wear it. I promise I won't ruin it. Plus, it won't be as hot in a few weeks."

"You may wear it since we don't have time to buy a dress. Who will you ask to stand up for you, to be your maid of honor? Since this will be a small wedding, you shouldn't have a big bridal party."

"I always thought Suze would be my maid of honor."

"That would be nice. If we only knew where she was. Even if we did, she wouldn't come home. I don't think she'll ever come back." Mary Ann began to cry.

Mary Margaret should have known better than to mention Suze. The weight of Suze's name had grown heavier over time, making it increasingly difficult for Mary Ann to hear her name. And with ML married and now Mary Margaret, Tricia would be the only daughter at home.

"Mary Ann, I'm sorry. Please don't cry. I'll ask ML to be my maid of honor, and Tricia can be a bridesmaid."

Joseph found refuge in several Scotches that night. It wasn't his favorite drink; actually, he didn't have a favorite drink. He'd drink anything: beers, red wine, white wine, Scotch, Manhattans, old-fashioneds, brandy, it really didn't matter. While Mary Ann's night continued like any other weeknight—cleaning up the kitchen, helping Mark and Trisha with their homework, bathing Patrick and reading him a story—Joseph drowned his misery in alcohol.

Mary Ann found Joseph late that night sitting in the den in the dark. Mary Margaret and Tricia's bedroom was right above the den, which had originally been a porch. When Joseph had it enclosed, he skimped on the insulation. Mary Margaret could hear every word spoken in the den below as she lay in her bed staring at the ceiling. Fortunately, Tricia was sound asleep and didn't hear a thing.

"I'd like to kick his ass," Joseph said.

"What good would that do? There's nothing we can do except make the best of it," Mary Ann said. "I just spoke with Don and he'll see if he can arrange for them to get married at St. Theresa's." She did her best to remain calm to prevent Joseph from getting out of control. Mary Ann was the quintessential Pollyanna.

"I told you she shouldn't go to visit him, but you wouldn't listen to me. I remember what it's like to be a nineteen-year-old boy."

"I'd like to think she wouldn't sleep with him unless she was married, so that's the reason they married."

"That motherfucker! Wait until I get my hands on that bastard."

Mary Margaret couldn't hear anything for a minute, but finally the sound of ice cubes clanking against Waterford crystal drifted through the floorboards. He was making another drink.

"Mary Ann, don't be so stupid, guys only have one thing on their minds at that age. If you were a better mother, you wouldn't have let her go and none of this would've happened. No wonder Suze got the hell out of here."

Mary Margaret couldn't believe he had brought Suze into this. It wasn't Mary Ann's fault that Suze ran away, and neither was this. He should be yelling at Mary Margaret, not her mother.

Mary Ann left the den and closed the door. Fights between them always ended that way. She would walk away in disgust, and he would drink more. But tonight was different. She didn't let him off easy. Mary Margaret heard the door to the den open again. Mary Ann was back.

Mary Margaret suddenly felt uneasy, yet she silently cheered her mother on.

"Joseph...don't...you...*ever*...talk to me like that again. I'm sick and tired of you belittling and blaming me. It's amazing I have any self-esteem left at all after being married to you. Did you ever think that the girls want to get away from *you*? You haven't exactly been the greatest role model. After hearing you speak to me the way you do for years, they must think it's okay to be treated this way by a man. No wonder they have such poor taste in men. Look at their father."

"Shut up, Mary Ann. Go to bed."

Mary Ann caught her breath and started at him again. "You think Billy is a motherfucker? Why? Does he remind you of yourself? Do you see a little of you in him? He drinks too much. He didn't go to college. He doesn't go to church. He treats Mary Margaret poorly, and he has no respect for women."

Mary Margaret clapped her hand over her mouth as she let out a sharp bark of laughter. She had never heard her mother use the F-word before.

This time, Mary Ann slammed the door shut behind her, something that surprised Mary Margaret almost as much as her cussing. When her parents fought, her mother kept it quiet and private, but tonight it was like she wanted Mary Margaret to hear.

Mary Margaret hated how her dad walked all over her mother and talk to her with so little respect. But tonight she was proud of her mother for standing up to him. For as long as she could remember, her mother had tolerated his ranting without fighting back. Mary Margaret didn't know why Mary Ann was afraid to stick up for herself or talk back; except once she heard her father threaten that he'd leave. Maybe that's why she kept quiet. Deep down, Mary Margaret didn't think her mother would mind if he left. But she also knew that her mother didn't want them to be one of those divorced families that she and her friends whispered about. Mary Ann's best friend, Carol, used to call her Elmer. For the longest time, Mary Margaret didn't understand the nickname, but then one year for her mother's birthday Carol gave her a bottle of Elmer's glue as a joke and Mary Margaret finally understood. Mary Ann was the bond holding the family together.

Joseph slept on the couch that night, rocking the house with his thunderous snoring, keeping Mary Margaret awake. It happened whenever he drank too much. In the morning, Mary Margaret heard him walk into her parent's bedroom and ask Mary Ann, "What's for dinner tonight?" She didn't answer him.

Damn! She finally stood up to him, and he doesn't remember a thing.

Mary Margaret's church wedding took place on a beautiful fall day. The colors on the trees resembled a forty-eight-count box of Crayola's. The air was crisp but warm enough. The bright sunlight was reflecting off the trees, and the soon-to-be-brown-but-still-vibrant-green grass made the air look and feel unusually clean. A perfect day for an imperfect wedding.

Mary Margaret, Billy, and their parents were able to keep the previous elopement a secret. Mary Margaret was a pro at keeping secrets. Even secrets she couldn't trust Billy with yet. If Suze was there, she would have told her everything, so in this case it was good she was gone.

She never realized how much she depended on Suze until she ran away. Keeping her secrets to herself felt like wearing a coat made of concrete—it slowed her down and wore her to the point of exhaustion. The nuns told her that keeping secrets unravels your moral fiber and prevents you from reaching your full potential. And that people only keep secrets about things they feel guilty about or are ashamed of.

She didn't care if her wedding wasn't perfect. She was used to putting up a front and acting like everything was hunky-dory. But it was all so exhausting. She told herself that all she needed to do was get through the wedding. Soon she'd be out of the house, on her own, and able to live life the way she wanted, without her father's claws hooked into her back.

Mary Ann and Nana wanted Mary Margaret to go through all the motions of a traditional wedding day. Mary Ann's bedroom became the bridal party's dressing room. When ML got married, they used the ladies locker room at the Shaker Country Club where Uncle Richard belonged, but he didn't offer it for this wedding. Mary Margaret couldn't have cared less. She loved Mary Ann's bedroom. It had the biggest, fluffiest, four-poster bed in the house. It also had periwinkle blue toile wallpaper, silk drapes, a full-length mirror, and was the only bedroom with wall-to-wall carpet, a television, and an attached bathroom. She was happy they were getting dressed there and not in a stuffy, snooty club locker room.

Mary Margaret's nerves were getting the best of her. After dry heaving for thirty minutes, she joined her 'wedding party' in the bedroom. ML was in the bathroom applying Mary Ann and Nana's makeup while Tricia watched. The wedding gown was suspended on a padded hanger on the end post of the bed. Its long train was draped over the bed like a bedspread. It was a size two, Mary Margaret's size.

She had been binge eating for weeks, her way of dealing with stress, and hoped the dress still fit. She said a Hail Mary, slid off her jeans and top, grabbed a girdle from her mother's dresser, and slid into the gown.

"Mary Margaret, is that you?" her mother called from the bathroom.

"Yes, it's me. Were you expecting someone else?" she replied.

"Don't get dressed until I do your make-up," ML said through the door.

"It's too late. I just need someone to help me with the buttons."

"I'll button you up," Nana said as she entered the room. "But first, I have a wedding gift for you. On your wedding day, you should wear something old, something new, something borrowed, and something blue. This can be your 'something new.' Uncle Don brought this mantilla back from Rome. The pope himself blessed it. A bride needs to cover her head in church."

"Nana, it's beautiful. It matches the lace on the train. Thank you." She gave Nana a hug, which turned into a long embrace. Nana wouldn't let go.

Finally, Nana pulled back and looked at Mary Margaret with tears in her eyes. Stroking the side of Mary Margaret's face with the back of her hand, she said, "You're a beautiful bride, my darling. You know how much I love you. I always have, and I always will, no matter what."

"No crying! Your makeup will run!" ML shouted. She was always loud. Leave it to ML, the family drill sergeant and event planner, to keep everyone focused and on task. No time for emotions. Those would have to wait until later.

Mary Margaret was grateful the wedding ceremony was short and sweet. Uncle Don officiated the Mass even though he knew she and Billy had already eloped. Like her parents, he didn't like Billy. Before the wedding, he gave Billy a mint to mask the alcohol seeping from his pores after the previous night's so-called bachelor party.

At the end of the ceremony, Don introduced them to the congregation as Mr. and Mrs. Malone. All Mary Margaret could think was that in five hours she and Billy would pull out of the driveway and officially, not secretly, start their new life. They would be the longest five hours of her life.

"Joseph, get up, someone's at the door!" Mary Ann tried to wake him.

Mom, I'm so sorry. You don't deserve this. I wish this didn't happen to you. Yes, this time it's happening to you. Be strong, Mom. I'm sorry. You were the best Mom, the best Mary Ann.

"Jesus Christ, it's two in the morning. It's probably one of Billy's drunken friends coming back for another beer. Don't they know the reception ended at midnight? Just ignore them and they'll go away."

Mary Ann pulled back the drapes and gasped. "There's a police car in the driveway. Joseph you have to go downstairs to see what they want. Now they're banging on the door. They'll wake everyone up."

"Alright, alright already. I'm going."

Brace yourself, Dad, and be strong for Mom.

Mom, don't stand at the top of the stairs. Go back to your room. Dad will handle this. Please, please don't stand there and listen to them.

"Mr. Von Guten, I'm Officer Haynes and this is my partner Officer McDonnell. There's been an accident. May we come in?"

Joseph stepped back and led them into the living room. "Did someone from our party have too much to drink? Is anyone hurt?"

"It's your daughter. She and her boyfriend . . ."

"Her asshole husband," Joseph interrupted.

Nice, Dad. No respect for the...

"I apologize, we didn't know she was married. Her license says Von Guten," McDonnell explained.

"Mr. Von Guten, she didn't make it. Neither did her husband. And we're sorry to say she lost the baby as well," Officer Haynes said. "We're very sorry for your loss."

...dead. At least sit down and act like you care, like you're upset. I'm trying to talk to Mary Ann, but she can't hear me. I see her, but she can't see me. I'm all alone, but I'm home, yet I'm not. I'm on the outside looking in. Is this heaven? Is this all there is? Or is it purgatory, or limbo—one of those vague in-between places the nuns told us about? The last thing I remember is Billy opening a beer while he was driving. I grabbed it from

him, and once again I became the punching bag. The last punch felt like a hammer going through my eye. And then I was wet. The frigid water was soothing—like an ice pack Mary Ann used to tenderly place on a boo-boo when I was little. Then, there was nothing more to endure. No pain. No sorrow. No anger. No resentfulness. No life. The water surrounded me. I was back in the womb, safe and protected from the perils of life.

Mary Ann fainted.

Mary Ann, wake up! Dad, help Mom! She's at the top of the stairs. Dad, she needs you! There's no use. They can't hear me. I'm gone, and it's just as well. I wish the cops hadn't told them about the baby. What they didn't know wouldn't hurt them. They lost a daughter, but they didn't need to know they lost their first grandchild, too.

"What happened to them? Where and when was the accident?" Joseph's voice was actually cracking. He broke down into tears before they began to answer. The cops were used to this. They continued to tell Joseph the details while he held his head in his hands, sobbing.

"They lost control on a curve on Riverside Road in Hunting Hills. The car rolled over several times and ended up in the river, upside down. They had their seat belts on which must have made it difficult for them to get out if they were still conscious," McDonnell said.

"Mr. Von Guten, we'd like you and your wife to come down to the coroner's to identify the bodies. The coroner has some questions for you. Your daughter was covered in bruises, and we don't think they're from the accident. He thinks they've been there for a while."

The weight of the world has been lifted from my shoulders. The lies and secrets are gone, and all that's left is peace and laughter. I used to carry the weight of the world, and now I'm weightless. I just want to spread my wings, fly, and laugh. God, it's been so long since I laughed. I forgot how good it feels to laugh again. Daddy, Mommy, I'm safe now. He can't hurt me anymore.

Dear Diary,

Suze is gone, Mary Margaret is dead, and I'm cursed. There's nothing to live for. I have failed. I can barely get myself out of bed in the morning.

I know I can't let myself get down, for the sake of my family, but I don't know if I have the strength or the will to move on.

What am I thinking? Where is my faith? My strength is in the Lord. "Surely goodness and mercy shall follow me all the days of my life…"

Hah! If this is goodness and mercy, I pray that evil and cruelty never cross my doorstep. I can't endure much more.

Why did she have to fall in love with that jerk? Maybe for the same reason I fell in love with my scoundrel? Would Billy have been another Joseph? If so, would Mary Margaret have been another me? Lord knows she was on the same path.

I must let it go. The Lord will be my rock.

I have the rest of my family who needs me.

I will be strong.

I will be strong.

Mary Ann

chapter

SIX

"Children begin by loving their parents. After a time they judge them. Rarely, if ever, do they forgive them."
Oscar Wilde

"Trip, you have mail."

Mary Ann was in the kitchen while he ruffled through today's stack on the hall table. *For God's sake, why is she always in the kitchen cooking? I wonder if she even leaves that room when no one's home all day.*

"I see it."

Joseph C. Von Guten, III. Jesus, I hate being called 'the third.' Mail with 'the third' on it is usually something I don't want to open. And I don't have to open this one; I know exactly what's in it. The color of the envelope gives it away. "Welcome. Your friends and neighbors have selected you to serve…" Should I open it or burn it? Throw up or open a beer? Just my luck, after a crappy day at work with Dad, I come home and find a letter from my friendly local draft board.

"What is it?" Mary Ann asked.

Trip walked into the kitchen. "I can only guess, and I'm not so sure I want to open it."

Mary Ann put down the knife, turned around, and stared. Her face was taut and pallid, and her knuckles turned white as she clutched the edge of the counter for balance. Recovering she turned back toward the kitchen window and began peeling potatoes, but Trip noticed her shaking hands. Her motherly duty was to act like everything was okay, like everything would be all right. Sometimes Mary Ann was easy to read. Trip could tell she was acting. Acting like everything was peachy keen. A dead give-away that she was trying to protect one of her brood from reality.

"Where's your father? I thought you drove to work with him," she asked.

"He dropped me off and went to the liquor store. He'll be back in a minute."

"You should open it before he gets home," she said.

"I don't need to. Garrett Gallagher got his yesterday, and he showed it to me last night at the Coventry Saloon. The crazy son-of-a-bitch was waving his envelope around like a flag. Sitting on the corner barstool he started shouting, 'drinks are on me!' We all knew what it was. When he passed out at closing time, I drove him home. I wasn't sure what was worse—him being drafted or his bar bill. He'd been buying drinks for everyone, even strangers, for hours. It was over three hundred dollars." Trip gave a low chuckle, as if remembering the night fondly. Mary Ann wasn't the only one who could act.

"Open it. Maybe you're on the reserve list or the waiting list and you won't have to report just yet."

"Mom, there's no such thing. Where do you come up with this stuff? I'm not opening it. I don't need to. I told you and Dad that if my number came up, I'm not going."

"Trip, you know how Dad feels. You owe it to your country to serve and protect, like he and his brothers did."

"This is different. Don't you watch the news and read the papers? Do you know what's going on over there? It's a jungle. This isn't like fighting in the countryside in the south of France. This has nothing to do with America. This isn't our war, and we have no business being there. Jesus, Mother, the Vietnamese are insane. When they take American soldiers prisoner they torture them. It's brutal. They rape women, kill children, and ravage entire villages for no reason at all. It's a fucking nightmare. There's no way I'm going. End of discussion." Trip threw the envelope down onto the kitchen table and made his way toward the fridge for a beer.

"Trip, don't use that language when you talk to me." Mary Ann swung around to face him, paring knife in one hand and potato in the other.

"Sorry, but I don't think you understand how bad it is. You don't want me to wind up like Mary Margaret, do you?" Trip immediately knew he had gone too far, but it was too late. He cracked the bottle cap off his beer and took a long, deep swig.

"Joseph Christopher, don't say things like that. You have no idea how that makes me feel. There's nothing worse than losing a child." Mary Ann's voice cracked as she turned back to the sink and began furiously scraping at the potato in her hand.

"No, I don't, Mom, but that *is* the point. If I go over there, you will most likely lose me as well. Have you thought about that? You need to. You won't know where I am. You won't be able to contact me. I'll wind up as one of the thousands of POWs, or worse yet, dead." Having finished his beer, Trip chucked the bottle into the trash and yanked the refrigerator door open to grab another.

"Trip, your father will be so angry if you become a draft dodger. He risked his life as a soldier. As far as he's concerned, his sons have the same responsibility. Please don't upset him. Don't upset *us*. Since Mary Margaret died, I struggle everyday just to get out of bed. Sometimes it's so hard to go on, but I do my best. If you go to Canada, it will be as bad as Suze running away. I can't handle much more of this."

"I know you miss Suze, and you're still mourning for Mary Margaret. But Mom, life goes on. You have to stop looking back and wondering what you could have done differently. I know you struggle, believe me."

"What do you know?" Mary Ann's voice had dropped to almost a whisper, and Trip could almost hear the flood of tears rising.

"Mom, it's *obvious*. You've hardly been out of the house in the past six months. You never talk to Mark, Tricia, Patrick, or me. We take care of ourselves because we know you can't. But you need to move on. You have other people in this house who need you. Mary Margaret doesn't need you anymore, we do."

She started to shake. *Here we go again.* Setting the unopened beer down, Trip walked over and put his hands on her shoulders. Mary Ann hung her head and cried. She wouldn't look at Trip. It had been months since he had been this close to her. He'd forgotten how much taller he was than her. *Hell, I still want to be her little boy. I want her to take care of me, and get me out of this mess. But today, the roles are reversed. I'm trying to help her, to give her the courage to pull herself out of her own mess of a life.*

"Mom, I'm sorry I upset you, but I need you now," Trip whispered into the top of her head. "I need you to stand by me, to give me your support. I don't believe you really want me to go to Vietnam. You say you do because that's what Dad thinks, not what you think. I know it. For once in your life, speak for yourself. Tell me how *you* feel. Please?"

She didn't say a thing. Trip suddenly felt very cold. For the first time in a long time he really studied his mother and saw how her shoulders slumped and her clothes hung off her malnourished frame. He realized he hadn't seen her eat a decent meal since Mary Margaret died, even though she did nothing but cook for the family. For the first time, Trip realized that maybe she couldn't speak for herself. Maybe she didn't remember how.

"Trip, of course I don't want you to go to Vietnam, but I also want you to do what's right. Dodging the draft by going to Canada is not the right thing to do. No mother wants her son to go to war. No mother wants to bury a child or have one run away. But I can't make you do what I want. And I can't give you a better answer, Trip. If that's what you're looking for, I don't have one."

"I'm not looking for a magical way out; I just want your support. I want you to stand behind me whatever decision I make. I'm not a child anymore. And I'm not going to put my life on the line for something I don't believe in. Isn't that what you taught me? To stand up for what I believe in?"

"Yes, I did as long as what you believe is valid. I may agree with how you feel about the war, but it doesn't give you the right to break the law. Dodging the draft is a federal crime. You, *we,* need to think this through and come up with a legitimate way to get you out of the war. There must be a classification that would keep you from being drafted."

"I've already looked into it, believe me. I don't qualify for any of them. I don't work for a company that's a government contractor, I'm not preparing for the ministry, and I've never served before. There are a bunch of other classifications, none of which apply to me. Trust me—I've tried to find a way. Mom, I know you're a rule-follower, but sometimes rules and laws are meant to be broken. I'm going to Canada. End of story. I hope you'll help me, but we'll have to talk about this later because Dad just pulled into the driveway."

Trip was in no mood to be around his father after spending the entire day working for him. While Joseph parked the car in the garage, Trip went into the living room, flicked his Bic and held the flame up to the unopened envelope. He tossed it burning into the empty fireplace and watched it go up in flames. The fire started out gray and smoky then blazed blue and eventually grew into bright orange and gold flames. Out of sight. Out of mind.

Trip wondered if he should have opened the envelope. Maybe he was planning on going to Canada in haste. What if his number *hadn't* been called? Would they have sent a letter telling him he *wasn't* being drafted? He didn't think so. His suspicions were confirmed by Roger Mudd on the CBS Evening News, who told him his number had been called. Number 210. The last number called for the draft that year. *Just my luck. Uncle Sam may have me by the skin of my teeth, but he'll have to find me first.*

He didn't want to go to Vietnam, and he didn't especially want to be a draft dodger and go to Canada. He didn't think of himself as someone who ran away from his problems. Nor did he want to stay home and work for his father in the family business. He thought Divine Candles was a death trap. Even Dr. Ferrari told his father that is was unsafe for Trip to work there. "Trip is extremely allergic to bees," Dr. Ferrari had told Joseph. "Just handling beeswax could cause Trip to go into anaphylactic shock."

What Trip really wanted to do was go to college. During his senior year in high school, the college counselor convinced his parents to go look at colleges. Because Trip was interested in architecture, the college advisor suggested they look at Catholic University of America in Washington, D.C. It was the only school his parents would consider visiting, most likely because it was Catholic. Since ML hadn't gone to college, this was new territory for them. It was an adventure for all of them, and off they went.

Mary Ann, the only college graduate on either side of the family, would have enrolled Trip right then and there on visiting day if she could have. Her excitement and joy over the possibility of her son going to college was real. She and Don choreographed every step of the visit to try to impress and convince Joseph that CUA was where Trip belonged. Don called the president of the university and told him they were coming, and they received VIP treatment during their visit. Both the president and dean of students implied that Trip would be welcomed as a student if he applied. Having an uncle who was a bishop, graduating from a Catholic prep school, and coming from a fourth generation family business that supplied the church with the most respected liturgical candles, all helped seal the deal.

During the campus visit, Trip tried not to let his enthusiasm show. He'd learned long ago that the more you wanted something, the less the chance Dad would let you have it. When Trip was fifteen, he wanted a pair of Jack Purcell tennis shoes so badly that he worked in the yard for a week straight to get on Joseph's good side. He also cleaned out the garage, washed the windows, detailed the car, and organized Joseph's workroom in the basement. But no matter what he did or how much he begged, Joseph wouldn't let him get the shoes.

To counter his father's perpetual reluctance, Trip used reverse psychology. He acted nonchalantly about going to college and hoped it would work to his benefit. Let it be his father's idea. Trip didn't say much during most of the campus tour. But when they walked inside the School of Architecture, only an idiot couldn't see how mesmerized Trip was by the massive studios, drafting tables, and miniature cities and building models displayed everywhere. He tried, but he couldn't hide his enthusiasm. When the student tour guide warned Trip that the workload in the school of architecture could be quite heavy and said that he'd have to get used to getting by with little sleep, Joseph turned and spoke.

"Trip, you're not cut out for this. You couldn't handle the pressure." Joseph shoved one hand in his pants pocket, the other fiddled with a model of the Louvre. He didn't bother making eye contact.

In that moment, Trip realized that regardless of how he chose to behave, his father would never allow him to go to college. During the seven-hour car ride home, Trip felt like a chemistry experiment gone awry, a lethal mixture of chemicals in a beaker about to explode. He sat in the back seat looking out the window as the world zoomed by. As the beautiful, modern buildings of D.C. flew past his window, he had to rapidly blink to keep his tears from falling. His fists clenched and unclenched on the knees of his blue jeans, and he stared at the back of his father's head as he drove, imagining punching him with all his might. *He pulled the rug right out from under me, and watched me land on my ass. Worst of all, he embarrassed and humiliated Mom and me when he told the director of admissions that I didn't need to go to college. That he had plans for me. That I would join the family business and one day become its president. I'd rather be boiled alive in a vat of beeswax.*

Trip wanted to vanish into thin air.

For days, he wouldn't leave his bedroom, let alone the house. His friends knew something was wrong with the social coordinator of the senior class. Without Trip making plans with the girls from Our Lady of Peace, they spent their weekends smoking cigarettes or watching Mannix re-runs. While his friends were celebrating their admissions acceptance letters from colleges, Trip was silent. He didn't have the courage to tell them that he wasn't going. That he would be stuck in this god-forsaken, smug suburb for god-knows how long, maybe eternity. After weeks of doing nothing because of the funk Trip was in, his friends finally asked him what was wrong. When he told them he wasn't going to college because he was *needed* in the family business, his friends were shocked. After all, Trip was the one with the brains, the one with the good grades. Trip was the one who wrote everyone's research papers, the one they went to for help with algebra, French, and history. If they were going to college, why wasn't he?

His friends understood him better than his family. He may have accepted the fact that he was stuck working for his father, but they wouldn't stand for it. They wanted to send a message to Mr. V.— loud and clear.

So they did.

On a Sunday morning in the spring of Trip's senior year, Mary Ann woke to an amazing sight. When she looked out the window, she thought it had snowed. Their house and yard had been tee-peed with three hundred rolls of double-ply Charmin Ultra. The trees were so covered with the country's most preferred toilet paper (by three to one), that it looked like it had been hit by a snowstorm. Mr. Whipple would have been proud. They didn't squeeze the Charmin, they simply tossed it high into the air over every tree branch, shrub, and roof peak of the house. Mothers throughout the parish complained that there was no toilet paper available to purchase within fifteen miles.

When my friends finally get off their asses to do something, they do it right.

Trip's mother stood in the front yard, bent over with stomach-cramping, tears-running-down-your-face laughter. She held her robe tightly around her as her shoulders shook and she wiped tears out of her eyes. It was the rare hysteria that only the most ridiculous of acts ever merit—the kind that happens too few and far between in the family. Mary Ann said she hadn't laughed like that since Carol was alive. Both Trip and Mary Ann knew that getting mad and damning those responsible for the mess would accomplish nothing. On the other hand, Joseph, as always, had a different view. He cursed those who did it and said that if he ever found out who they were, they would be cleaning his toilets for the rest of their lives. The tee-peed springtime snowfall made a great photo on the front page of the weekly *Sun Newspaper*. And since it was a slow news day, it was also the ending story on the six-o'clock news. For the first time in the life of the Von Guten Family, 2822 Devonshire Road had its thirty seconds of fame.

Trip was mistaken. His father hadn't gone to the liquor store after he dropped off Trip. He had made another stop, and it wasn't for flowers. Joseph strutted in the front door, and he *never* used the front door. In addition to making an entrance, Trip was sure his father wanted to catch the attention of his brother, Richard, across the street.

"Mare, Mare, where are you?" Joseph only called her *Mare* when he was trying to get on Mary Ann's good side or appease her.

Trip could hear his father's voice from his bedroom in the attic. Just the sound of him calling his mother by her pet name made Trip's stomach turn. As much as he didn't want to see his father any more that day, he went to see what it was all about.

Joseph was standing in the front hall, holding a white nylon garment bag with a zipper. Mary Ann came up from the basement with freshly folded laundry in her arms.

"Cikra's? What's this?"

The bag was from Cikra's Furs. The Cikra family belonged to St. Theresa's parish and owned and operated the most prestigious fur store in Ohio. A Cikra fur was a statement piece, a status symbol. Only members of old blue-blood families and the wives of newly successful Clevelanders wore Cikra furs. Mark came up behind Trip and they both stood unseen at the top of the stairs watching the show. Or more precisely, the *transaction.* And that's what it was, a cold business transaction. Mary Ann did her best to act grateful as she accepted his gift. But she had a few things to bring to his attention.

"Joseph, I don't know what to say. It's absolutely beautiful. I love it, but can we afford this? We should be sending Trip to college, and the house needs repair. Just look at the carpeting on the stairs. Thank you, but I think you should take it back."

Trip was sure his father would blow his top. Instead, he just gave her one of his looks. *The* look. The one that said, "*Don't cross me. Don't second guess me.*"

Watching his father's mouth thin and his weight shift, Trip suddenly realized how his father had come across the coat. His father hadn't paid *money* for the coat. He'd won it in a card game. There was no way Joseph would have bought a mink coat just because he loved his wife. This was a showpiece. It was his opportunity to falsely display his success to the community. To let everyone think that business was good. Mary Ann read Joseph's body language, changed her tune, and hugged him, whispering her thank-you in his ear. She set aside the laundry, put the coat on, and began to walk up the stairs to their bedroom. Joseph followed. Mark and Trip quickly and quietly ran up to Trip's room, staying out of sight.

Trip tried hard not to think about what would happen next.

Nancy Kaufman

Dear Diary,

I do not understand the curse of gambling. I understand adultery. I even understand a man drinking to forget the pain of responsibility he is born into. But gambling? Losing money on a bet? Betting that certain cards will show up in your hand? That certain other cards won't show up in the hand of another?

I don't understand why Joseph thought I would like a fur coat that belonged to another woman. Does he think I'm stupid? It certainly wasn't an act of love or kindness. We need new carpeting for our house, but instead it's hanging in my closet. Why do I love him?

That's a far better and more important question with a far more important answer.

Mary Ann

chapter

SEVEN

1975

"Family love is messy, clinging, and of an annoying and repetitive pattern, like bad wallpaper."
Friedrich Nietzsche

Mary Ann was caught off guard by Trip's letter. He'd been good about writing to her from Canada, but she had come to accept the fact that he was gone. She prepared herself for the worst—that he'd never return, just as Suze hadn't. In his letter, he asked her not to tell anyone he was coming home, especially his father. But he didn't say why. *Is he afraid of his father's reaction? Or does he want to surprise him?* Trip said he'd be home for the Fourth of July. The irony of her draft-dodger son coming home on the most patriotic day of the year made her head spin.

For weeks Mary Ann had been looking for a reason to have a party, an excuse to do something special for her family. Now she had it. Trip's homecoming was worth celebrating, at least to her. She wanted to do more than have another Von Guten backyard cookout, but her creative juices weren't flowing.

After reading Trip's letter, she picked up the phone.

Please answer. I hope you're not saying Mass. Don, answer the phone.

"Hi, Mary Ann, how are you? I've been meaning to call, but I've been..."

"That's okay, I'm just glad you answered." Mary Ann cut him off. "Trip's coming home and he asked me not to tell anyone, but I figured I could tell you."

"Don't worry, my lips are sealed. Your secret is safe with me, as always."

"Don, I know it's not a reason to celebrate, a draft dodger sneaking home, but I want to do something. Not just for him, but for the family. Do you have any suggestions? I don't want to just have another a cookout?"

"I don't know why not, your cookouts are legendary. But why don't you go somewhere? Take a vacation? When was the last time, if ever, you went away with the kids? You could go to the beach, Cedar Point or Geneva-on-the-Lake. Anywhere on Lake Erie would be fun, and the kids would love it."

"I knew you'd have an answer. I'll call you later and let you know what I come up with. Love you!"

She wanted to tell Patrick that Trip was coming home, but she didn't know if he could keep another secret. Patrick was eight years old when Trip left, and a day didn't go by without him asking when Trip would be home. Patrick and Mary Ann were the last family members to see Trip. Reluctantly, Mary Ann drove Trip to the entrance ramp of Interstate 90. She knew that if she didn't, he'd find a way there anyway. The less hitchhiking he had to do to get to Canada, the better. Since she couldn't leave Patrick home alone that afternoon, she brought him along for the ride. Mary Ann made Patrick promise not to tell anyone that they drove Trip to the highway. "It will be our little secret," she'd said, clutching his small hand in hers and promising ice cream on the ride home.

Before Trip got out of the car that day, he gave Patrick his rabbit's foot. "Hold onto this for me, little buddy. Rub it when you think of me, and it will bring you good luck," Trip told Patrick as he ruffled his curls and lightly chucked him on the chin.

On the way home from the interstate, Patrick said, "Mom, I wish we were rich. You know why?" She couldn't answer because of the lump in her throat. "Because if we were, we could buy Trip a car, and he wouldn't have to hitchhike." Her heart stung like nail polish remover on an open wound.

First on the list of things to do: 'pillow talk' with Joseph. But she needed him to go to bed at the same time she did, and sleep in the same bed. For the past three months, Joseph had been sleeping on the couch, claiming he fell asleep watching the news. Or he'd be out late playing cards, and on those nights she wasn't sure if he slept at all.

Luck was on her side. Joseph caught a cold and wanted to go to bed early. This was her chance. Mary Ann set up the vaporizer, pulled down the shades, and brought him a glass of water and a dose of Nyquil. "We need to go on a family vacation," she said as she rubbed Vicks vapor rub on his chest.

"You know how I hate it when you say 'I need,' or 'we need.' *I need this. I need that. The kids need these. We need whatever.*" He tried to imitate her using a high-pitched, whiny voice. "When is enough ever enough for you?" he asked, pushing her hands from his chest and pulling up the covers.

"Joseph Von Guten, that's not true. I'm hardly materialistic. And I rarely say we need something that isn't a necessity. Sometimes I think you have no idea what it takes to raise a family. Do you realize that we've never taken the kids on a family vacation?"

"Wait a minute. What about all those trips to Cape Cod?" Joseph asked.

"Those weren't family vacations. First of all, you rarely came with us, and if you did show up, you flew there by yourself and only stayed for a weekend. I drove thirteen hours by myself with the kids. Second, my mother rented those houses, not us. It didn't cost you a dime. And third, we weren't all there at the same time. It wasn't a family vacation. I took some of the kids up there to visit my mother. She intended to create vacations for us, but you wouldn't set aside the time. So I'm planning a trip, whether you like it or not."

"And where do you plan on going? Disneyland? Did someone die and leave you a fortune?"

Joseph coughed without covering his mouth. Then he sneezed. Mary Ann was sure she'd catch his cold as his mucous landed on her cheek. She turned away from him in disgust and briefly wondered if he had been raised in a barn or orphanage. But she knew better. Joseph's mother was polished and polite and expected nothing less than perfect etiquette from her sons. From the stories Mary Ann heard, they were raised in a house with rules and routines similar to the Von Trapp family, but with a father *and* a mother. They even had a nanny who made them matching outfits. Instead of blowing a whistle to call the boys when it was time to do homework, chores, or come to dinner, Mr. Von Guten would ring a bell. The only difference was the Von Gutens couldn't sing—Joseph had the voice of a rusted steam engine. However, they were the greatest dancers in the parish. All the girls in high school would stand at a dance with their fingers crossed, hoping that one of the Von Guten brothers would ask them to dance. Caroline, Joseph's mother, made sure they could waltz, swing, fox trot, tango, shag, boogie-woogie and jitterbug like no one else.

"I'm going to rent a cottage at Geneva-on-the-Lake. It's not a long drive, and we can take food and eat our meals at the cottage. Patty Snider's family owns cottages on the lake and I'm going to call her to see if she has one available. And you're coming. So make sure you're available. I'm thinking we'll go for the Fourth of July." Mary Ann sat back down on the edge of the bed and pulled down the comforter to spread another glob of Vick's on Joseph's chest. She knew that physical contact would make Joseph more compliant.

The older Mary Ann got, the more confident she was becoming and the less intimidated. Normally, Joseph wouldn't want to continue the conversation, especially if he felt lousy, but maybe Mary Ann's confidence made him a bit more aggressive in response.

"I feel like there's a conspiracy against me. Have you been talking to my brothers?"

"No, why do you ask?"

"I'm not sure I believe you. This is too coincidental. Today, they took me out for lunch and told me that they were worried about you. That they hadn't seen you, or us for that matter, in a long time. They said people have been talking about how depressed you've been since Mary Margaret died. And that our kids are always sleeping at friends' houses. Did you know there was a mandatory parent meeting for the basketball team last week? Peter said no one could believe we didn't show up, especially since Mark is the team captain," Joseph said.

"Really? People are talking about me? About us? We need to do something!" Mary Ann's voice was filled with panic. She stopped rubbing Joseph's chest and stood up, her Vicks-covered hand flying to her cheek.

"No, *you* need to do something," Joseph said, leaning up on his elbows. "I work every day to pay the bills. You take care of the kids. That's your job. If you want to plan a trip, it's fine with me as long as it's not expensive. Now, I'm going to get some sleep."

Joseph rolled over and closed his eyes. Within minutes, his body twitched then quickly jerked; it was a sure sign that he had fallen asleep. She used to joke with Carol about how it always seemed like he was being electrocuted in the moments before he fell asleep, like a prisoner being executed.

Why is it so easy for men to fall asleep, even when something is bothering them? I wish I could turn my brain off like that and fall asleep whenever I wanted.

Mary Ann went to the bathroom to wash her hands and face before quietly climbing under the covers and switching off the bedside lamp. She forced her eyes closed, but even though she tried to sleep, she lay in bed for hours. She wanted to toss and turn, but she didn't want to wake up Joseph. He was snoring particularly loudly because of his cold and had snatched up the entire comforter. Mary Ann didn't mind as her head was spinning with the imaginary conversations she was sure women in the parish were having about her. She could easily imagine what they were saying about her.

If they only knew what I've been through; if they could walk in my shoes for a day, they'd be sympathetic. Burying a daughter, having another run away, and aiding a draft-dodging son is enough to make anyone crazy or depressed. Still, it's not very Christian of them to talk behind my back. But, who am I to judge?

The kids couldn't believe it when Mary Ann told them they were taking a vacation.

"A real vacation? Out of town?" asked Patrick.

"Well, sort of. We're going to Geneva-on-the-Lake. It's only a two-hour drive and we're renting a cottage," Mary Ann explained.

"Why can't we stay at a hotel? I've never been to a hotel," Tricia said.

"Because there are too many of us. The cottage sleeps ten people, so ML and Stan can come up and…stay for the weekend, too." Mary Ann almost let the cat out of the bag and said ML and Stan were bringing Trip. ML promised to keep her secret and wait for Trip to come home.

"Can I bring a friend? Please, Mom? Can Francis come with us? You said it sleeps ten, so there's enough room for him. It will be so boring for me without a friend. I'm not hanging out with Tricia and Patrick," Mark said.

She couldn't tell Mark there wasn't room for Francis because Trip would be there. *One of the boys will have to sleep on the sofa bed.* And she couldn't say no because Francis's parents took Mark with them on their trip to Geneva-on-the-Lake last summer before that damn drunk driver killed them. Now that Francis lived with his older brother Kevin, who was married to ML's best friend Angela, Mary Ann felt she should include him. "If it's okay with your father, it's fine with me."

Mark, Frances, and Tricia helped Mary Ann pack the car Friday morning. Most husbands would have loaded the car but not Joseph. He didn't want to have anything to do with this vacation. He agreed to go, but he told Mary Ann she needed to make all of the arrangements. "You make the plans. I'll do the driving and grilling," he told her. This wasn't going to be much of a vacation for her, just a change of scenery. She still had to shop for groceries, pack everyone's bags, arrange for the cottage rental, put gas in the car, and cook. She was beginning to wonder if it was worth it all.

The cottage was nicer than Mary Ann had imagined. But then again, she didn't expect much. She imagined that the hardwood floors had once been beautiful, but time and sand had worn them down and any luster they once had was long faded. As the family unloaded the car and carried bag after bag of food and clothing across the kitchen floor, the sand scrunched under their shoes.

The kitchen wasn't fancy, but it was more than sufficient for a lake cottage. The living room had a wall of shelves scattered with random paperbacks that previous renters had read and left as gifts for those who came after them. There were no great works of literature, like *To Kill a Mockingbird* or *The Grapes of Wrath,* just beach reading—romance novels, murder mysteries, and a few fantasy books. Mary Ann made a mental note to take a closer look later to see if she could find something worth reading. The large bay window in the living room looked out over the lake. The beach was narrow because of erosion, but there was ample room to set up lounge chairs, and plenty of room for skipping stones, building bonfires, and roasting marshmallows.

"Mom, which room should I put my stuff in?" Tricia shouted from the second floor.

"I call the room with the big bed," Mark shouted back.

"Mark, your father and I will take that room. You, Patrick, and Francis can stay in the room with the bunk beds. Tricia, you're in the room that looks like a porch. It's called a sleeping porch," Mary Ann answered.

"But, Mom, there aren't any curtains. I won't be able to sleep in."

"Sorry, honey. There's nothing I can do about that. Keep your head under the sheets."

They should be here by now.

Trip's letter said he would be home by four this afternoon if the bus from Detroit were on time. ML and Stan planned to leave work early to meet him and drive to the cottage.

What's taking them so long?

Early that morning, Mary Ann prepared everything for dinner so she wouldn't be stuck in the kitchen when they arrived. She tried to pass the time by looking for an interesting book on the living room bookshelf, but it was like waiting for a caterpillar to turn into a butterfly. It was nearly seven o'clock. She stared at the books, but the titles weren't registering. All she could think about was Trip.

How will Joseph react? Will he be mad at me for not telling him? Will he be angry at Trip for dodging the draft? Or will he be happy to see him?

Joseph was making drinks at the makeshift bar in the living room when the car pulled into the driveway. Mary Ann turned around quickly when she heard the gravel crunching under the tires, just as Joseph handed her a drink. "Cheers," he said.

"Cheers!" They clinked their glasses together. "To family. To a family vacation." Her hands fluttered around, and she began straightening the seashells on the coffee table. She was as nervous as a whore in the Sistine Chapel. "Why don't you go outside and see if they need help with their suitcases?" she asked Joseph.

"They're only staying for the weekend. How many bags can they have?" Joseph asked.

Mary Ann couldn't bear waiting any longer, but she didn't want to be the first to see Trip. She walked into the kitchen so Joseph could be alone with Trip when he walked in.

From the kitchen, she heard the screen door creak open, but no footsteps. "Mary Ann, come look at this. Tricia and Patrick are beating Mark and Francis." Joseph was looking out the window at the kids playing badminton, a drink in his hand and his back to the door.

"Ahem, ummm." Even though she was in the kitchen, Mary Ann knew it was Trip. Mothers have the unique ability to recognize the sound of their children's coughs, sneezes, and throat clearings.

"Jesus Christ," Joseph mumbled. "You son-of-a-gun."

Mary Ann walked into the living room as Joseph held out his hand to shake Trip's. But Trip was having none of that; instead he took one step closer and put his arms around his father. They held each other for a few moments until Trip saw Mary Ann over Joseph's shoulder.

"Mother."

Mary Ann ran into his arms. She couldn't talk. She knew if she tried it wouldn't sound like English. She just rocked back and forth and held on to Trip for dear life, tears dribbling down her cheeks.

"Let me look at you! Your hair is so long." She didn't know what else to say. He looked different. His hair was down to his shoulders, and he had a mustache and short, uneven beard. He looked like a hippie from an anti-war rally.

"Do you like it?" he asked.

"Not really. Are you going to keep it?" She ran her fingers through the tips of his hair and over the scruff of his beard.

"No, I let it grow because I didn't want to pay for a haircut. Don't worry, Mother. I'll get it cut tomorrow, and I'll shave this off," he stroked his face.

"Is this why you wanted to take a vacation?" Joseph asked, turning back to Mary Ann.

Mary Ann and Joseph made eye contact and both could see that the other had been crying tears of joy. Instead of answering, Mary Ann laughed and gave Trip another hug.

ঌ৺

After dinner, Mark and Francis wanted to go to the strip. Francis's family had been to Geneva-on-the-Lake several times, and he knew his way around the town. "Mrs. V, they have the best donuts at *Jimmy's* on the strip. If you like, we can bring some home for breakfast," Francis said. He was a lot like Eddie Haskell, truth be told. Mark knew his mother would fall for it. Donuts for breakfast would mean one less meal to cook, one less mess to clean.

"You can go if you take Tricia and Patrick with you. And you have to be back by ten-thirty," Joseph said.

"Ahh, come on Dad, not Patrick. Tricia can come, but I'm not babysitting Patrick."

"I'll take Patrick to get ice cream and for a spin around the go-cart track, and the three of you can go off on your own," Trip said.

"Yessssss, let's go," Patrick said, already scrambling to put on his blue-and-white sneakers.

"Dad, can we stay out later? It's already nine o'clock," Mark asked.

"Okay, but only because I'm in a good mood. Just don't get into any trouble, and keep an eye on Tricia."

The strip was as lively as an amusement park on a summer Saturday afternoon. Cars cruised Main Street back and forth and back again. The main drag was only about a third of a mile long with unofficial turnarounds at both ends of the strip. From eight until midnight, there was a constant parade of cars, bumper to bumper in both directions, being driven by local teenagers and summer visitors. Every five minutes, the same cars would cruise by, hoping the scene had changed since the last lap. Like in the movies from the 50's, they'd drive back and forth looking for a familiar face or a piece of action. The sidewalks on both sides of the street were crowded with loiterers and kids smoking cigarettes mixed in with clean-cut tourists from the suburbs. Mark and Francis walked ahead of Tricia, but told her not to get too far behind. Mark didn't want his little sister tagging along, but he didn't have a choice.

Several bikers on Harley Davidson's rode by slowly; they were so loud that Mark couldn't hear what Tricia was saying.

"I said, I want to turn around and go back to the candy store we passed," Tricia shouted.

"No way. We're not getting candy," Mark shouted back.

"But I saw some girls I know from cheerleading camp. Maybe I can hang out with them while you go to the arcade." Tricia planted her feet and put her hands on her hips.

That was music to Mark's ears. They quickly turned around and walked Tricia to meet her friends. They watched through the window as Tricia waved, indicating she could hang with them until they were to meet at the car.

Mark and Francis made their way down the strip, hands in their pockets, sauntering down the sidewalks like townies. Francis was afraid their polo shirts and short haircuts made them stand out—they looked too clean-cut. He didn't want to be seen as just another tourist. "Let's get some beer," he said.

"Are you crazy? My father would kill me. And he'd call your brother, too," Mark said.

"How will he find out? He's half in the bag as it is. He'll probably be passed out by the time we get back, and your mother is clueless."

Mark grimaced at Francis's taunts, but he knew he was right. Still, he didn't want to drink. "There's no way we can buy beer. I don't have a fake ID, do you?"

"No, but I bet Trip will buy some for us. He seems like a cool dude. Let's go find him and ask."

"I don't think that's a good idea. Maybe he will, but if he doesn't he might tell my parents that I asked. I'm not taking a chance."

"Jesus, Mark, you're such a wuss. No one comes up to Geneva-on-the-Lake and hangs without drinking. I should have brought some from home and hid it in my suitcase."

They continued walking the strip in silence. Francis spotted some kids he knew on the other side of the street.

"Wait here. I'll be right back." He ran across the street, weaving between the cars until he reached the group of boys.

Mark stood awkwardly by himself, shifting from foot to foot and running his fingers through his hair. He watched as Francis talked with the boys. He must have known them from his previous trips there. They all turned to look at Mark from across the street. He turned to look into the hardware store behind him, as if he was interested in something in the window.

Shit, they're talking about me. He's probably telling them I don't want to drink. Damn him.

Mark jumped as Francis sneaked up on him and slapped his back a little harder than what would be considered friendly. "Mission accomplished. We don't need to ask Trip after all." Francis opened his jacket to reveal a six-pack of beer. *Psshht.* He popped one open, spraying himself with foam, and handed it to Mark. *Psshht…gulp, gulp, gulp…*Francis chugged half of a beer before Mark had a chance to take a sip. "Drink up, buddy, or I'll have to drink all of these by myself. Which is fine with me, by the way."

Mark reluctantly took a sip and was surprised by how good it tasted and how refreshing it was on the hot summer night. Two blocks later Mark had finished his beer, and Francis was on his third. There were only two left, one in each of Francis's windbreaker's pockets. Francis didn't bother to offer another one to Mark, nor did Mark ask for one. Either Francis wanted them for himself, or he knew Mark didn't want more. *I hope Mom doesn't smell beer on him.*

Francis had a nice buzz going and was ready to take on the arcade. They made their way to Woody's, the newer of the two arcades on the strip. Newer or not, it smelled of cigarette smoke and spilled beer, made worse by the summer heat. *Ping. Ping. Pang. Clank. Clank. Ping.* The bells, music, sound effects, and lights of the pinball machines were as entertaining as the games themselves. Red-eyed teenagers—mostly locals with nimble thumbs and fingers—played the machines as if they were concert pianists, onlookers mesmerized by the performance. The summer tourists, largely on vacation from Pittsburgh, favored the Skee-Ball machines, which spit out tickets like water from a hose. The highly prized tickets were turned in for stuffed animals, pocketknives, plates, and a variety of other knick-knacks for players to take home and show off to friends who didn't have the luxury of leaving the Iron City suburbs. The locals had won almost every prize imaginable and were more interested in getting the highest score in pinball than collecting tickets from the game preferred by the summer cone-lickers.

With these two factions—locals and tourists, ruralites and suburbanites—engaging in such a small place, the potential for rowdiness, mayhem, and confrontations was high. There were rough, macho bikers on Harleys; non-rebel middle-class bikers on Hondas and Kawasakis; grungy and drunk young locals; and somewhat preppy and clean-cut visitors. While their differences alone were enough to spark fights, it rarely came down to that. The groups kept to themselves, because at Geneva-on-the-Lake they all had the same intention: to have a good time.

Mark and Francis were well on their way to their second hundred tickets when they saw Trip and Patrick across the arcade. Patrick was pulling Trip by his arm, weaving in and out of the crowds looking for the ticket machines. Trip looked exhausted. Francis was in the middle of a Skee-Ball winning streak, even after finishing five beers within an hour.

"Hey hipster Tripster! Oveeeer here!" Francis slurred loudly across the arcade.

Mark left Francis and quickly walked over to give Patrick two-dozen tickets. "Get yourself a prize, and let Trip take you back to the cottage," he said to Patrick. "Or, better yet, hold onto the tickets until tomorrow, and we'll come back and win some more. The more tickets you have, the bigger the prize you can get." Patrick thanked Mark for the suggestion.

"Is he okay?" Trip asked Mark, motioning over to Francis. "It looks like he's having a little too much fun. Mark, don't get in trouble."

"I told him we shouldn't drink, but the next thing I knew he got a six-pack from some guys and was chugging it," Mark explained. "Don't worry, it's gone, and I'm driving. Please don't tell Mom or Dad."

"I won't. Just come home soon."

"Oh, gross!" a tourist nearby Francis shouted. Trip and Mark looked over to see Francis throwing up all over the Skee-Ball machine.

"What's the matter with Francis?" Patrick asked.

"Oh, shit," Mark said. "Trip, will you pick up Tricia at the candy store and drive her home? I'll get him cleaned up and bring him back soon."

"Are you sure you can handle him?" Trip asked.

"Yeah, just get Tricia for me. We'll meet you back at the cottage."

The screen door slamming over and over again woke Mark from a deep sleep. He later learned that Patrick had been running in and out of the house to tell his mother about all the games and toys he had found in the garage. First, he found a net to throw baseballs against that bounced the balls back to you. Then he found a box of roller skates. The next time he ran into the kitchen, it was to tell his mother about the golf clubs, tennis rackets, and inner tubes for swimming. And finally, he had found lawn darts, a bow with arrows, and a croquet set.

"Francis, get up. Let's go for a run," Mark tried to wake him, forgetting that he might not be in any shape to run. Moments later, Francis finally sat up in bed and hit his head on the bunk above him.

"Crap! Are you crazy? I thought this was a vacation, not boot camp. Oh fuck, my head." He moaned as he slowly lowered his head back down onto the pillow.

"We need to get in shape for basketball, so let's go for a run. Coach said we need to stay in shape. Or in your case, get back in shape."

Francis had torn his ACL at the end of the last season and had to have surgery to repair it. He had two pins in his knee and an eight-inch-long scar that looked like it belonged on Frankenstein's forehead. He was supposed to go to physical therapy twice a week and do exercises on his own, but Francis was stubborn and lazy. Of course, he was also a natural athlete who could easily score twenty points a game without a problem. Mark, on the other hand, had to work hard to stand out, to stay in shape, and to make the team.

"I'm sleeping in, go without me. Maybe we can find a pick-up game later at the park." Francis turned over and went back to sleep.

Mark had already laced his shoes and slipped into shorts, so he decided to run alone. He knew that he couldn't go without training. Unlike Francis, Mark didn't have natural speed or endurance. He resented the fact that Francis didn't work to be a good athlete. He slammed the bedroom door as he left the room.

"Where are you going so early?" Mary Ann asked as she sipped a mug of coffee at the kitchen table.

"I'm going for a run. Francis wants to sleep in," Mark replied.

"Do you know your way around?"

"Mom, don't worry. It's a straight shot from here to the strip. I'll be back in an hour."

"ML went to get donuts since you forgot to last night, so you might see her along the way. Be careful," Mary Ann shouted, but Mark was out the door before she was finished talking to him.

He stretched his leg muscles in the driveway, wearing his basketball socks, Converse high-tops, and satin-like basketball shorts leftover from last year's uniform. Players were required to turn in their uniforms at the end of the season or get billed for them along with tuition. But Fr. Gellin favored Mark and told him he could keep the uniform without charge since they were getting new ones next season. Gellin wasn't just Mark's coach but also a friend of the family. Gellin had been a classmate of Uncle Don's in the seminary and had been to the Von Guten's for dinner many times. Whenever Don had dinner at his sisters', Mary Ann encouraged him to bring a friend from the priesthood for a home-cooked meal. If they didn't know the Von Guten's through Bishop Don, they knew of them because of Divine Candles. It was awkward for Mark to be the coach's favorite, but he'd do whatever it would take to be on the team as a starter. Gellin was also Mark's Chemistry teacher and high school advisor, and it was known by all that Mark was his favorite student. Mark often stayed after school to help Fr. Gellin set up lab experiments for the following day.

Downtown, such as it was, was closer than he thought. Either that or he was running exceptionally fast this morning. Within twenty minutes he was at the strip, running down the now-empty sidewalks. Geneva-on-the-Lake was a ghost town compared to the crowds ten hours ago. The only signs of life were in front of Jimmy's Donuts. As Mark ran by, he could taste the sweetness of the donuts. The smell of cinnamon and fresh dough seeped out of the exhaust vent and onto the strip, pulling customers into the store like a magnet. Mark ran by and saw ML bent over and talking with Jimmy, who was in a wheelchair with a beer in his hand. Everyone who visited Geneva-on-the-Lake knew Jimmy, and if they were new to the town, he made a point of introducing himself. Jimmy slept during the day and worked nights making donuts. When most people were drinking coffee, Jimmy was having his after-work beer. ML didn't see Mark run by because she was focused on her conversation with the town's donut maker. For a second, Mark thought about turning back and riding home with her, but his endorphins had kicked in and he was enjoying the rush.

He ran another ten minutes and turned around at the pier to head back to the cottage. When he passed through the strip again, the donut shop crowd had diminished, and only a few cars remained in the lot across the street. ML's car was still in the lot. *Maybe I'll ride home with her after all.* He started to run toward her car and saw that she was standing intimately close to someone next to the car, giggling and tossing her hair while arms suddenly wrapped around her and she was engaged in a kiss. Stan had been swimming in the lake when Mark left the cottage. *Who does she know from around here?* Mark stopped suddenly, panting, trying to catch his breath. He couldn't believe what he was seeing. *No, that can't be her. Shit, it is.* He was stunned. He doubled over, gasped for air and held onto his stomach to catch his breath.

ML didn't notice Mark as he ran off the strip and behind the stores, cutting back to the main road that led to the cottage about two blocks down. It took him less than ten minutes to get back to the cottage, half the time it took him to run to the strip.

At the end of the gravel driveway, he stopped, plopped down onto the grass, and laughed at himself. He didn't know he could run so fast. While he was sitting there trying to catch his breath, ML pulled into the driveway and rolled down her window.

"I have donuts," she said.

"Yeah, I know," he said warily.

❧

The old-fashioned percolator gurgled and filled the kitchen with the aroma of a diner. But Trip needed something stronger than coffee.

"Mom, how do you put up with him? He's like Dr. Jekyll and Mr. Hyde," Trip said.

"What are you talking about?" Mary Ann asked.

"Dad is what I'm talking about. Last night he was happy to see me. He even gave me a hug and told me he loved me. That was a first. And today it's the same old crap. I went to bed thinking maybe he changed while I was away, but I guess I was wrong. It must have been the liquor talking."

"Trip, don't talk like that. What happened? What did he say to you?"

"I wasn't awake for more than ten minutes when he started with me. *De Fuhrer* wants me to get my haircut and shave before lunch. No ifs, ands, or buts about it. Just do it. Then he laid into me about going to work at Divine as soon as we get home."

"He's just happy you're home. He doesn't want you sitting around without a job. And you even said last night that you were going to get your haircut," Mary Ann said.

"It's not what he says; it's how he says it. It's never a conversation. It's always one-sided—his side. Does he really think I'm so lazy that I don't plan to work? And, the tone of his voice… he's always angry when he talks to me. But when he talks to Tricia or Patrick, he's all sweet and nice."

"Trip, he's not angry with you. Because you're older, he expects more from you than he does from Tricia and Patrick. He wants the best for you. He wants you to work with him and someday take over the company," Mary Ann replied.

"But what if I don't want to work at Divine? It's never about what I want; it's always about what he wants."

"Trip, what do you want? What do you want to do with your life?" Mary Ann asked.

"Never mind, it doesn't matter anyway." Trip poured his untouched coffee into the sink and grabbed the keys to his father's car. "I'm going into town to find a barber shop. Snip away any residue of me being a draft dodger, let it land on the floor, sweep it into a dust pan, and toss it away so it can be forgotten."

"There's one next to the donut shop," Mark said. He had been sitting at the kitchen table reading the sports page while he listened to Trip and Mary Ann.

Trip kissed his mother on the cheek. "I love you, Mom. You're a saint."

The phone rang, startling Mark.

"Mark, my hands are wet. Answer that, please. I don't know who it could be. Probably someone looking for the cottage owner. Just tell them we're renters," his mother said.

"Hello? Hey, Uncle Don. Are you coming to Geneva? Yes, she's right here. Hold on," Mark said.

The phone cord had obviously been stretched too many times across the room as it hung in one big clump just off the receiver. Mark untangled the pea green cord as much as he could and walked the phone over to his mother.

"Hi. How'd you get this number?" Mary Ann asked Don. "I don't even know the number."

Mark watched his mother closely as her body language morphed. She slowly walked slowly across the room and sat down next to Mark. Her elbows were on the table, and one hand held up her head while the other held the phone.

"Oh my God, Don, no! Please tell me this is a joke. Oh, God, no. This can't be happening. I just saw her two days ago…she was fine."

"Mom, what's wrong? What happened?" Mark asked his mother, but she didn't answer. She couldn't look up at Mark. She just sat there and sobbed on the phone with Don. Mark got up from the table and went to find his father.

"Dad? Dad?" Mark called up the stairs.

"What? If you want to talk to me, come upstairs. I'm getting dressed," Joseph yelled back.

"Dad, something's wrong. Mom's on the phone with Uncle Don and she's crying."

Within seconds, Joseph was in the kitchen with Mary Ann. She couldn't talk. She just handed the phone to Joseph.

"Don, what's wrong?" Joseph asked. "Jesus, when?" After a few seconds of listening to Don on the other end of the line, Joseph said, "We'll be home as soon as we can. Do you want Trip to pick you up at the airport? Yes, you can stay with us. We'll see you later. Bye."

Mark took the phone from his father and hung it up. "Dad, what happened?" Mark asked.

"Nana died. We need to go home." Joseph held Mary Ann in his arms as she broke down.

❦

Dear Diary,

I don't know how much more bad news I can handle. I'm trying to hold myself together as best as I can, but my world is falling apart. Not only have I lost my mother, who was my soul mate and only source of real support, but today I also received some news that has made me sick to my stomach. News that I can't talk about with anyone, not even Don or another priest in confidence.

For years, something about Gloria Mooney bothered me, but I couldn't put my finger on it. I used to feel sorry for her and pray for her since she lived in such a pathetic house with an abusive and rarely employed husband. But today it became clear to me why she and her son Kevin have had a weird obsession with my family. A year ago, Gloria and her husband were killed in a horrible car crash. Gloria's sister recently sorted through her personal items and found an old letter addressed to me and marked with instructions to deliver to me only upon her death.

As I'm writing this, I'm wondering if what Gloria wrote is true, but then again why would she lie about this? She never asked us for money or help.

Gloria's letter said that when Don was a young priest, he was her spiritual advisor, and he often went to her house to help her with odd jobs since her husband was never around or sober. She claims they had a brief dalliance, and that Don is Kevin's father. She also said that no one else knows this, including Don and Kevin. She was well aware that Kevin was jealous of our family as a young boy, and as he grew older and after he became a detective, he became vindictive toward us. And to make matters worse, he married ML's best friend Angela. At the end of Gloria's letter, she asked me to burn it after reading, which I would have done even if she didn't ask.

Ashes to ashes, dust to dust.

Dear Lord, my troubled heart has driven me to you, my protector in time of need. You know all my failings, faults, and sins, as well as the torment gripping my soul. Help me, O Lord, to find the strength to carry this cross, for alone I can do nothing.

Mary Ann

chapter

EIGHT

"Anyone who thinks sitting in church can make you a Christian must also think that sitting in a garage can make you a car."
Garrison Keillor

Mary Ann hesitated before she opened the jewelry box. The powder blue leather box was trimmed with a gold-leaf scroll around the perimeter and topped with a brass plaque monogrammed MVA, Mary Ann's initials. She remembered clearly the moment her mother gave it to her on the eve of her wedding years ago. *"It's not much, but it's something new and something blue. Look inside and you might find something old."* Mary Ann could hear her voice as if she were standing next to her today. Inside the box she found a strand of pearls. They were her grandmother's pearls that had been passed down for generations. They were Catherine's most valuable possession, and she gave them to Mary Ann on her wedding day. She knew her mother didn't have much, especially in the way of valuable jewelry. She never had a wedding ring. Mary

Ann's father promised Catherine one, but she never received it. Then he disappeared when Mary Ann was two, and they never heard from him again.

She lifted the lid of the box and there they were, Catherine's pearls. She slowly caressed them with the pads of her fingertips and thought of her mother. Her best friend. Her safe harbor. Her Rock of Gibraltar. Tears ran down her face, and dropped onto the jewelry box mirror, blurring her reflection. *Don't cry,* her mother would have told her. *I'm with Mary Margaret, and we're having a pajama party.* Catherine always had at least one grandchild sleep over on Friday nights, and they would have parties in their pajamas. They would build forts with blankets and seat cushions, eat coffee ice cream out of fine china bowls with sterling silver spoons, and dance to the sounds of Tommy Dorsey on the phonograph.

Sobbing, Mary Ann clasped the pearls around her milky white neck and looked in the mirror as she held them up to her lips. *Mother, I'm sorry. Last night I broke down, sobbed, and even cursed God. I was crying for Mary Margaret, not for you. I had blocked out anything about her funeral, but with your death it's all coming back to me. My first death...They say that there's no death like the first death. I was in shock when Mary Margaret died and wasn't able to grieve. Now, I mourn for her more than you. It's not right.*

❧

Mark kept a close eye on his mother. He knew how close she was with Nana and how devastated she was. At the funeral home the night before, Mary Ann lost control of her emotions. As the funeral home began to close the casket, Mary Ann threw herself toward Nana and shouted, "Don't take her from me! You can't take her. Mom, don't leave me. Please don't leave me!"

Mark was afraid she'd do it again during the funeral Mass.

The church was standing room only, which was quite a tribute to Catherine, and to Mary Ann and Don as well. Even Earl the milkman was there. He knew Catherine from his weekly deliveries to the Von Gutens. She was always there helping Mary Ann, and went out of her way to ask Earl about his ailing wife and his son at Princeton. Bishop Snider of Cleveland met the family, pallbearers, and the casket in the church vestibule where he began his prayers in Latin. An altar boy handed him a silver aspergilium filled with holy water. The Bishop shook it over the casket, sprinkling it to call to mind the deceased's baptism.

"When we were baptized into Christ Jesus, we were baptized into his death. We were buried with him by baptism into death, so that as Christ was raised from the dead by the glory of the Father, we too might live a new life. For if we have been united with him in a death like his, we shall certainly be united with him in a resurrection like his," the bishop recited.

As Bishop Snider led the procession up the aisle to the altar, Mark was shocked to see the number of priests there to assist. St. Theresa's rarely had the honor of the Bishop of Cleveland officiating Mass, but today there were two bishops and six prominent priests from the Cleveland Diocese. Fr. Burns came down from the altar and ceremonially put a vestment on his old friend, Bishop Don. An altar boy handed Don a thurible, a brass censer with smoke rising from it, emitting the strong smell of burning incense. It's a scent that Mark despised – a deep, dense aroma, thick with spirituality. It seeps into your lungs, almost causing a high or hypnotic feeling of sadness. You can taste death as the incense permeates your senses.

The congregation finished the third verse of "Joyful, Joyful, We Adore You" when Don walked slowly around the casket, mumbling prayers in Latin. He blessed the casket and the soul of his mother with the thurible by swinging it like a pendulum, releasing more and more of the entrancing smoke. He swung it vertically twice and a third time horizontally, making the sign of the cross. The three swings symbolized the Holy Trinity: the Father, the Son, and the Holy Spirit.

Patrick impatiently tugged at Joseph's sleeve. "Dad, what is Uncle Don doing, and why does it smell so bad?" he whispered.

Joseph ignored Patrick without giving him an answer, most likely because he didn't know the real meaning behind the ritual.

Mark bent over and whispered in Patrick's ear, "He's honoring Nana and showing her respect. The smoke represents her soul going up to heaven."

While the family stood around the casket waiting for Don to finish his prayers, Mark began to waver and was about to fall. And he might have if Trip hadn't grabbed him and helped him into the pew.

"Are you okay?" Trip asked.

"I didn't eat breakfast, and the incense is making me nauseous."

"Here, have a lifesaver. It will make you feel better."

During the funeral, Mark sat without participating. He didn't rise when the congregation stood to pray, and he didn't kneel when they showed reverence and humility. Even though it was cool in the church, he began to sweat profusely. Trip handed him two more lifesavers.

I have to get out of here.

Mark's heart was pounding so hard he thought it was going to burst from his chest. He looked all around him trying to figure out an escape route. He was in the middle of the row, and there was no way out without causing a scene. Bent over with his elbows on his knees and his head in his hands, he tried to catch his breath, but his breathing remained short, quick, and shallow. He needed air.

I need to get the fuck out of here.

"Mark, what's wrong? You're sweating like a pig. Are you sick?" Tricia asked. "That damn incense."

"Shhh, don't talk like that in church," Tricia whispered.

"It's making me nauseated. I have to get out of here before I throw up," Mark whispered back.

"You can't just leave."

"Do you want me throwing up on you?" he muttered.

Tricia let Mark squeeze by her and followed him out of the pew. They were in the second row from the altar so they had to pass the entire congregation to get outside. He ran. Tricia walked. Luckily for her, by the time she got outside he had stopped throwing up.

"Fuck, I don't know what's wrong with me. I feel like I'm having a heart attack, whatever that feels like," Mark said. "Look, I'm soaking wet and my heart is racing."

"Mark, watch your mouth. We're in front of church, for Christ's sake," Tricia said.

"Oh, but it's okay to take the Lord's name in vain?"

"It's not as bad as your language. I think you're having a panic attack. Want me to get you a paper bag to breathe into?"

"I'll be fine. Do you think they'll use incense again? If they do, I can't go back in there. Damn priests."

"You're not making any sense."

"You wouldn't know. Nobody knows."

"What are you talking about?"

"Nothing. Forget it. I just wish *I* could."

"I give up. You're really beginning to scare me. You sound like you're going crazy."

"If it were only that simple."

Mark stayed in his room all day after they returned from the cemetery. Mary Ann checked on him once and was convinced he had the flu. He told her not to worry about him. "I'll be fine. I'll come downstairs later."

"I'll have ML bring you something to eat. I know how you get without food," Mary Ann said. Mark was known for his fainting spells. When he was little, Mary Ann always had candy in her purse to keep him from passing out during church. On a road trip to Cape Cod years ago, he fainted in the turnpike rest area because he didn't eat breakfast before they got on the road. And he fainted his first time as an altar boy.

"Knock, knock," ML shouted from the other side of his bedroom door.

"Come in, it's open. Can't you knock? What's with the 'knock knock'?"

ML pushed open the door with her foot. "Can't you see my hands are full? Here's a sandwich. Mom said you need to eat."

"I'm not hungry. Just leave me alone," Mark rolled over in bed, hoping she'd leave.

"Mark, what's wrong? Is something's bothering you? Talk to me."

"Why do you care?"

"Did something happen? Or, is it about Nana?"

"Yeah, it's about Nana," he snapped.

"Don't BS me. It's more than that."

"I'll keep it to myself. Thank you anyway for your *concern,*" he said.

"Hmmm, do I detect a hint of sarcasm? What are you hiding? It's not good to keep secrets."

"You should know."

ML sat at the end of his bed. "What are you talking about?"

"Nothing, leave me alone. Get out of here."

Nancy Kaufman

D*ear Diary,*

I wonder why we don't see the signs in ourselves that others see so clearly. Is it true of everything? Is it the splinter in yours that's easier to see than the log in ours? Is it the forest for the trees?

Do they think that throwing up in the morning without a reason or a fever is something that's unconnected? Why do we not recognize consequences when we see them? Eventually, I know we do. But certainly not in time to prepare us for the results of our actions. Not in time to reduce the surprise from a sledgehammer's blow to a tiny tap from a child's toy hammer. Is that what keeps us going on? Being stupid, naïve, oblivious to what surrounds us?

Sometimes I just wish I didn't know. Keep me ignorant, oh Lord. I already know too much for my own good.

Mary Ann

chapter

NINE

1977

Where secrecy or mystery begins, vice or roguery is not far off. (Unknown)

"Come on, let me pierce your ear," Missy said.

"They are pierced," Tricia replied.

"I mean a second hole."

"No, that will hurt."

"Drink a few shots and I'll hold ice on your ear, you won't feel a thing. Tommy will think it's sexy."

"I'm done with Tommy. Maybe I should say he's done with me," Tricia said. The last time Tommy and I went out..."

"You mean two-and-a-half months ago?" Missy asked. "You need to get over him."

"It seems like yesterday. Anyway, he dropped me off, went back to the party and was with Katy. He asked her to go to the

Michael Stanley Band concert at the Agora that weekend. I guess I didn't meet his expectations."

"You mean when you had your little rendezvous in *my* bed?" Missy asked.

"I can't believe I did it with him."

"You've had the biggest crush on him for a year."

"It was more than a crush to me, but now I feel like a fool. I never should have said '*I love you.*' That must have scared him away."

"Forget about him. He was absent the day God passed out brains, but he was first in line for testosterone. He's so stupid that his idea of math is counting beer bottle caps," Missy said. "Now you know why I gave you that poster that says '*Boys are Grief.*'"

Tricia and Missy sat on the Von Guten's screened-in porch. It was after school, and Tricia was surprised to come home to an empty house. Her mother was probably golfing—her new pastime.

"Just hurry up. I have to be at Carson Pontiac by four o'clock or I'll lose my job. You promise it won't hurt?" Tricia had no idea what it felt like to get her ears pierced; the family dentist had done it the first time and sedated her. Mary Ann had a low tolerance for pain, both for herself and her kids. She was completely knocked out during the births of her first six children, and she's had never had her own ears pierced.

"Calm down, you won't feel a thing," Missy assured. Trisha's ear was numb from the ice, and the room was beginning to spin from the shots. Missy sterilized the sewing needle by holding it in the flame of a candle they lit on the porch.

"Tell me when you're about to do it," Trisha insisted.

"I'm already done. Give me the earring and I'll put it in."

Trisha couldn't believe she didn't feel a thing, but then again, that's what Missy promised. "You're the best. It didn't hurt at all," Trisha said.

"What? You didn't believe me? I told you it wouldn't."

"Shit, I'm going to be late for work. Will you drop me off?"

"Only if you promise to call me later with the answers for math," Missy said.

"Carson Pontiac, Mercedes, and Toyota, how may I direct your call?" Tricia enunciated, trying not to slur her words. She had been on the switchboard, her part-time high school job, for about thirty minutes. The vodka was beginning to hit her, and her ear was throbbing while she tried to work.

"This is Officer Mooney. I'd like to speak with Mr. Carson."

"Please hold while I connect you," Tricia said. She looked fixedly at the numbers on the switchboard, but her contacts felt like they were covered with olive oil. *Shit.* She wasn't one of *those* girls who belonged to the *Wednesday Club.* She didn't need to break up the week on Wednesdays by drinking during lunch. She used to be friends with those girls, but by the time they got to high school, things had changed. Her former middle school friends had a reputation now, one that Tricia didn't want. She was in a fog, unable to find her way out of a paper bag, or push a flashing button on the switchboard. *Damn it. Why did I let Missy talk me into this?*

The lit up buttons looked like one giant light. She hit a red one, struggled and said, "Thank you for holding, here's Mr. Carson." She disconnected the call. Seconds later the buttons lit up again. She did her best to say "Carson Pontiac, Mercedes, and Toyota. How may I help you?"

"This is the Cleveland Heights Police and this is official business. You disconnected me." She recognized the voice. It was Detective Mooney, ML's best friend's husband.

"I'm sorry if I discollected you. Pleeeease hold on for Mr. Carolson." Tricia's tongue felt like a leather belt in her mouth. She was sure this would be her last day. Or maybe she'd be lucky and Mooney wouldn't tell her boss. She must have hit the right button, because he didn't call back. Tricia looked at the clock and was relieved to see that the showroom was about to close. She paged her brother Mark who worked in the service department and asked him for a ride home. He went home for dinner on Monday nights before going to a night class at the seminary. He had dropped out a while ago but was trying to get back in by taking a few classes.

On the way home, Tricia talked non-stop. She told Mark about Missy piercing her ear and that the police called twice because she hung up on them. At this point, she was laughing so hard she thought she was going to pee in her pants. "Do you believe I hung up on the police?"

Mark on the other hand didn't laugh. "What did they want? Whom did they ask for?"

"How would I know what they wanted? They asked for Mr. Carson. Why do you care?"

"I don't, I'm just curious. Did you hear Mr. Carson on the phone with him?" Mark ran his fingers through his wavy dark chocolate hair.

"No, I told you I don't know anything. Carson's office door was closed. All I know is that Detective Mooney sounded mad, probably because I hung up on him."

"Shit, it was Mooney who called?" Mark slammed his hand on the steering wheel, making the car swerve slightly.

Tricia gracefully swayed with the car. "You sound like you know why he was calling. What's going on?" Tricia asked.

"I heard someone in the parts department talking about a break-in and a bunch of tires were stolen. Mooney probably thinks I did it. For some reason he hates me, and he's out to get me. But don't repeat that. You probably will, since you're drunk."

"Oh, shut up. Since when did you become you such an angel?" Tricia snapped back, then smirked as she surfed her hand in the wind out the rolled down window.

Tricia dragged herself out of bed and crawled down the hall to the bathroom to throw up. Her ear-piercing buzz wore off late last night, and she woke feeling like someone had pumped helium into her head. She thought she was finished puking, until she got a whiff of her mother's perfume oozing through the crack under the bathroom door. The smell of Estée Lauder made her gag again, but this time nothing came up. She dry-heaved until her stomach was as tight as a washboard. The sound of her retching echoed off the tile walls of the bathroom.

"Tricia? Are you okay?" Mary Ann asked through the bathroom door. "Are you sick to your stomach?"

Sick to my stomach? Why can't she say puke or vomit? She always sugarcoats nasty things.

"I'm okay. I think the pudding I ate last night was spoiled. I feel much better now. I'll be downstairs in a minute." *I'm never drinking again. Ever.*

During study hall, she got a hall pass to go to the college counseling office. She was only a junior in high school and hadn't looked into colleges yet, but she thought about getting out of Cleveland, and the sooner the better. The college counseling office was full of information about universities, mostly Catholic ones, but it was also a source of information about exchange programs and semesters away. Tricia didn't know of anyone who had gone away for a semester, but she knew it was an option. She was bored with school, and tired of her friends drinking their way through the weekends. She was tired of her friends in general. She had gone to school with the same kids since kindergarten. After eighth-grade graduation from St. Theresa's, the boys went to Xavier and most of the girls went to Our Lady of Peace. She hadn't met anyone new in the past ten years. She lived in a bubble, with air as stale as an old man's breath, and she was dying to burst out. Tricia was a voracious reader, so she knew there was a huge world out there waiting to be explored. None of her brothers or sisters went to college, and she was determined not to follow in their footsteps. She was not going to turn down that road to hell with the cruise control on.

I'm not going to be like them and stay in this god-forsaken excuse of a town for my whole life. Each day, I see myself becoming more and more like them. What was I thinking? Drinking after school, then going to work? I'm such a loser. If that's what I'm resorting to for a 'good time,' I need to get out of here.

Ms. Gallagher, the college counselor, wasn't in her office, so Tricia browsed the shelves until she came across a section on alternative high school programs. There were only five books on the shelf, and three of them were Catholic boarding schools in California.

Perfect. Mom went to college in California and talks about how they were the best four years of her life. She'll let me go. I just have to convince Dad.

She opened a booklet titled *Villanova Preparatory School* and began reading:

"Located in the Ojai Valley, about an hour from Los Angeles. A co-ed Augustinian boarding school." *Perfect. Boys.*

"The curriculum provides students with the skills necessary for admission to any university." *Sounds better with every sentence.*

"Emphasis placed on effective communication and study skills, critical and interpretive thinking, and the ability to make rational, informed judgments." *I wish I had that ability when I was with Tommy.*

"Catholic core values are stressed…"

"Seventy-five percent of faculty consists of Augustinian priests and nuns." *Ugh, but a selling point for Mom and Dad.*

Scholarships given to honor students schooled in the Catholic tradition." *This school is meant for me!*

"Can I help you? You're Tricia, right?" Ms. Gallagher asked as she slid behind her desk and crossed her long legs.

Tricia jumped. "Oh, sorry, I didn't hear you come in. I hope you don't mind that I was looking at these."

"You're welcome to come in here anytime. My door is always open. You can come and just hang out if you'd like, even if you don't need to talk about college. Think of my room as a safe harbor. Let me know in advance if you need a hall pass, so you don't get a demerit." Ms. Gallagher was wearing a well tailored, emerald green pencil skirt and a silk button-up top. Her red curls bounced off her shoulders when she moved.

Hmmm. She's cool. Maybe I will hang out here. It can be my escape from the dimwits around here.

"Ms. Gallagher, do you know anything about boarding schools?" Tricia asked.

"Yes, what do you want to know?"

"Everything. Are they hard to get into, and do they cost a lot of money? Can you enter mid-year for the second semester?"

"It depends on the school. Do you have one in mind?"

"Not really, but what do you know about Villanova Prep in California? It sounds nice."

"Do your parents want you to go to boarding school? California is a long way from home."

"I'm not sure how they'd feel. I haven't talked to them about it, but I'm one of seven kids, so they might like the idea of lightening the load at home. I doubt they'd miss me. Since I'm the sixth out of the seven, I usually—no, I *always*—go unnoticed."

"Tricia, I doubt your parents want you to go to boarding school because you have a big family. If anything, they should want you to go for the education, discipline, and experience. It's also a great stepping-stone to college. Unlike what many people think, boarding school is not a place for troubled kids or kids whose parents don't have time for them. Some of the most successful, brightest people in the country went to boarding schools. Did you know that Jacqueline Kennedy went to boarding school? And boarding schools have great success getting students into the most prestigious colleges. It's a privilege to go to boarding school," Ms. Gallagher said.

"Don't tell that to my father. He doesn't want me to be privileged. He says that we aren't from the privileged class; we're from the working class. He wants us to work for everything we have."

"You can work your way into boarding school. You can earn the right to go there if you have good grades. Applying to boarding school isn't much different than applying to college."

"No one in my family has gone to college, so my father won't understand."

"What about your mother, will she?"

"Maybe, it depends. She went to college in California, so she might be more open-minded. She usually wants the opposite of what my father wants, so she might be on my side. If my uncle Don, her brother, thinks it's a good idea, then she'll definitely want me to go. She thinks anything he says is the gospel," Tricia said.

"Why does she have so much faith in her brother? I don't know about you, but my brother and I never agree on anything."

"My Uncle Don is Bishop Maloney of Philadelphia. So he's kind of like God in our family," Tricia explained.

"Bishop Maloney? Really? He could be your admission ticket to almost any Catholic boarding school in the country, if not the world. If your grades are good and he writes a letter of recommendation, you can pack your bags faster than you can say 'supercalifragilisticexpialidocious.'"

"Can I take this brochure home? I'll bring it back later this week," Tricia asked.

"Of course, but don't worry about returning it. I can get more. Anyway, in the years I've worked here I've never had a student interested in boarding school, so I usually end up throwing them away. Let me know if you want me to talk to your parents. That is if you're serious about this."

"I think I am, but I have to talk to my parents, and of course Uncle Don."

"If you want to go next semester, we have to move quickly to get the paperwork done. We only have about six weeks, but we can make it happen."

The bell rang, indicating that it was time to move onto the next class.

"Thanks, I'll let you know."

"Tricia, wait." Mrs. Gallagher called to her as she was nearly out the door. "You asked if I knew anything about Villanova, but I didn't answer you. I went there for two years and then to Notre Dame College in South Bend and Harvard for grad school. I moved back here to take care of my parents. I'd be happy to write a letter of recommendation for you."

ML picked up the phone on the first ring. "What?"

"ML? It's me. Why did you answer the phone like that? Is something wrong?" Tricia asked.

"I'm sorry, I was preoccupied when the phone rang. I'll start over. 'Hello.'"

"Hi, can I come over tonight? I need your help with something," Tricia said.

"Sure, Stan is out of town on a business trip. I picked up some Chinese food on my way home if you want to eat with me."

"Great! I'll be there soon."

Tricia could have found her way to ML's apartment blindfolded simply by following the trail of Chinese food. The aroma of peanut oil, Szechuan peppers, and garlic permeated the hallway as soon as she stepped off the elevator. It was far from aromatherapy and the furthest thing from Feng Shui. The air made the muscles below her earlobes tighten, and saliva quickly accumulated in her mouth—a sure sign that she was on the verge of vomiting. She took a deep breath, bent over, and put her hands on her knees until the feeling passed.

"You only eat Chinese when Stan's not home, but you also eat it when you're depressed. Talk to me, big sis. Is it something at work, or with Stan?" Tricia asked.

"I got my period."

"And Chinese food makes your cramps go away? Or were you hoping to get a fortune cookie that reads *'in three to five days your disposition will change for the better. Period.'*" Tricia laughed at her own jokc, almost falling off the shiny metal barstool she was perched on.

"It's not funny, Tricia. I've been trying to get pregnant for three months. I'm beginning to think I'm never going to have a baby." ML was bracing herself with both hands flat on the kitchen counter across the bar from Tricia, opening and closing the various cartons of Chinese food.

"I'm sorry, I didn't know. Don't worry, you'll get pregnant. I'm sure Mom passed her fertility genes on to you. Look at *her.* Once I heard her tell Aunt Carol that she could get pregnant by just looking at an erection."

"Tricia, I can't believe you said that."

"What? I'm just repeating what I heard. You have to admit, it's kind of funny to know that Mom talks like that when she's not around us. If she knew I heard her, she would have flown into a confessional faster than Sister Bertrille."

"Who?" ML asked as she opened another white carton with red Pagodas and sniffed at the contents. "You know, Sally Fields, the flying nun. Oh my God, that stuff stinks."

"But it tastes sooooooo good. Want some? It's Kung Pao Chicken."

"No, I don't feel well. That smell…it's making nauseated. I haven't felt good since I drank some of Dad's vodka the other day. That stuff ripped out my stomach. But do you like my new earring? Missy pierced a second hole after I drank a shots."

"It's cute," ML said, spearing a particularly big and shiny piece of chicken with her chopsticks.

"I think I'm about to get my period, so I'll soon be joining you in your misery."

"I'm miserable for a different reason. I don't want a period, and you do," ML said. "Pass the hot mustard, please."

"You got that right. I haven't had a period in two months, and I'm bloated. When I do get it, it's going to be heavy. I just know it." Tricia rubbed her abdomen thoughtfully.

"Tricia, are you pregnant?" ML paused, a piece of chicken dangling midway to her mouth.

"God, no! I'm not pregnant! I skip periods all the time, and then Aunt Flow visits for more than a week. The last time this happened I bled through every outfit I wore," Tricia said with disgust.

"Are you sure? You've felt sick for days, the smell of Chinese food is making you queasy, and you're late."

"Yes, I'm sure."

"Have you had sex?" ML asked. Tricia couldn't look at ML. Her face turned red and hot, and she began to perspire. "Tricia? Have you? Don't tell me with that jerk, Tommy."

"What do you know about him? He's a nice guy. And to answer your question, yes, I have. And yes, with him. But we only did it once."

"Once? Tricia, you can't be that stupid. It only takes one time."

"Duh, I know that. But I also know I'm not pregnant."

"Prove it. I have a pregnancy test in the bathroom. I was hoping to use it, but I'll gladly waste the ten bucks on you instead. Take the test. You have to pee in a cup then use the medicine dropper to put it into the test tube. Put the test tube in the plastic holder and attach mirror. In two hours, if a brown circle appears in the mirror, you're pregnant."

"I'll bet you fifty dollars I'm not."

"Deal, but I want proof," said ML.

"I can't believe I'm doing this, but what the heck. I'm about to be fifty dollars richer!" Tricia shouted nervously as she walked down the hall to ML's bathroom. "Someday, we'll be laughing about this."

Two hours later, Tricia returned to the bathroom to check the tube that she was convinced would put fifty dollars in her pocket.

"Oh, shit! Shit, shit, shit! ML, come here!" Tricia yelled from the bathroom.

ML jumped up from the kitchen table so quickly that her chair tipped over. Without picking it up, she ran to the bathroom where Tricia was sitting on the floor, knees bent, holding her head, and rocking back and forth. The test tube with a dark brown circle was sitting in its holder on the sink.

"I'm sorry, ML. I'm so sorry. I can't believe this is happening," Tricia cried like a child. "Mom's going to hate me, and Dad's going to kill me. Oh my God, what should I do?"

"Shhhh, we'll figure something out. " ML was on the floor holding onto her little sister like she used to when Tricia was a toddler. ML was practically her second mother. She helped care for Mark, Tricia, and Patrick almost as much as their mother did. "Don't cry, I promise I'll figure something out. Let's go into my bedroom."

Tricia curled into a fetal position on ML's queen-sized bed. She was still in her school uniform: white blouse, navy and white plaid kilt, blue knee socks, and saddle shoes with Algebra equations scribbled in pen on the sides. Her mascara was running down her cheeks onto the white pillowcase. Normally, ML would have thrown a fit, but she had bigger worries. She handed Tricia a tissue and lay down on the bed facing her.

"Can it be wrong? I've heard of false positives. Maybe I should do it again, just to make sure," Tricia said.

"I bought the expensive test, the one that's 98 percent accurate. False positives rarely happen. If anything, it would be a false negative. The faster the plus sign appears, the more accurate it is. If it took more than two hours to appear, then I'd question it," ML said. "You can get a blood test to measures your hormone levels, which will confirm if you're pregnant."

"Where can I get a blood test? I can't just tell Mom I need to go to the doctor. And since I'm under eighteen, won't they tell Mom and Dad?" asked Tricia.

"We can go to Planned Parenthood. They won't charge you, and they won't call parents."

"This parenthood definitely wasn't planned. Crap, what am I going to do? I can barely say the word abortion, let alone have one. Right? I could never kill a baby and live with myself. Plus, if anyone found out, I'd be the town whore. I can't put Mom through that."

"I agree, an abortion isn't an option. But stop worrying about Mom and worry about yourself. Not to change the subject, but why did you want to come over tonight?"

"Never mind. If I'm pregnant, it's irrelevant."

"Tell me anyway. You said you needed my help with something."

"I wanted your advice about going to boarding school next semester. I've been so miserable at school and at home. They don't even notice me; it's like I'm invisible. The school counselor said I might be able to get a scholarship, especially with Uncle Don's help. So I thought...but it doesn't matter now." Tricia began silently sobbing into the pillow, her blonde ponytail and small, narrow shoulders shaking.

"Tricia, this could be the solution to your problem. You'd be out of town for about five and a half or six months, and no one will know you're pregnant. If you're far enough along, you might be able to have the baby and put it up for adoption before you return home for the summer," ML said.

"I don't know, ML. I don't know if I can keep a secret like this."

"Yes, you can. Secrets between friends are hard to keep, but one of this magnitude won't be. It will be easy to keep because you won't want anyone to know. Believe me, I know. If something means a lot to you, and if you think people will talk about how your moral fiber has unraveled, then you'll do whatever it takes to keep the secret."

"But what about my birthday and Easter? Mom will want me to come home or she'll want to visit me," Tricia said.

"You can say that a schoolmate asked you to her house for Easter, and I'll find a way to keep her from visiting you on your birthday. I'll offer to visit you. I'll convince her that she can't leave Patrick and that I really need the vacation. And with her fear of flying, it won't be difficult to keep her from you. Don't worry, we'll make it work. I promise."

"You said something about adoption. I saw a movie about a girl who gave up her baby for adoption, and she felt guilty for the rest of her life. She never learned how to cope with giving her baby away. I don't know if I can do that. Oh, God, but I also know I can't take care of a baby. ML, God works in mysterious ways, right? Will you…will you take my baby?"

"Stay with my for a few days, while Stan is out of town, and we will figure something out. You may be the answer to my prayers, and boarding school may be the answer to your prayers."

chapter

TEN

1978

"If you cannot get rid of the family skeleton, you may as well make it dance."
George Bernard Shaw

Trip walked into the office of Divine Candles with a pile of mail.

"If you come across any checks," Joseph said, "put them on my desk, and put the bills on Uncle Richard's. It's his turn to worry."

"Dad, the lawsuit is over, I promise. There's no way an appeal will be granted. Then it's business as usual," Trip said.

"I hope you're right. Do you know how much money we've spent on lawyers? Hundreds of thousands of dollars. We don't make that much to begin with, and this lawsuit not only cost us money, but our reputation as well."

“Anyone who knows anything knows that a candle maker can’t be blamed for a fire. It’s not our fault St. Michaels forgot to put out their candles on Christmas Eve. It was human error, not a manufacturer’s defect.”

“Apparently our customers don’t know that...or should I say our *former* customers? Just look at the sales figures for the past six months. For generations this family has dedicated its business and its life to the church, and what do we get in return? Stupid, baseless litigation so they can build a new church with *our* money.”

“Dad, they lost. It’s over. They lost in court, and they won’t get an appeal.” Tripp began rubbing his forehead. The conversation was beginning to wear on his nerves.

“Trip, don’t trust lawyers. They’d love a new trial. That’s more money for them. Meanwhile, I’m slowly drowning in debt, and your mother has no idea how far behind I am paying bills.” Joseph threw his fist into the desk for emphasis.

“Does that mean we can’t hire Mark?” Trip asked.

“Mark? He can’t work while he’s in the seminary. What are you talking about? Oh God, from the look on your face I can tell something’s wrong. Don’t tell me...he got kicked out?”

“No, he left, and this time he said he’s not going back. He came home last night when you were out playing cards. I was up until four a.m. talking with him. He’s still in bed.”

“Jesus Christ, what did he say? Why did he leave *this* time?”

“He wouldn’t say why.”

“Father Gellin left Xavier and is now teaching at the seminary. I’ll call and ask him if he knows what happened. Better yet, I’ll have your mother invite him over for dinner. Maybe he’ll talk some sense into Mark.”

“Dad, don’t call Father Gellin. I have a feeling he might be one of the reasons Mark left.”

“That doesn’t make sense. Gellin’s been a mentor to Mark for years. Wasn’t he the one who convinced Mark to join the seminary in the first place?”

“I don’t know for sure, but something must have happened between them. Mark said he couldn’t live in the same building as Gellin. I’ll talk with him after work—when he’s sober. He was at the bars on Lee Road last night, and everyone was buying him drinks. He ran into detective Mooney, who told Mark to watch his back and that ML should watch hers, too.

"Mooney blames Mark for Francis not making the team senior year. Francis didn't go to college because he couldn't afford it. He was planning on a basketball scholarship," Joseph said.

"Mark is not to blame for Francis being cut. Francis played like shit after his surgery. Mark worked hard for his spot while Francis took his for granted. But why would Mooney say ML should be careful? What does she have to do with any of that?"

"He blames Mark for Francis's problems. And he thinks Mark was the one who broke into Carson Olds and stole tires a few years ago, but he could never prove it. About ML, he had a crush on her in high school, and she wouldn't date him. I don't trust him. He's dirty."

"I never met a cop who wasn't," Trip said.

"Great, not only do I have to worry about Mark, I have to add him to my expenses. He can work for room and board, but I'm not putting him on the payroll. I can't believe he's throwing a cushy future out the window. Look at Uncle Don's life: he gets a new Cadillac every year, he lives in a mansion with a secretary and a personal assistant, people offer him their condos in Florida, and he never has to worry about meals, clothing, or paying bills. He'll be taken care of for the rest of his life."

"You forgot 'no heavy lifting,'" Trip joked. "On a happier note, here's a letter from Tricia."

Joseph read Tricia's letter out loud. "'*Dear Dad, I love Villanova. Augustinian nuns aren't as strict or as old fashioned as Notre Dame nuns, and the girls in my dorm are really nice.*' At least I don't have to worry about *her*."

❧

"The Virgin Mary has blessed you with this adoption," Mary Ann said. "ML, I'm so happy for you and Stan. This truly is a blessing. When will the baby be here?"

"Someone from the adoption agency is bringing her to Cleveland on Friday. We'll meet them at the airport," ML said.

"Are you nervous? Excited?"

"Both! I can't believe I'm finally going to be a mother. I hope I know what to do."

"As soon as you hold that baby in your arms, you'll know exactly what to do. Trust your instincts, trust yourself. Have you chosen a name for her?"

"She's already named. Her name is Ashley." There was silence on the other end of the phone. "Mom? Are you there?"

"Yes, yes, I'm sorry. I was just thinking . . . she's not named after a saint. Maybe you can give her a baptismal name when you christen her."

"She's from a Catholic adoption agency, Mom. I'm almost sure she's already been baptized. They wouldn't let her fly if she wasn't."

"Oh, then I guess I can put away your Christening dress. I took it out of the attic as soon as I heard I was going to be a grandmother. Who chose the name?"

"I didn't ask," ML lied.

"It's too bad this didn't happen when you were in California visiting Tricia. You could have flown the baby home yourself."

You're right. I could have.

"Yeah, well, I guess adoptions don't always go as planned. The agency never knows for sure if the mother is going to give the baby away until after it's born. Often, the birth mother changes her mind after delivery. Then there's paperwork that needs to be done and medical tests to be performed. I won't believe it myself until I have her in my arms." *If she never finds out about this, she'll never forgive Tricia and me.*

"ML, can you do something for me?"

"Of course, Mom."

"Can we have a formal baptism at St. Theresa's with Uncle Don? Then we can invite family and friends over for a christening party. Please? Do this for me?"

"That's fine, Mom. Especially since I didn't get to have a baby shower."

"Who will be the Godparents?"

"I'm going to ask Tricia and Mark."

❧

Tricia peeled the bubblegum-pink polish off her nails while she waited to switch planes in the Denver airport. Flecks of pink lacquer speckled her black pants. She dug into her purse to find the Pepto-Bismol. Her nerves were wreaking havoc on her stomach. She had a lot to be nervous about—she hated to fly and she was scared to go home, but mostly she was petrified to see Ashley in ML's arms. She had never seen Ashley. Once the cord was cut, her baby was whisked away to the nursery, which was probably just as well. She couldn't bear to look at her or have Ashley see, touch, or feel her.

"Flight 1258 to Cleveland is now boarding at gate ten." The announcement made the butterflies in her stomach flutter at an unsettlingly high-speed. She didn't have a choice. She had to get on that plane, go home, and begin to pretend. Pretend for the rest of her life that everything was normal. That she had spent a typical semester at boarding school. Well, she didn't *have* to lie. She just wouldn't tell them *everything* that happened. *What they don't know.... No harm in omitting a few details.* During her time at boarding school, Tricia had become a master at rationalizing her thoughts and actions.

She dreaded getting on the plane, but she zipped her red and black Le Sport Sac duffle and sauntered to the gate.

As she waited in line to board the plane, she thought she heard a familiar voice behind her. *I must know someone on this plane. Out of the hundred and fifty passengers flying to Cleveland, I'm bound to recognize someone.* If she did, she'd have someone to talk with to make the flight go by more quickly. On her flight from LA to Denver, she finished reading the last two issues of *Seventeen* magazine. If she didn't find someone, she'd have nothing to do for the next two and a half hours.

Seat 17C was an aisle seat. After an elderly man dropped his bag on her head as he tried to lift it into the overhead compartment, Tricia tried to settle in. She'd much rather be sitting next to the window. She was more at ease during landings if she could see the ground.

Something smelled good, like fresh-baked pastries, which made her hungry. She looked up from reading the flight safety instructions for the second time today to see a woman getting into seat 16D, diagonally across the aisle. She was carrying a Le Cordon Bleu Cooking School canvas bag, which obviously held the baked goods.

I wish I were sitting next to her. Maybe she'd share.

Forty minutes into the flight, the stewardesses rolled their carts down the aisle to serve drinks. The cart stopped and locked into position next to Tricia for what seemed like forever. The attendants served the rows in front of her and behind her. It was the woman-with-the-goody-bag's turn to order. "I'll have a coke and milk, please," she asked. She had to repeat herself because the attendant didn't believe what she'd heard.

That's a Von Guten drink. Who else drinks coke and milk? I have to meet this person.

Click. Snap. The cart brake was released and moved back.

"Would you like a drink?" the stewardess asked Tricia.

"I'll have what she's having. A coke and milk."

"I've never heard of that before, and now I'm serving two. Are you together?" the stewardess asked.

"No, I heard her order it, and I haven't had one in a long time. Try it, it's much better than you'd think," Tricia said.

The woman in 16D dropped her cocktail napkin. It was the perfect opportunity for Tricia to get her attention.

Tricia leaned forward and tapped her on the arm.

"Excuse me. You dropped your napkin."

"Thank you."

Briefly, the two women looked at each other. Then back at their drinks.

Tricia's butterflies were back, this time in a full-fledged frenzy.

Is that…? No, it can't be.

Out of the corner of her eye, Tricia saw 16D turn around. Tricia could feel the woman's eyes on her. She felt too nervous to look up, but was ultimately too flustered not to. She found herself staring at a brunette woman with one brown and one blue eye. Seven years had gone by since she'd last seen her. It was her tenth birthday, and one of the worst days of her life. Although she told Father Burns she forgave her for running away that day, she never really did.

"Tricia," the woman whispered under her breath.

My throat's closing up. My chest is tightening. My palms are sweating. Breathe, Tricia, breathe. I can't, I can't breathe. Hail Mary, full of grace…

She closed her eyes and practiced breathing like she was taught in Lamaze class. It was the only thing she could think of doing. With her eyes closed, she couldn't see her. Maybe it really wasn't her after all. Tricia heard 16D unbuckle her seatbelt and put her tray table up. *Please don't come over here.* Tricia gripped the arm of her chair, holding on for her life. She felt something warm on top of her hand. Another hand, a soft, familiar hand. She could feel the woman breathing inches from her face.

"Tricia, it's me…Suze."

Tricia opened her eyes to find them already flooded with tears. She could no longer avoid looking at her sister.

"How were you planning to get home? That is, if you're planning on going home," Tricia asked Suze while they waited for their luggage.

"I told Mom I'd take the train to University Circle and call her from there."

"Mark's picking me up, so come with us. Wait, Mom knows you're coming home?" Tricia was shocked.

"Yes, we've been talking a lot lately. She told me that ML was adopting a baby, and I thought it was a good reason to come home."

"You needed a *reason* to come home? Why didn't you come home years ago? Weren't my eighth-grade graduation or Mary Margaret and Grandma's funerals good enough reasons for you? Why now?"

"It's just time. I'm in a better place in my life now. Someday, when you're older, you'll understand."

"Right, right, I forgot. I'm just the little sister who doesn't get it. You're the *worldly* older sister who knows it all, who has experienced life to its fullest." Tricia started to get angry all over again. "There's not much to get, Suze. You ran away when you were fifteen. You broke Mom's heart and made her crazy worrying about you for years. You have no idea how what you did affected Mom. Maybe someday when you have your own daughter, you'll understand."

"Bringing up the past isn't going to make the situation any better. What happened to all that Catholic school teaching they've been brain washing you with? Like forgiveness, tolerance, acceptance, turn the other cheek, and don't judge others? Tricia, please forgive me. Mom has. I can't change what happened, and I'm *truly* sorry for leaving on your birthday. I don't want to ruin this for ML. Can't we just be happy, or at least act happy for her and the baby?"

"*Truly,* I'll forgive you when I'm ready. You can't just appear on an airplane and expect me to be all happy and excited to see you. I need some time, and this isn't it. Mark's here, that's him in the silver Maverick. He's going to shit a brick when he sees you."

"What happened to the cherry tree? Remember how we'd climb it to see who could get to the highest branch? I always won, because you were all too scared," Suze said.

"It was struck by lightening years ago." Tricia said as she purposely brushed Suze aside to get her suitcase out of the trunk

"Suze, I'll get your suitcases," Mark said. "Stay in the driveway for a minute while Tricia and I go in the house. Wait a few minutes before you come in. It looks like everyone is here, and they're going to be shocked when they see you."

Mark and Tricia carried the suitcases into the front door and plopped them down on the terracotta herringbone tiled entrance hall. Tricia could hear everyone in the kitchen. And then suddenly, the cries of a baby. *The* baby. Her baby.

"Let me hold her. She needs to get to know her grandma," she heard Mary Ann say.

Tricia started to get that feeling again—racing heart, tight throat, light-headed and weak. *I can do this. I know I can do this. Pull yourself together, walk in there, and smile. Be strong.*

Mark walked into the kitchen ahead of her. Tricia paused for a moment, took a deep breath, shook out her arms like a swimmer about to race and walked in behind him.

The first person she saw was her father in his signature Irish cardigan sweater, standing at the bar mixing drinks. "Hey! Whadaya say? Look who's here!" Joseph exclaimed.

"Hi, Dad, I missed you," Tricia said as her father gave her a good old-fashioned bear hug, along with some side-to-side rocking. In the corner of her eye, she saw Mary Ann holding Ashley wrapped in a pink blanket and a small satin bow in her fine blonde hair.

She walked over and kissed her mother on the cheek.

"Look at your niece. Isn't she beautiful?" Mary Ann said as she adjusted the satin blanket around the baby's arms. "Here, hold her while she's happy. I just got her to settle down." Mary Ann handed the baby to Tricia without giving her a chance to back away. Before she knew it, Tricia was looking into the eyes of her daughter. She involuntarily kissed Ashley's forehead.

"She's beautiful," Tricia replied. She started to sway like a mother does out of instinct and habit. All eyes were on her. Uncle Don, ML, Stan, Mark, Mary Ann, Joseph, Mark, Trip, and Patrick were all staring at her silently. Mark broke the awkward silence.

"For this my daughter was dead, and is alive again; she was lost, and is found. And they began to be merry," Mark said.

"Luke, chapter fifteen, verse twenty-four," Don said. "Mark, it's the prodigal *son,* not daughter. And why are you quoting Luke? You're not referring to the baby, are you?"

"Who's here? I heard someone come in the front door," ML interrupted.

"In a second, you'll understand why I chose that verse," Mark answered.

"Holy shit," Joseph said.

"That's not the reaction I was hoping for, but I know I don't deserve much more than that. Hello, Dad," Suze said.

Suze and Joseph stood motionless, firmly planted four feet away from each other. Silence fell upon the room. Eyes darted from face to face as everyone waited anxiously for Joseph's reaction. Would he blow up, yell, scream, and tell her she wasn't welcome home after what she put them through? Or would he forgive and forget and welcome her with open arms? Seconds seemed like hours while they waited for him to make a move.

Joseph put down his drink, took a deep breath, and grabbed Suze like she was a soldier returning home from war. They hugged, rocked, and cried. "Oh my God, oh my God. Thank you, God. Thank you, thank you, thank you," Joseph cried through his tears. Then he picked Suze up off her feet and twirled her around like she was his little girl. One of her Birkenstocks flew off. A huge sigh swept through the room at his joyful reaction.

"We should make merry and be glad; for this thy *sister* was dead, and is alive again; and was lost, and is found. Amen!" Don said.

"Luke, chapter fifteen, verse thirty-two," Mark replied.

Tricia woke early the morning of the Baptism. She didn't sleep well the night before, as she had dreamt that she heard a baby crying. When she woke, her nightgown was soaking wet. She had been wearing a tight bra around the clock for a week to keep her breast milk from coming in, even though they gave her a pill that was supposed to 'dry you up.' Her postpartum nurse, Sister Ann Marie, told her a tight bra or an ace bandage wrapped around her chest would help keep her from leaking. She thought after ten days she'd be able to sleep without a bra, but the milk was seeping out of her breasts. She rummaged through her unpacked suitcase and found the ace bandage from the hospital at the bottom of the bag and wrapped herself up like a mummy before throwing on a shirt. She went downstairs to the kitchen and found some Tylenol to relieve the pain. Sister Ann Marie also said two Tylenols and a few Hail Mary's would help. She expected to find someone in the kitchen, but no one was around. Joseph's car was gone; she assumed that he, Trip, and Mark were at work. Mary Ann's car was gone as well. Suze announced the night before that she planned on sleeping in.

Tricia was restless and decided to take a walk. Two blocks later she found herself standing in front of St. Theresa's. She remembered that the sacrament of Penance was offered Monday, Wednesday, and Friday mornings from nine to ten in the morning, so she decided to take Sr. Ann Marie's advice and say a few Hail Mary's, along with confessing her sins.

The confessionals consisted of three carved wood doors. The middle door, the largest of the three, was where the priest entered and waited for the penitents, the sinners, to come and secretly admit their weaknesses. The doors to the left and right were for the sinners. Each room was about the size of a public bathroom stall. To talk with the penitent, the priest would slide open a small screen about the size of a milk chute. The rooms were dimly lit so the priest couldn't see the penitent's face, but the penitent could see the profile of the priest. Tricia thought the whole scenario was ridiculous. The purpose of the closed doors, dark rooms, and screens was to shield the identity of the confessor, yet she knew darn well that the priest recognized the voices of most of the parishioners.

What the heck, I'm going to do to this even if Fr. Doyle knows it's me. He has to keep my sins a secret, no matter how serious they are.

Tricia was kneeling in the confessional waiting for the priest when she heard him slide back the screen to the penitent on the other side, his cue for the sinner to begin.

"Please bless me, father, for I have sinned, it has been four months since my last confession," she heard a woman say. Tricia wasn't comfortable listening to someone else's confession. She tried to tune it out, but could still hear.

I'm glad she's going first. I don't want anyone to hear what I have to say.

"And these are my sins," the woman continued.

Shit, it's Mom. I can't listen to this, but I can't just get up and leave, or can I?

Tricia was paralyzed. She knew she should do something, but she couldn't move. She was frozen in place, her hands clenched in prayer. She began to lose circulation in her fingers, her knees locked on the padded kneeler.

"Father, I have fallen."

For a moment, there was silence. "I know that you haven't been to church in a while, Mary Ann, but God will forgive you for straying if you show him you are truly sorry and atone for your sins," Fr. Doyle said. "Tell me why you stopped coming to Mass."

He knows it's Mom.

"Father, I haven't come for many reasons. Since my daughter's and mother's death, I've been angry and have lost faith in God. I was blaming him for taking them away from me."

"And how do you feel about falling from the Church?"

"When I said I have fallen, I wasn't referring to not going to church. The sin that I am confessing is much more serious than that."

"Is your sin mortal or venial?"

"Perhaps you can answer that question."

"I can absolve you from your sins, mortal or venial, once you confess, profess the act of contrition, and resolve to live a better life with Jesus Christ."

Mary Ann broke down and began to cry. “Father, I’ve committed a sin, and I have knowingly received the Eucharist for many years before confessing.”

“Mary Ann, receiving communion without confessing a mortal sin is a serious matter in the eyes of the Church. That itself is considered a mortal sin. Tell me about the sin?”

“Father, the sin I’ve committed is so awful that I can’t get myself to say it out loud. But I’ve examined my conscience, and I know I must confess. I know I did it willingly, but the circumstances surrounding the act were such that at the time I didn’t think it was wrong. It felt so right. Yet, now I know it was wrong. I can’t live with myself or my sin any longer.”

“If you know what you did was wrong and you repent, God will reconcile you through the Holy Spirit and give you peace. Do not be afraid to talk about your sins here. I am not here to judge you, neither is Jesus Christ. Mary Ann, your sin is a personal matter between you and God, no one else. God is all-mighty, all-powerful, and all-forgiving.”

What could she have done that is so horrible?

“I want my faith back; I need my faith back. And I know I cannot have it without confessing. Father, please forgive me for I have committed adultery.”

Holy shit.

“You said that for many years you have been receiving the Eucharist without confessing. When did this happen?”

“Almost twenty years ago.”

“That’s a long time to carry a cross of that magnitude.”

“Although I haven’t confessed to a priest, I have had many conversations with God asking for his forgiveness.”

“How many times did you commit this act?”

“Once, Father. Only once. However, I became pregnant and had the child. I never told Joseph he wasn’t the father, and of course my son doesn’t know that someone else is his father.”

“As you know, your actions have affected the lives of others, even if they aren’t aware. Does this man know the child is his?”

“Yes, I believe so. Although we have never spoken about it, in my heart I think he knows. He is a good man, and he would never do or say anything that would hurt my family or me. If he ever claimed to be the father, he knows it would devastate my husband, our son, and the rest of my family."

"You said that the circumstances at the time made you feel like it was okay to be with another man. Can you explain?"

"My best friend died after a long battle with cancer. I was at her bedside with him, her husband, for a week before she died. The day after she died, I was at her house helping him go through her things. We were both grieving. We held on to each other for support. While we consoled each other, one thing led to another."

"Is there anything else you want to confess at this time?"

"No, Father."

Thank God. I can't bear to hear any more.

"You may now say the Act of Contrition. Let us bow our heads."

"O my God, I am heartily sorry for having offended thee, and I detest all my sins because of thy just punishments, but most of all because they offend thee, my God, who art all-good and deserving of all my love. I firmly resolve, with the help of thy grace, to sin no more and to avoid the near occasions of sin."

"May our Lord Jesus Christ absolve you; by His authority I absolve you from every bond of excommunication and interdict, so far as my power allows and your needs require. Thereupon, I absolve you of your sins in the name of the Father and the Son and the Holy Spirit. Amen."

"Amen," Mary Ann repeated.

"For your penance, say the rosary daily for six months. Attend Mass on Sundays, and show acts of kindness toward your husband. You may go in peace."

"Thank you, Father."

❧

Dear Diary,

I know parents who have a favorite child, and they readily admit it. I don't have a favorite, and if I did I certainly wouldn't admit it. Each of my children is different, and I love them individually. I used to think that Don was mother's favorite. He made her proud by becoming a priest. But then there were times when I thought I was her favorite. It could have been the mother-daughter relationship, which is so different than the mother-son. When mother shared her secret with me about Don, it didn't change my respect or love for her. It just made it stronger, deeper. When I found myself in the same situation with Patrick, I wanted to tell her, but I was too ashamed. Although I know she would have understood and not judged me or loved me less.

And now I've passed this family weakness down to Tricia, God bless her. And may God forgive us for our sins. Three generations of weak women with broken hearts. But broken hearts are what give us strength, wisdom, and compassion. A heart never broken is cold and indifferent and will never experience the tenderness of fallibility.

I can't say Tricia is my favorite child, because I don't have a favorite. Although, I do feel like I have a special connection with her. I hope that someday she will feel the same about me.

If the pope knew that Don was a bastard, would he still have been made a Bishop? But who are we to judge one another? That's a job for God only.

I have a new granddaughter who has two mothers. Ashley should have no excuses in the mothering department. But I do. I have sinned twice, three times, maybe more.

Because I didn't ask for forgiveness, my sins are compounded. I wonder if my sins have caused the sins of others. If I had sought forgiveness earlier and paid for my redemption sooner, could I have saved my children from their pains?

I'm not sure how Tricia will handle the new realities of her life. But I will do my best to help her without revealing that I know her secret. If she wants me to know, she will tell me herself.

And I will do the same for ML. I will be there for her, no matter what.

Birth and death are so intertwined.
I wonder which will be next.
And what it will mean. If anything.

Mary Ann

chapter

ELEVEN

The face is the mirror of the mind, and eyes without speaking confess the secrets of the heart.
St. Jerome

"Bless me Father, for I have sinned. It has been one year since my last confession, and these are my sins."

Tricia paused, not sure if she was able to spill her guts about the dirty deed to a priest. *After Mom's confession, this will sound like I stole a cookie out of the cookie jar.*

"Father, I had sex with a boy." *Duh, of course it was with a boy.* Fr. Doyle stroked his forehead as though he were trying to rub away his thoughts. "According to the Bible, sex before marriage is a sin in God's eyes. It is an act that should only be performed between married couples for the purpose of reproduction. Are you sorry for your sin?"

I wouldn't be here if I wasn't.

"Yes, Father."

Four Hail Mary's and five Lord's Prayers later, Tricia was absolved of her sin, her conscience was as clear as it was going to get, and she was ready to take on the role of being Ashley's godmother. Now she needed to get back home to help get ready for the Christening party. And to start pretending.

"Hi, ML, when are you coming over?" Tricia twirled the mangled telephone cord between her fingers as she waited for a reply.

"I don't know...maybe an hour or so before the Baptism. It depends on when Ashley wakes up from her nap. Why?" ML said.

"I was just wondering. I could use the company. This family is more messed up than you know. I feel like you and I are the only normal ones."

"What do you mean?"

"Never mind. Come over as soon as you can. Ashley can nap here. I'll talk to you when you get here. Bye."

"Who was on the phone?" Mary Ann asked Tricia as she hung up.

"Oh, hi Mom. I didn't know you were in the room. How long have you been standing there?"

"I just came downstairs, why?"

"Nothing. You just startled me. I was talking with ML."

"Would you be a sweetheart and iron the Christening gown while I put together the crudités?" Mary Ann asked.

"Mom, let me do the crudités," Suze said.

"Well, good morning. I didn't expect you up so early," Mary Ann said to Suze as she dragged herself down the stairs.

"Have you ever had a party without serving crudités? You should do something different," Suze said while yawning, covering her wide-open mouth with the crux of her elbow.

Mary Ann was well known for her beautiful vegetables and dip baskets. She would spend hours carefully carving radishes into roses, turnips into daisies, and carrot sticks into perfectly straight rectangles. Then she'd meticulously arrange them along with other vegetables to look like a basket of flowers.

"Let me make an appetizer," Suze said, grabbing a coffee mug out of the cupboard.

"Thanks, dear, but since when do you know how to cook?" Mary Ann asked.

"I was going to tell you last night, but we were so wrapped up with ML and the baby that I didn't have a chance. I've been studying to be a professional chef at the Cordon Bleu Cooking School," Suze said.

"That explains the bag you had on the plane," Tricia said.

"That's wonderful! We'll have a chef in the family. Does that mean I won't have to cook anymore? Is that why you came home, to get me out of the kitchen and take over for me?" Mary Ann joked, smiling broadly.

"Maybe for a short time, but I have to get back to Portland in a week to meet with producers from a cable network."

"You're only home for a week?" Mary Ann asked, her smile wavering.

"I wish I could stay longer, but I have an unbelievable opportunity. At Cordon Bleu they call me 'Lazy Susan' because I always use shortcuts and simplify recipes and techniques, yet the dishes still taste great. At first they threatened not to let me graduate, but then they realized I was on to something that would appeal to the average cook—quick and easy meals."

"So, what does that have to do with producers?" Mary Ann asked.

"One of the cable networks is thinking of doing a cooking show, and they want to talk to me about being the on-air chef. Get this…they want to call the show 'Lazy Susan Cooking.'"

"A chef *and* a celebrity in the family," Tricia said. "Can I have your autograph?"

"Very funny. Keep your fingers crossed that the interview goes well and they like me."

"If you don't have a stylist to help you prepare for the interview, I suggest you get rid of your moldy Birkenstocks and buy some real shoes," Tricia dug in.

"Of course they'll *love* you," Mary Ann said. "Have either of you seen Mark today? I want him to set up the bar on the side porch."

"I think he's still sleeping, but I'll wake him," Tricia said as she quickly rushed out of the kitchen, thankful for the excuse to leave.

Tricia knocked on Mark's bedroom door. She was sure he was still asleep, but just in case she didn't want to walk in. No answer. She slowly opened the door and was smacked in the face with the stench of spoiled beer leaching out of his pores.

"Jesus, Mark, this room smells disgusting. You smell disgusting. Get up! Mom needs your help getting ready for the party."

"Get out of here! I don't feel good. I'll get up when I want."

"If I drank as much as you, I wouldn't feel well either. Get up. You need to set up the bar. While you're at it, maybe a little hair of the dog that bit you will cure your hangover. And *please* take a long shower and use some Listerine so you don't reek at the Baptism."

"Have you ever thought about how many times we've been in this church? We've spent almost as much time here as we did at school," Tricia asked ML as they unsuccessfully tried to find comfort sitting on the hard oak pew with Ashley in the last row of St. Theresa's.

"I'm sure it's thousands," ML said. "I can recite the entire Mass from memory, including the priest's prayers."

"I hope uncle Don drizzles the water over her forehead and doesn't dunk her head in the baptismal font. I'm afraid I'll drop her."

"Don't be ridiculous. You won't drop her. And don't worry, I asked him not to put her head in the water. Right, Ashley? We won't let you get all wet. Aunt Tricia will take good care of you." Tricia drifted her fingers over sleeping Ashley's baby-down hair as ML rocked her in her arms.

"What should I do if she starts crying? I mean if she cries and I start to leak?" Tricia whispered.

"Stop worrying. She probably won't cry, but if she does, will you be okay? You won't cry over spilled milk, will you? I can't handle both of you crying." ML jabbed her elbow into Tricia's ribs, grinning.

"Very funny, ML. It won't be the most comfortable thing in the world, but I'll deal with it."

"I'll be right next to you if you need me, but you won't."

"Speaking of crying, don't look now, but Mom is at the altar with Fr. Doyle and it looks like *she's* crying. I told you this family is a mess."

"She's must be apologizing for not coming to church in a long time. I don't think she's been since Nana died. Maybe today will make her want to come back."

"If you only knew," Tricia said under her breath.

"What did you say?" ML asked.

"Never mind."

"You've been saying that a lot lately. I hate it when you do that."

Mary Ann, Fr. Doyle, and an altar boy walked down the aisle of the nave and joined the family in the back of the church by the Baptistery. After exchanging hellos with the family, Fr. Doyle unlocked the wrought-iron gates to the white Italian marble baptismal font, and the altar boy lit the candles.

"Bishop Maloney will be here shortly, he's in the rectory getting ready. ML and Stan, who have you chosen to be the godparents?" Doyle asked.

"Tricia and Mark," ML answered.

"Tricia and Mark, are you aware of the responsibilities that go along with being a godparent?"

"Yes, Father," they answered in unison.

"Mary Ann, is everyone here?"

"Yes, ML wanted only family," Mary Ann said.

"Well then let's take our places. Grandparents—Joseph and Mary Ann—stand next to ML and Stan. Tricia and Mark, stand on the other side of the parents. Tricia, please hold the baby. The rest of you can gather around the font. ML, what name have you given her?" Doyle asked.

"Ashley."

"Very well. Here comes the Bishop."

"Good afternoon, everyone," Don said. "I hope you didn't stay up too late last night after I left. Mark, you look a little under the weather."

"I'm fine, just a little tired. But don't worry, I'll get my second wind for the party," Mark said.

"ML and Stan, this is a very special day for you. We're welcoming your daughter Ashley into the Catholic Church and freeing her from original sin so she may have life everlasting. Let us begin," Don said.

After Tricia and Mark denounced Satan and professed their faith on behalf of Ashley, Don placed his stole over the baby to introduce her into the church. More prayers and blessings were said and motions made over the baby's ears, nose, and eyes.

"Ashley, I baptize thee in the name of the Father and of the Son and of the Holy Spirit," Don made the sign of the cross three times, and a stream of holy water poured over Ashley's small head.

Startled by the water, Ashley flailed her arms and legs and cried. Tricia could feel the rush of heat in her chest. Whenever she heard Ashley cry, or even heard the cries of a baby on TV, she could feel milk escaping through her nipples. By now she had learned to wear nursing pads under a tight bra. If only she had a way to conceal her tears. As they pooled in her eyes, she looked across the font and saw her mother staring at her with tears in her eyes as well. *Does she know I know her secret? Does she know mine? There are too many skeletons in the family closet.*

"Nice to be home?" Joseph asked.

"Yes, it's nice to sleep in my own bed and finally eat some real food," Tricia replied.

"Is everything okay? You don't seem like yourself."

"It must be jet lag. The time change has thrown me off a little."

"You've been so quiet since you've been home, and your face is really red," Joseph said.

"Really? I feel a little warm."

"Let me feel your forehead. Tricia, you're burning up. I knew something wasn't right."

"But I feel fine for the most part. I'll take some Tylenol."

Tricia went upstairs to her parents' bedroom to find the Tylenol that Mary Ann kept in her bathroom cabinet.

"Hey, ML, I didn't know you were in here," Tricia said.

"I needed to change a poopy diaper and get her out of the Christening dress before she throws up on it. What are you doing up here? I thought you were helping Mom in the kitchen."

"I think I have a fever from being so damn engorged. Maybe I should just breastfeed her and get this milk out of me. I don't know if I can take this much longer. I'm in so much pain."

"Be patient, you'll dry up soon. Besides, if you start nursing, your body will just produce more milk. And if you did and someone saw you? That would definitely be the end of our secret. Lay down in your room and I'll bring you an ice pack. But first I want to show you something. You know that birthmark you have on your back that you hate so much? Look, she has one on hers too, in the same place."

"Poor thing," Tricia said, tracing the whale-shaped birthmark in little circles.

"Last night, Mom said she looks just like you did as a baby. She even got out your baby book to show me."

"Oh God, do you think she suspects something?"

"I don't think so. I brushed it off by saying that it's nice that she has some of our family's traits so that when she's older she'll feel like she belongs with us."

"Shhh. Do you hear that? Who's playing the piano? Uncle Jack isn't here yet, and no one in *our* family plays," Tricia said.

"It must be Patrick. While you were gone, he sat down at the piano one night and started playing like he had been doing it forever. He doesn't even know how to read music. He plays by ear," ML said.

"That's crazy. We're all so tone-deaf we couldn't carry a tune in a bucket."

"Maybe it's because he's so into music and is always blasting the stereo. It's become ingrained in him from listening to it all the time." ML finished putting a clean diaper on Ashley, picked her up, and began nuzzling her neck.

"Or maybe he listens to it all the time because the music is ingrained in him naturally," Tricia said before tossing three Tylenol into her mouth and chugging an entire glass of water from the tap.

"Another great Von Guten party." Joseph kissed Mary Ann on the cheek. "And it's all because of you."

"Joseph is that Scotch I smell? It's not even five o'clock," Mary Ann asked.

"No, it's not Scotch. Loosen up, we're finally grandparents. Isn't that reason enough to celebrate? What's the difference between having a drink now or in twenty minutes? I helped Mark set up the bar and showed him how to make a few different drinks. So he practiced on me and gave me an old-fashioned. He's a little heavy with his pours, but besides that, he knows his way around a bar."

"That's what I'm afraid of. He's been drinking too much. I think something's bothering him, and he won't talk about it. I asked Don to convince him to go back to the seminary, but he said Mark wouldn't talk about it. He told Don 'it's history,' and he's moving on with his life. The problem is I don't think he's moving on. He's stuck and he doesn't know what to do—besides drink," Mary Ann said.

"Did I hear someone say something about a drink?" Don walked into the kitchen.

"Yes, you've come to the right place," Joseph said.

"Joseph, make Don a drink," Mary Ann said.

"Abracadabra, you're a drink." Joseph waved his hands in the air, sloshing some of his drink onto the carpet.

"Very funny, Joseph. How many have you had? Did the party start without me?" Don asked as Mary Ann turned to get a paper towel.

"No, let's get a drink on the porch. It's getting too hot in the kitchen." Joseph walked away.

"Mary Ann, do you want a drink?" Don asked, watching her blot the orange puddle off the floor.

"No, thank you. Someone in this house has to stay sober."

"Mom, let me help you." Suze appeared with a large glass of wine in her hand.

"Saved by Chef Lazy Susan! Don, did you hear that Suze is a professional chef?" Mary Ann asked.

"She told me in the car on the way back from church," Don said. "Are you sure you don't want a drink? I'm heading to the bar now."

"Speaking of drinks, here's our bartender," Mary Ann said. Mark opened the refrigerator, grabbed some limes, and slammed the door shut. "Mark, will you get uncle Don a drink?"

"Mom, what the hell are Detective Mooney and his wife doing here? He's such an asshole, and I'm sure he feels the same about me," Mark said.

"Angela Mooney is one of ML's best friends, and she wanted her here for the party. Mark, please don't ruin this day for ML."

"Angela is just as bad as her husband."

"Stop that right now. Angela is a nice person. Don't pass judgment on her just because you don't like her husband. She's never done anything to you, has she?"

"ML and Angela deserve each other. They both have bad taste in friends. If you only knew..." Mark turned and left the kitchen, the two limes squeezed in his left hand.

chapter

TWELVE

1999

The thing about family disasters is that you never have to wait long before the next one puts the previous one into perspective.
Robert Brault

Suze was in a hurry to get down the escalator to baggage claim. It had been ten years since she had been back to Cleveland. She wasn't planning on visiting anytime soon, but when Mark called to tell her to get on the first plane home, no matter what the cost, she complied. Even though Suze ran away when she was fifteen, and Joseph considered her dead for many years, and even though she lived two-thousand miles away, the two had developed a close-knit relationship over the phone. Growing up, Suze hated her father. Joseph never understood the mindset of the peace, love, and rock n' roll movement of the '60s and '70s that despised all things corporate and middle class. Ironically, she had become the epitome of what she had once so vehemently despised—a successful businesswoman, entrepreneur, and celebrity chef. The one-time hippie turned her life around 180 degrees. Suze and her father talked to each other at least twice a week, and he and Mary Ann had visited her in Portland several times in the past five years. When friends would ask Joseph about his family, he mostly talked, no, mostly *bragged* about Suze and her TV show.

A week ago, Suze was talking to Mary Ann on the phone when Joseph picked up the line in another room and interrupted their conversation. "All I have to say is *come home*!" he yelled into the phone.

"Dad, maybe I'll come home for Thanksgiving," Suze said.

"No, I mean come home for good. Come home to your family. You're out there all alone. With all the money you're making, you can build a television studio here," Joseph said.

"Dad, don't make me feel bad."

"Then come home," he said and hung up the phone.

Suze wasn't surprised that Mark didn't recognize her. The Hollywood producers and image-makers had completely made her over to fit their celebrity profile. Her mousey-brown hair was now golden chestnut, long, and smooth. Her John Lennon glasses gave way to blue-tinted contacts, and her clothes were now sophisticated-chic. No longer the second-hand bohemian duds she once favored. She even walked differently—tall and confident, as though she had gone to finishing school. Nana would have been proud.

"Mark, over here!" Suze stepped off the escalator.

Mark looked at his sister; tears filled his eyes as he slowly shook his head left and right. The airport commotion around them disappeared as he walked toward her, never breaking eye contact until they stood inches apart. He didn't need to say anything. The look on his face said it all.

Suze dropped her carry-on. "No, no, please don't tell me he's gone. Please, oh God, Mark, tell me he's okay." Suze cried as passengers bustled their way around her, grabbing their luggage from the baggage carousel, anxious to get away from this unexpected and unwelcome emotion.

Mark held her in his arms and softly said, "He's with the Lord, Jesus Christ."

"Don't feed me your religious shit. God can't have him yet. He can't take my dad away from me. It's not fair. I didn't get to say good-bye. I didn't get to tell him I love him. For a family so devoted to religion, it hasn't done us much good has it, Mark? So don't feed me your holiness crap. We lost Mary Margaret, Nana died when she wasn't even sick, and now Dad. How do you still have faith, especially after the church obviously fucked you up? I don't understand. I don't get it."

"We tried to get him to hang on until you arrived. I told him you were on your way. Suze, don't be mad at God for this. He works in mysterious ways," Mark said.

"Fuck, excuse my French, but there's no mystery here, Mark. Dad is dead. I can't believe he's gone. He's really gone?"

"Come on, let's get your bags and go home. Everyone's at the house."

They were quiet during most of the thirty-minute drive home from the airport. As they entered the Heights and passed all of the neighborhood landmarks, Suze spoke up.

"Dad begged me to move back home, and I was seriously considering it. Damn it. I don't know if I can go back into that house without hearing 'Hey, whadaya say? Look who's here!'"

"I know what you mean. It already feels weird knowing he won't be walking in the door ever again. And he won't be sitting in the den when we walk in the back door. The house will never be the same."

"That house is more than just a house. It's the fiber of our family, the gathering place for our celebrations, with Dad and Mom leading the way. It's where I got drunk for the first time, and Dad caught me. It's where I lost my virginity while Dad was passed out on the couch in the next room. It's where Mary Margaret had her first driving accident in the driveway. It's where all of our baptisms, first-communions, confirmations, and graduations were celebrated with Dad grilling burgers on the patio. It's where the annual Memorial Day picnic and Von Guten lawn darts tournament was held, with Dad staking money on ridiculous bets. It's where we had our own fireworks show on the 4th of July in 1970, when the house was struck by lightning. It's where we all snuck out late at night, climbing out my bedroom window and down the pear tree. Even though Dad almost always caught us before we reached the street. It's where all of us were brought home to after we were born. And Dad was always there. Always," Suze said, sobbing into Mark's shoulder and clinging to his shirt.

"I haven't seen Mom shed a tear. Don't you think that's kind of weird?" Tricia asked.

"She's probably in shock. I don't think it has hit her yet," ML said.

Tricia, ML, and Angela were riding in the car behind the limousine that followed the hearse to the cemetery. The pallbearers—Patrick, Trip, Mark, Stan, Tricia's husband Scott, and *Uncle* Jack—rode in the lead limousine with Mary Ann.

"Angela, thanks for having Kevin stay at the house today. He's getting good at that," ML said. "Damn, we've had too many funerals in this family, and this is the worst one. To bury my own father…." ML broke down and began sobbing. Angela took her hands into her own to comfort her.

"Angela, you're a good friend to ML and to our family," Tricia added. "ML, don't you think it's weird that Uncle Jack is riding in the car with all of them?" Tricia tried to change the subject to calm ML.

"No, he's one of the pall bearers. What's so weird about that?" ML asked.

"I guess you're right. But, I was thinking, he's the only non-family member in that car."

"You think too much. Anyway, Mom was with Uncle Jack when Aunt Carol died. I'm sure he just wants to do the same for her."

"Wouldn't it be funny if they ended up together, Mom and Uncle Jack?" Tricia asked.

"I can't believe you're thinking about that when we haven't even buried Dad yet."

"It's not that far-fetched of an idea. Think about it. They're good friends; they know each other well; they're both alone…."

"Tricia, I'm sure that's the last thing on Mom's mind right now. There's going to be a lot to do in the next week to get Mom up to speed with bills, expenses, the future of Divine, Dad's will, life insurance, and so on. So don't get carried away, and *don't* say anything to Mom about Uncle Jack. She has enough to deal with right now," ML said.

"Did you put anything in the casket like Mom suggested?" Tricia asked.

"Stan and I put a Lucky Strike in his hand. Dad always said that if you can't smoke and drink in heaven, he didn't want to go. What about you?"

"My college diploma. I tried to give it to him the day I graduated, but he wouldn't take it. Patrick put in Oreos. I hope they have milk in heaven. Mark put in a deck of cards. Do you know if Mom put anything in?"

"She wrote him a letter and put it in his pocket. I'd love to know what she wrote."

"Me, too," Tricia wondered while staring out the car window at the passing landscape. The evaporating dew on the rolling lawns created a haze that put her in a thoughtful trance.

Unlike the previous Von Guten trips to the cemetery, the sun was shining and tree branches were dotted with buds waiting to spring to life. After a long winter of record-breaking low temperatures and snowfall, a new season was finally upon them. When the car doors opened, Tricia heard the heart-rending sound of the bagpipes that Detective Mooney had arranged. Tricia tried to keep the funeral expenses to a minimum for her mother, and told him it wasn't necessary to have a bagpiper since her father wasn't Irish or Scottish. However, Mooney explained that it was customary for bagpipers to play at funerals for those who served in the armed forces, and that the bagpiper offered to play free of charge.

Once the pallbearers were in position to carry the casket, the bagpiper led the procession to the gravesite. The powerful and poignant sounds made it impossible for Tricia to keep her emotions at bay. Until now she had held herself together. She fought the tears and tightening of her throat, but she couldn't keep it in any longer. Her eyes were hidden behind sunglasses, but her chest heaved in rhythm with the resonant Scottish instrument. Fittingly, the heartbreaking and soul-searching music melted into a cacophonous slide of silence, the air leaving the bag like a soul leaving its body.

Assisted by Fr. Burns, Don led the service with Mary Ann, her children, their spouses, and grandchildren at his side.

"Let us pray," Don began. "Dearest brothers and sisters, we pray for Joseph, whom the Lord has called forth from this world and whose body has been given to us this day for burial. May the Lord receive him into his peace, and when the day of judgment comes, raise him up to be gathered among the elect and numbered with all the saints at God's right hand." Burns continued by blessing the casket and grave with holy water and incense.

Although they were in the open air, the smell of the incense lingered too closely to Mark and he felt himself fainting in slow motion. When he realized he was about to go out like a light, he slowly bent his knees, knelt by the edge of the grave, and lay down in the grass. Tricia pulled a vial of smelling salts out of her pocket. Don had given it to her earlier, knowing that Mark had a tendency to faint. Burns paused until Tricia assured him that Mark was going to be okay. She was able to bring Mark back almost immediately, and Fr. Burns continued as if nothing happened. Unlike church where they had eulogized Joseph, celebrating his life with funny stories and relived memories, the graveside service was simple, somber, and straightforward. Don and Burns took turns reciting the prayers and leading responsorial psalms routine at graveside services, inserting Joseph's name when appropriate.

"Eternal rest grant unto him, O Lord, and let perpetual light shine upon him. May he rest in peace. Amen," those attending said together.

"With longing for the coming of God's kingdom, let us pray," Don said and began to lead the family and friends in the Lord's Prayer:

"Our Father, who art in heaven, hallowed by Thy name;
Thy kingdom come;
Thy will be done on earth as it is in heaven.
Give us this day our daily bread,
And forgive us our trespasses
As we forgive those who trespass against us;
And lead us not into temptation,
But deliver us from evil."

In the distance, the sound of *Amazing Grace* on bagpipes announced the end of the service. As Tricia looked out over the hills of tombstones, she saw the bagpiper walking away, into the depths of the cemetery, taking with him the music that would continue to haunt her long after this day.

"What are you doing up here?" ML asked Tricia, who was shuffling through the top drawer of Mary Ann's dresser. "I've been looking all over for you."

"I saw Mom make a Xerox of the letter she wrote to Dad in the funeral home office before the wake. And there's only one place Mom hides things – in her underwear drawer. I had to read it. Listen to this," Tricia plopped herself down on the bed and began to read aloud:

Dear Joseph ~

Although I've always contemplated our mortality and wondered which one of us would die first, I never truly expected this day to come. Perhaps I thought we were immortal. One regret I have is that I didn't get to say good-bye to you nor you to me. That's why I'm writing this letter. I can't say these things to anyone else but you, for no one would understand where my heart is or where it was when we first met.

Fifty years ago, you made my heart flutter and my knees weak with your romantic demeanor, your soft lips, and your gentle touch. And to top it all off, you had a unique ability to sweep me off my feet and dance the night away, cheek to cheek. The first time I laid eyes on you, I knew you were the one, and that I had to break my engagement to Charles Stone.

"She was engaged to someone else? How come we never knew about this?" Tricia asked.

"I didn't know either. Keep reading before someone walks in the room," ML replied.

You were the man of my dreams, the one I wanted to be with for the rest of my life. When I wasn't with you, my heart ached. Even when I slept, I missed you. Joseph, you mesmerized me with your dreams for the future and your lust for life. Your enthusiasm and passion for everything you did was contagious and spellbinding. You were the life of every party, and I was so proud to be the one on your arm. All the other girls wished they were with you—with Joey V, the handsome Von Guten boy—but I was the lucky one. You had two hearts—yours and mine. I gave mine to you willingly, knowing it was in good hands. I trusted you with my heart because I knew that one day we would be one.

And then we became one, and we were determined to be a team, unlike our parents. Nothing made me happier than having you next to me in bed each night and seeing your face first thing every morning. We were living in Camelot, and you were my knight in shining armor.

As we began our family with the arrival of ML and soon after Trip, Camelot faded away. At first I thought it was just part of being a parent. But I was determined to keep our love alive. I wasn't going to let children change our special relationship. Our marriage was the labor of my love. But you grew further and further away from me, distancing you from the children and me. I tried to get you to love me as you did before. I was starving for your love, but you weren't willing to give me an ounce of it. You looked at me differently and didn't include me in any decisions. We were supposed to be a team, but you put me on the bench. As fast as I fell in love with you, I fell out of love with you. Then I reminded myself that I… we… took an oath 'for better or for worse,' and I convinced myself that it was just a phase you were going through.

When you pushed me out of your life, you filled the void with gambling, drinking, and late nights out. By then we had seven children, and as our family grew larger, you moved further away from me. Still, you had my heart. I may have fallen out of love with you, but I still loved you, because I could never forget who you were when I married you. For better or worse, I wasn't walking away from the father of my children.

Gambling and drinking were your worst demons. They were your hell on earth. And you brought it into our home. You were stripped of your senses, and as a result you tried to strip everything away from me—my dignity, my passion for life, my self-esteem, my confidence, and my good nature. But no one would ever have known. I exhausted myself holding up a façade that everything thing was 'peachy keen,' that our life and our family together was wonderful. I did this for two reasons: the children and myself. I hope you never thought my Pollyanna ways were meant for you, although I'm sure you benefited from my outlook on life. I was determined to keep peace and normalcy within our family, for the children's sake.

I laid down all the joys in my life, all of my dreams of working for Procter and Gamble, to help you follow your dream. But you threw away your dreams as you gambled and drank your salary and nights away. Together, as young lovers, we had a dream: to raise a family, become grandparents, and one day travel and see the Seven Wonders of the World. We were a team, until suddenly you gave up on me. It was you, and not I.

I'm not mad at you. I don't resent you. And I don't have any regrets. We raised seven children to become responsible adults, except for our tragic loss of Mary Margaret. They are your legacy, and they are proud you were their father. I watched them closely the night you died. They cried for you; they laughed about you; they told endearing stories of memories they have of you. In your own way, you left an indelible mark on their souls. It was also wonderful for me to see how close they are with each other. Although there were many years of slamming doors, screaming, and sibling rivalry, they've grown to love and respect each other, even if they don't always like each other. They are what got me through these past two days, and they will be my reason to continue living without you.

Living without you. Those are words I never thought I'd say. For some reason, I always thought we would leave this world together. So now it's my turn to do things my way. I've never said this before, and still I'm not saying it. I'm writing it: damn you, Joseph. Damn you for belittling me. Damn you for making me believe that I was worthless. Damn you for calling me an idiot and a dumb bitch. Damn you for taking my heart and throwing it away like it was garbage. Damn you for leaving me home night after night, alone with the children, waiting and hoping for you to walk in the door. Your constant reminders of how worthless I was made me weak and vulnerable; so weak that I betrayed you and our vows. I've concealed my infidelity from everyone, including you, for many years, and it will continue to be the cross I bear for the rest of my life.

I won't miss your drinking. I won't miss your gambling. I won't miss your lies. I won't miss the pile of newspapers you left on the floor. I won't miss making you fresh squeezed orange juice every day. I won't miss you pissing away your paychecks. And there are a million 'no mores' to add to the list. No more coupon clipping. No more lying about you being sick and not going to church on Sundays. No more shopping sales at Sears. No more cigarette butts in every room in the house. No more picnics and barbecues held just so you'd have an excuse to drink at home. No more crudités baskets. No more, no more, no more!

Now I know how you felt. After saying these horrible things, just like you said to me over the years, I still love you, and I believe that you still loved me. May God forgive me for writing, let alone thinking, these thoughts. I will always love you. You were my knight in shining armor, my Romeo, my lover, my best friend, my dance partner, my valentine, and my soul mate for many years.

I believe that one day we will be together again, Mary Ann and Joey V, dancing the night away, cheek to cheek, my heart in your hands, just as we were, once upon a time.

Until we meet again,
I remain your ever-loving wife.
Goodbye, my love.

Mary Ann

chapter

THIRTEEN

I don't care how poor a man is; if he has family, he's rich.
Dan Wilcox, M*A*S*H

On the surface, the party at 2822 Devonshire didn't look any different than a typical Memorial Day, 4th of July, or Labor Day at the Von Gutens. The cars of all the regulars lined the streets—parish priests, friends, and family. But while it may have looked familiar, there were a few unexpected firsts.

It was the first time that Joseph's card-playing buddies had ever been to the house. For the first time, the bar was set up in the backyard while the lawn darts remained in the garage. For the first time, Mary Ann wasn't in the kitchen in an apron preparing the food, which meant there were no crudités. And, for the first time, Joseph wasn't there.

Mary Ann felt strange not preparing for the guests, who arrived carrying bottles of wine, beer, Canadian Club, and Wolf Schmidt, along with platters of Cleveland Heights traditional post-funeral comfort food—mostly deli trays from Corky and Lenny's. The dining room table was overflowing with the Jewish deli's infamous clock-shaped foil platters of sliced meats and cheeses, fanned perfectly and spaced evenly on a carpet of rippled lettuce. In the center was a bull's-eye of potato salad, crowned with a carved tomato and a jeweled black olive pierced with a toothpick and tipped with a quarter-inch of curly, red cellophane. Swiss cheese lay at the top of the clock, corned beef between one and three, Muenster from three to five, smoked turkey from five to seven, Swiss again from seven to nine, and rare roast beef from nine to 11 o'clock. The trays were garnished with green olives stuffed with pimentos, baby gherkins, and Don Herman's Kosher pickle spears. Baskets of Jewish rye, with and without seeds, were placed randomly on the table, as were plastic containers of Plochmans and Hellmans. A lonely Hamilton Beach Crock Pot of Swedish meatballs sat on the corner of the table, its extension cord dangling from the plug in the wall, a half-opened and spilled box of toothpicks next to it.

This hodgepodge buffet was not at all what regular guests were used to seeing on Mary Ann's dining room table. The regulars knew Mary Ann hated ham, deli trays, and cold cuts. If Carol had been there, she would have arranged for freshly made lasagna, manicotti, and chicken cutlets to be delivered from Guarino's Restaurant in Little Italy.

The industrial-sized stainless steel coffee maker, gurgling in the corner of the room brewing coffee that mostly went unused, was also an unusual sight. Regular guests of the Von Gutens were more interested in the drinks being served outside at the bar near the swing set than the coffee being served in the dining room. But Mary Ann let the neighbors plug it in anyway.

When the fifth honey-baked ham arrived, wrapped in gold foil and dripping sweetened ham juice, Tricia took it pleasantly from the sympathetic well-wisher. Out of the corner of her eye, Mary Ann saw her heading with the ham down the stairs to the basement refrigerator. She went to the door and called, "Tricia, while you're down there, take the beef burgundy out of the freezer to defrost. We'll have it when everyone leaves."

When she turned around, two men dressed in Armani suits, Gucci and Farragamo loafers and reeking of aftershave greeted her. "You have a lovely home. It's exactly as Joe described it to us. I'm sorry I didn't introduce myself. I'm Hugh Hepner. This is Teddy DeWold. We play cards with Joe on Wednesday nights. That is, we *did*." Mary Ann got a sharp, roiling pain in the pit of her stomach as Joseph's two worlds collided right in front of her. They were in her own sacred place, her family's home.

She had heard of Hugh Hepner. When Joseph told her his name years ago, she had immediately visualized Playboy bunnies and centerfolds standing around the players at the card game, hands on their shoulders, breasts barely covered. Since that first image, she had always hated the thought of Joseph playing cards on Wednesday nights. Who knows? Maybe she wasn't crazy. Maybe they did have hookers at the game. Maybe there was a lot about Joseph she didn't know.

"We're going to miss Joe." Mary Ann shivered at the non-family-like familiarization of his name. It made her uncomfortable just hearing it. He let them call him Joe?

"Even though he hasn't played with us on a regular basis in a while, we still kept in touch," Teddy said.

"Thank you for coming. I'm sorry our first meeting had to be today," Mary Ann lied. She never wanted to meet them. She made it clear to Joseph that he wasn't allowed to mix his gambling friends with their family. They would never be welcome in her home. In fact, she wished they hadn't come today. But, begrudgingly, she had to give them credit. They were doing the right thing by being there. She told herself to be polite or to at least try.

"Are you gentlemen married?" Mary Ann asked.

"Yes," they replied, slightly out of sync.

"Well, then, I have a question for you." Mary Ann paused and looked at DeWold, then at Hepner. "How do your wives feel about you playing cards and gambling?"

"They don't mind," Hugh said broadly. "At least mine's never said anything about it. We each have our separate lives, you know, like most married people do these days."

"I've noticed that happening more and more. How do you feel about that change, Mr. Hefner?"

"It's Hepner. I get that a lot, but my name's Hepner. I'm not lucky enough to be the *real* Hugh. But seriously, I think it's a great thing for a husband and wife to have separate time. At least for me, it is. Being the breadwinner is a demanding job. Wednesday night is my time to howl, to relax with the boys. Get away. Makes me a better husband in the long run, I think."

Hepner looked satisfied with his answer and turned to DeWold to hear his reply.

"Actually, I think my wife is happy to get me out of the house," Teddy laughed. Hepner chuckled, too.

"What does she do, your wife, when you're out howling with Mr. Hefner, here? Sorry, Hepner."

"I don't really know. I guess I never thought to ask her what she does. As long as she doesn't mind me being out, I don't care what she does."

Both men continued to smile, waiting for Mary Ann's next question. Mary Ann tilted her head and looked down at the floor, her hands clasped together in front of her. She began speaking, her voice barely audible, causing the two men to lean in. The three were huddled; heads down, looking almost like a scene from Picasso's Blue Period.

"I minded, a lot. Once Joseph started playing cards on Wednesday nights, I lost him. As far as I'm concerned, the life drained out of him and it never returned." The muscles in the faces of the two men grew slack, their smiles fading to blank, wary visages.

"At first I blamed the two of you and all the others. Not by name, you understand. Joseph, or Joe, as he seemed to be called by his pals in the world of Kings and Queens, never brought up the names of the men with whom he spent his family-less Wednesday nights. Occasionally, when one of *your* family members had trouble in school or with the law, he'd be forced to identify you by name as card-playing *friends* of his. So, over time, I got a pretty fair view of all of you. I could tell who was most likely cheating on his wife; whose children were running wild; who was having financial troubles. I got to know all of you far too well."

Mary Ann looked up and into the eyes of one, then of the other.

"Eventually, I realized that it wasn't *your* fault my Joseph was hanging out with you. It was his fault and mine. Somehow, Joseph and I lost, or maybe we never really had, our close relationship. The relationship a happily married man and woman have that says they are the two most important people in the world to each other."

Both men began to squirm. Mary Ann was sure her conversation reminded them of similar exchanges they'd had with their wives, probably far too often for their comfort.

"But you know what I never understood? What I never got to know?"

Mary Ann waited for them to shake their heads meekly and raise their eyebrows questioningly.

"I never understood why losing his money, our money, his family's money, why losing money was more important to him, more fascinating, more fun, than spending time with us. Can either of you answer that?"

After a short pause, Mary Ann raised her voice and went on.

"Can you? Do you have an answer why men like you, and that includes my Joseph, why men like you would even *bother* being married and raising a family in the first place if the minute life got difficult you bail out? Go out gambling and drinking? And who knows what all else? WHY? Why would you do that? And why did you have to take my Joseph with you when you did?"

Don and Fr. Burns walked into the kitchen and, while not having heard a word that had just been said, Don immediately intervened before Mary Ann lost her temper completely.

"Mary Ann, dear, ML is looking for you in the living room," Don said.

"Please excuse me. I need to go check on something. It was a pleasure meeting the two of you," Mary Ann lied again, and began to walk away. Then she stopped and turned back.

"The other thing I never knew?"

The four men waited silently, knowing a response on their part was not required for her to continue.

"Which one of your wife's fur coat is hanging in my closet? Tell her she can have it back. It's a gift from me."

Mary Ann wheeled around and walked away. ML wasn't looking for Mary Ann. Don was simply trying to prevent her from losing her cool. She was grateful he did, or she may have said something she'd regret. But Don was right. She needed to calm down. She went upstairs to her bedroom to get away, maybe lie down for a few minutes, and maybe freshen up a little. As she walked toward the bathroom, she noticed a powder blue envelope on her nightstand with 'Mary Ann' written on it. She recognized the handwriting immediately. His handwriting was unlike any other man's. It was as flowing and artistic as his piano playing. She held the envelope, and stared at the writing trying to decide if she should open it. She wanted to read it, but didn't know if she had the strength at the moment. She was angry and hurt that Hepner and DeWold showed up at her house. And she wasn't sure how she would react to what was inside *his* envelope. She wasn't sure what *kind* of note it would be. *Maybe it's a simple condolence card. Maybe it's something that will make me laugh. Maybe not, maybe it's more.*

Mary Ann looked out the window and saw him standing at the bar in the backyard. He had one arm around Patrick's shoulder and they were looking down at the grass, apparently talking about something serious. The sight of the two of them together resurrected one of her worst fears. *He wouldn't, would he? He wouldn't tell Patrick without talking to me first. Jack, please don't tell him, not yet.*

She and Jack never spoke about whether or not they'd tell Patrick the truth one day. Their reticent love and implicit bond was strong enough that they didn't need words for reinforcement. Like soul mates or an old married couple, they could read each other's minds, making it unnecessary to verbally agree. Mary Ann worried about many things but never about Jack confessing to Patrick's that he was his father. He loved her too much to complicate her life.

Watching them from the window, her heart ached for Jack. He would have been a wonderful father, but he never had the chance. And there he stood, holding that lost chance in his arms. Although Patrick looked more like Mary Ann's side of the family, the two had obvious similarities. She thought about how different Jack would have been as a father to Patrick. More compassionate, more reasonable, more sensible, and more loving than Joseph. Then she felt guilty: guilty for not giving Patrick what he deserved, guilty for not being honest, guilty for not letting Jack be the best role model for Patrick, guilty for her infidelity, guilty for years of wishing she could be with Jack, guilty for chastising those men who were guilty of the same sin.

Jack looked up and saw Mary Ann standing at her bedroom window. Their eyes locked for a moment, until Mary Ann couldn't take it anymore and turned around. The blue envelope was still on the nightstand waiting to be read. She sat on the edge of her bed and held it, shaking. A tear rolled off her cheek and onto the card, making the ink in the tail of the 'y' bleed; her name looked like it was crying too. Reluctantly, then hurriedly, she opened the envelope.

Dear Mary Ann ~

When I was a young boy, my mother once told me to be careful what I wish for. At the time, I wasn't sure what she meant. She always told me that I could be whatever I wanted and do whatever I dreamt of. She encouraged me to dream big, so why should I be careful of what I wish for? Now I know what she meant. For more nearly thirty years, I've wished for us to be together, but I never wished for something bad to happen to Joseph. Unfortunately, I know too well about the pain and suffering of losing a spouse. I wouldn't wish that upon anyone, especially you.

Without you, I couldn't have coped with losing Carol. You were her best friend—our best friend—and your love, support, and encouragement helped me get through it all. I was weak, and your friendship made me strong. I remember those days like they were yesterday. Yet, here we are decades later, and you are walking in my shoes.

Things are much different than when Carol died. You are blessed to have six wonderful children and a loving brother who will help you get through these difficult times. Nothing can compare with the power of family at a time like this. Even if you don't always like each other or get along, families come together and strengthen their bonds when tragedy or loss occurs. You are very fortunate to have such a strong support system.

Over the years, I've tried to let you live your life without interfering. Although unspoken, your decision to stay with Joseph was the right thing to do. We made a mistake, a big mistake, by crossing the line years ago. We were both weak but that doesn't excuse our actions. I've tried to rationalize our behavior and tell myself that it was acceptable for many reasons. Two of these reasons are that you deserved better than Joseph and that our love was real, not just a fling.

I'm going to take a chance, go out on a limb, and tell you that I still ache for you and for what we could be together. I constantly crave you. Your laugh, your smile, your scent, your presence, your aura, your voice, your mannerisms, they all mesmerize me like a drug, and I'm addicted. I've dreamt of the day that we could finally be together without hurting anyone in the process, and I hope that day is in the near future.

This may not be the best time to tell you this, but for years I've been waiting for the chance, and I couldn't wait any longer. I'm not asking you to make a decision today. I'm just asking you to think about it—think about giving us a chance. If you don't have the same feelings for me, I will respect your decision and quietly move on with my life without you.

Forever yours,
Jack

❧

Besides the occasional "we're sorry for your loss," not much was said about Joseph that afternoon. It felt and looked like any other Von Guten party. Just as much alcohol was consumed as during a Labor Day picnic, birthday party, or holiday celebration. There were only two differences. It was mid-day in the middle of the week, and Joseph was dead.

Later in the evening, when the guests were gone and Mary Ann was alone with her family, they talked about Joseph. They sat at the dining room table, comforted by the reheated beef burgundy and several bottles of Merlot. Tonight, Mary Ann pulled out the German crystal wine glasses that had been in the Von Guten family for generations.

"Mom, why are you using those? We only use them for special, *happy* occasions," ML made a point to stress the word.

"That was your father's rule, not mine. Why not use them? We should enjoy them. They make the wine taste much better, and for once we're going to do things my way."

"Mom, do you mind if I sit in Dad's chair?" Trip asked

"I think it would be nice for you to sit there. You're the oldest son and his namesake."

"Then I'd like to make a toast. Here's to Dad. To the greatest father, we'll miss you," said Trip, raising his full glass.

"Cheers!" They all clicked glasses with one another.

"Trip, I think he was the greatest father, but I know there were many times when *you* didn't like him," Mark said.

"Of course I didn't like him all the time. Who could? I bet we all feel the same way. But overall? He was an incredible man. To be a good parent or father, you're not always liked by your children. Right, Mom?"

"You're right. He wanted to be your father more than he wanted to be your friend. It's almost impossible to be both. Mark, you'd understand better if you had children. Hopefully some day you will," Mary Ann said.

"Our would-be-priest as a *real* father?" Tricia said. "That would be something to see."

"That might be sooner than you think," Mark said.

"Yeah, right," Trip said. "I'd drink to that."

"I always wished Mary Margaret had been able to have children," Mary Ann said, putting her wine glass to her mouth, sipping gently. "Of all of you, I think she might have made the best parent...no offense intended. I think you're all doing a great job. And Mark, when your day comes, if it ever does, I'm certain you'll be wonderful too."

Mark took a slug of his Coke, put down the glass, stood up and began pacing around the dining room table, head down, hands in his back pocket.

"I don't know how to say this any other way than to just say it. That day has come."

"What are you talking about?" Mary Ann asked.

"I am the father of a beautiful baby girl named Louisa."

"Jesus Christ, Mark, you've got to be kidding," Tricia said. She slammed her glass on the table, sloshing red wine onto the white embroidered tablecloth. Mary Ann reached over silently and blotted the red stain with her white cloth napkin.

"Pass the bottle. I'm going to need more wine to listen to this," Suze said, standing up to reach over the table for the bottle of wine.

"Pour me some while you're at it," Mary Ann said. She refolded her napkin and placed it on the table, as if it were being set aside an invisible plate.

"I'm glad Dad isn't here to witness this. He'd flip out," Trip said, leaning back in his chair and smiling into his glass.

"I disagree. He would understand better than all of you. He wasn't a racist like some of you," Mark said.

"Whoa, whoa, whoa," ML said. "What does racism have to do with this?"

"Mark, don't tell me you got that girl pregnant? The one who calls in the middle of the night? That Tina?" Mary Ann asked, her voice quivering.

"Who's Tina?" Tricia asked.

"Some girl he helped to get off drugs. He met her at an AA retreat last year, and since then she won't leave him alone," Mary Ann said. "Is she the one?"

"Yes, she told me earlier this week that I'm the father of her three-month-old baby."

"Do you believe her? Did you sleep with her?" Patrick asked.

"Yes, I slept with her, and I believe her."

"Does the baby look like you?" ML asked.

"What kind of question is that? Of course she looks like me. Well, it's kind of hard to tell at three months."

"Does that mean she doesn't look like you but you don't want to say so?" Suze asked.

"No, it doesn't mean that. The baby doesn't look a lot like me, but I slept with her mother, she got pregnant, and Louisa's my daughter."

"Looks don't necessarily mean anything," Trip said maliciously. "Look at Patrick. He doesn't look like *any* of us and he's our brother."

"What the fuck do you mean by that?" Patrick asked. "You're the biggest prick. So that must mean *you're* adopted because none of us are assholes like you."

"Trip and Patrick, stop that right now!" The boys glared at each other but did what their mother said. Mary Ann continued. "Mark, maybe that Tina girl *said* you're the father so you'll take care of them. You need to find out for sure if that baby's yours, and if she is? Well, then you love her like anything. Do you hear me?"

"What the fuck were you doing sleeping with *that* kind of girl?" Patrick asked.

"Patrick, watch your language. I've had enough of your foul mouth," Mary Ann commanded.

"It was a year ago, when I was drinking and getting high every day. I don't remember when it happened, but I know when we'd get high together we'd end up in bed."

Trip shook his head. "Dad is already rolling over in his grave. How did you let yourself get messed up with that kind of person? I don't understand why you would hang out with drug addicts and people from the ghetto."

"Enough of this! Mark, until you find out for sure that you're the father, please don't burden us with this. And I agree with Trip. Dad would be seriously pissed about this. It's not how we were brought up," Tricia said.

"Until we know for sure if you're the father, let's keep this between us. This conversation doesn't leave this table, understood?" Mary Ann said.

"Mom, I don't think this is something we'd go brag about," ML said.

"I sure as hell won't tell anyone," Suze said, finishing her glass of wine and hiccupping. "My lips are sealed."

Mary Ann felt as shitty inside as the weather was outside. She sat at the kitchen table with a glass of wine while the girls cleaned up the dinner dishes. She was staring out the window at the glow of St. Theresa's illuminated steeple in the distance, hypnotized by the rain and wind that was ushering in the night, a paradox of the sun that inaugurated the day. The ice-cold droplets that clung to the tree buds looked like tiny crystals reflecting the floodlights in the backyard. For more than an hour, she'd been unable to motivate herself to start going through Joseph's files to confront the sad state of their finances. The stack of papers in front of her was overwhelming. So much so that she didn't know where to begin.

Earlier in the day, Suze spoke to Mary Ann about not wasting time finding out what she could or couldn't afford. Tricia and ML wanted to wait a few days, but Suze wanted Mary Ann to get to the bottom of it before she went back to the west coast.

"A penny for your thoughts?" Suze asked.

"Huh? My mother always said that. I miss her." Mary Ann took a drink of her Nuevo Beaujolais. "It's so dreary outside. This morning was sunny and warm, and now it's rainy and cold," Mary Ann said.

"They say if you don't like the weather in Cleveland, wait ten minutes and it will change," Suze said. "Mom, while I'm in town, let me help you with this. Do you even know how much money you have?"

"I have no idea. Your father always took care of paying the bills and balancing the checkbook. I'm embarrassed to say that I've never paid a bill in my life, and I don't know how much money we have or even where it may be. I know our checking account is with Central Bank, but besides that? I don't know about our investments or savings."

"Well, I'm not surprised. We gave Dad a lot grief about a lot of things, and he may not have been a perfect father, but he was the one who handled the bills," Suze said.

"You're right. Even I didn't really realize how much he did for us or how much I needed him."

"Well, I know what dad would say right now. He'd say, 'let's roll up our sleeves and get started.' So, that's what we'll do," Suze said.

"Where did ML and Tricia go? They wanted to be here when I did this."

"They'll be back in a minute. They went to Tricia's house to check on Ashley. She took Tricia's kids home hours ago. It's weird, but after the funeral I sort of noticed how much Ash likes playing with Tricia's kids. They're like the brother and sister she never had. They even look alike," Suze continued. "Mom, let's start by going through your insurance file. You'll need to get copies of his death certificate to send to the companies he had policies with." Suze opened the folder marked 'John Hancock Life Insurance' and began shuffling through the papers. "Put your John Hancock on a John Hancock," she sang as she flipped the pages. She found what she thought she was looking for—the page that stated the value of the insurance policy.

"Mom, do you know how much life insurance Dad had?"

"I told you that I have no idea. But he always said that he was worth more dead than alive, whatever that means. What did you find?"

"It looks like he had a policy for $500,000, but its marked 'surrendered.' This doesn't make sense." Suze continued to read the file.

"What does 'surrendered' mean?" Mary Ann asked. "It doesn't sound good...."

"I'm not sure."

ML and Tricia came in the back door laughing like two schoolgirls.

"You're both soaking wet. Were you dancing in the rain or did you forget an umbrella?" Mary Ann asked.

"Both," ML answered.

"Where's Patrick?" Tricia asked.

"I'm in the dining room. I'm going through Dad's leather box of mementos. You girls can go through the important stuff," Patrick yelled in response from the other room.

"Did you start going through Dad's things without us?" ML asked.

"We just started, and already we have a question for Tricia. You should be in charge of this since you're the businesswoman of the family. I don't know anything about life insurance and investments. Look at his insurance policy and tell me what this page means," Suze said, handing Trish the wrinkled paper.

Tricia sat down at the yellowed, speckled Formica table that had been in the house since the day Mary Ann and Joseph moved in. The table had a fifty-year history, and the events of their lives were etched in its wear and tear. It had been host to thousands of nights of spelling homework, science projects, term papers, book reports, state projects, and leaves pressed and ironed between wax paper. It was home base for the annual Easter egg dying, Christmas cookie decorating, pumpkin carving, and valentines' construction. It was center court for balled-up napkin 'hoops' into glasses of milk for Mark, Tricia, and Patrick who ate dinner there nightly after their older brothers and sisters had moved out. For years it was the craft table for paper-mache, scratch art, oversized coloring books, paint by number, Spirograph, Lite-Brite, tie-dye, Play-Doh, finger painting, Silly Putty on newspaper cartoons, and Mary Ann's decoupage purses. It was the site of snow cone making with Snoopy and cake baking with the Easy Bake Oven. It was the game table for many late nights of Yahtzee, Scrabble, and Monopoly. It's where school pictures were unveiled, report cards were read with care, and birthday presents were wrapped. It was where Mark told his parents he wanted to be a priest and Carol told Mary Ann she had breast cancer. And it was where Mary Ann learned that Joseph was not worth more dead than alive. It's where she found out he had no worth at all. And neither did she.

Mary Ann couldn't believe what she was hearing. All she heard was something about the policy being surrendered for cash in 1995 and cancelled. Her loving Joseph had left her something she could have ever imagined. He left her nothing. Nothing at all.

ML, Suze, and Tricia riffled through files, frantically looking for another policy, perhaps a new one he'd bought since cashing the other one in. *Of course he had life insurance. There must be another policy in this pile somewhere.* The room began to spin. The sound of the girls' voices buzzing and arguing made her head feel like it was about to explode. She couldn't take any more surprises. No more unexpected nothings.

From the dining room, Patrick could easily hear what was happening. At times like this, most of the Von Gutens would pour themselves a drink but not Patrick. Alcohol was not his drug of choice. Music was.

Patrick sat down at the aging piano and played some random, seemingly unconnected notes for a few moments. No one spoke. Soon, the notes coalesced into a tune and Patrick started singing as he played.

"Papa was a rolling stone.
Wherever he laid his hat was his home.
And when he diiiiiiiied . . .
All he left us was alone."

"ML, give me your keys. Give me your car keys now!" Mary Ann's forceful demand made Patrick stop playing.

"Why? Why do you need them?" ML asked

"Your car is the last one in the driveway, and you're blocking me. Now, give me your keys. I need to go out. I need to get out of here. Give them to me now!"

Mary Ann was angry and trembling. She grabbed the keys out of ML's hand, walked outside into the cold rain without a coat or handbag, and drove away.

Dear Dairy,

Joseph, Joseph, Joseph. You know I never understood the gambling. I wish you were here to see how your bets finally paid off. With a great big zero. Nothing. That's what you left me. Nothing. Oh, I do have memories. Good ones and bad ones. And now, I have nothing in my hands, nothing in the bank, and no plan to save Divine. And no way to save our house, our home.

Now, I have nothing in my heart for you. My heart is full of sorrow. I am sorry you died. I truly am. But I am more sorry for your children. Especially when they find out the things I have known about you and about us for all these years. Somehow I know I will go on. Somehow, we will survive, no thanks to you. I had planned on growing old together. Now, I'm the only one getting old.

And Joseph?

I may not do that by myself. I may not go softly into the night alone. I may not.

Mary Ann

chapter

FOURTEEN

There is little less trouble in governing a private family than a whole kingdom.
Michel Eyquem de Montaigne, (1533-1592)
French philosopher

She was supposed to be in mourning, but she was more resentful than mournful. Mourning is sorrow. The pain she felt in the pit of her stomach wasn't sorrow but anger and fear. Her pain came not from being a widow, not from being left alone, but from being left with nothing. No cash, no savings, no life insurance, no income, nothing but a mess.

And now Mary Ann was caught in the middle of her sons feuding over who would be in charge of Divine Candles. Trip and Patrick worked for years under their father's direction. Not being taught and not learning so much as simply doing what they were told. Mark was working again in the family business for the umpteenth time. When Joseph died, Trip's ego grew tenfold. He insisted that he should become president since he was the oldest and his father's namesake. It was the logical thing to do, and he thought it was what Joseph would have wanted. Patrick didn't want to take orders from Trip, who was bossy and condescending. Mark, by his nature and with Mary Ann's pleading, tried to keep peace between his older and younger brothers but failed.

Joseph never created a succession plan for Divine Candles. Apparently, his operative plan was to live forever. Well, that failed. Nothing about continuing the business had been talked about, considered, or even tentatively sketched out, except the distribution of ownership. Joseph's brothers retired from the family business years ago, so Mary Ann received Joseph's stock in the company—sixty shares—while Trip and Patrick were each given twenty. But as far as day-to-day operations, no one was given a thing. There was no plan for how decisions were to be implemented, much less how they were to be made or by whom. The resulting confusion and conflict was too much for Mary Ann. She did her best to ignore it, along with the rest of the chaos that persistently surrounded her, taking over her every thought, her every waking moment, and her entire life.

There were piles of bills to pay, files of paperwork to become familiar with, and most importantly she needed to come up with a solution to the business mess Joseph had left her. But nothing seemed to motivate her to tackle her problems, to get things done, to make decisions. She was in a deep funk accompanied by complete procrastination and complete paralysis, and the longer she let things go the more difficult it became. There were thank you notes to write and phone calls to make to friends and family who helped her get through Joseph's funeral. But she didn't have the energy to pick up the phone or a pen. So she did what she could—minimal though it was.

Mornings, Mary Ann spent hours working on the daily crossword puzzle and drinking coffee at the kitchen table. Afternoons, she crawled back into bed. Most evenings, she endured time with her children who were taking turns keeping her company. By nine she was back in bed.

The next morning, she did it all again.

During this morning's trek through her daily routine, a new wrinkle in her life appeared. Well, not new exactly. Something thirty-four years old could hardly be considered new, but it was certainly a familiar scenario with a new twist. Since Joseph's funeral, she had managed to relegate Jack and his letter to the far back subconscious portion of her mind with relative success. Today, however, twenty-one down in the crossword puzzle brought his image into her mind, and their situation hit her full force in the middle of her awareness. It was the four-letter answer to the clue "*Man who can hold up a car.*"

When she left the house in ML's Toyota the night after the funeral, she had no idea where she was going or what she was doing. After fifteen minutes of driving aimlessly through Cleveland Heights' side streets, she found herself coming to a stop in front of Carol's house. Jack's house, really, although she still thought of it as Carol's. Either by intent or inertia, Jack was still following the customs, habits, and routines that Carol had established for their house. Turning the front porch light off and the lamp in the den on, as they were at the moment, was Carol's way of saying that no one was up. That everyone was in bed asleep. *Please call tomorrow.*

Mary Ann sat in ML's car and wondered if she should wake Jack. He wouldn't mind. It was, after all, what he said he wanted. But did she? Why did sitting in front of Jack's house make her feel like she was sneaking around? Thinking about having an affair? They were both single, unmarried, but she questioned whether it was moral. There she was, the day she watched dirt cover her husband's casket, in front of the house of the husband of her best friend and the man she'd secretly loved for almost as many years as she had known him, thinking about knocking on his door and asking him to let her stay with him till tomorrow, or longer.

If she were the one who'd died, would Joseph have felt the same? Would he be out celebrating, playing cards with his buddies?

A bright light suddenly shone in Mary Ann's eyes. She turned her head away and reflexively covered her eyes with her left hand. She looked through the driver's side window at the man shining a flashlight in her face, Detective Mooney. He indicated she should roll down her window. She complied.

"Good evening, Widow Von Guten. Your first night out alone? Where's ML, with a friend? This is her car, isn't it?"

"I'm sorry, Kevin, ML's at my house. I took her car and went out for a drive. You know, to shake out the cobwebs from the funeral? And I got so tired that I just had to stop. I wouldn't want anyone to think I had been drinking, especially not on a day like today."

"Certainly not. You *haven't* been drinking, have you? One can't be too careful, you know. Maybe it's time you moved along. Wouldn't want to wake up the neighborhood, would we?"

Jack. The answer was Jack. She filled in twenty-one down, laid the pencil on the table, and got up and opened the refrigerator. Maybe it was time for lunch. It was too early to go back to bed. Too soon to wonder if, indeed, Jack *was* the answer.

❧

"We've got to do something to get Mom to take control. We can't do everything for her. It's her job, and her responsibility to take care of these things," ML said to Tricia and Suze on a conference call. "If it were one of us in this situation, she'd *make* us be in charge. She'd help, but it would be up to us. You know that."

"I know she would, and she'd be right. And I know I should do my share of helping her out, but I don't know what I can do from Portland. Can't the two of you talk to her? Go over to the house, and *make* her do these things? Set up a system for her, and show her how to pay the bills? I think she needs someone to give her a push," Suze said.

"Don't you think I've been pushing her?" Tricia said with an obvious edge to her voice. "It's not as simple as it sounds out there in Portland. Just because you don't live here doesn't mean you can't help. It's going to take all of us. I'm afraid this is only the beginning of years and years of making sure she's okay. And the first thing she has to do? She has to sell that huge house and move into something smaller, something that doesn't cost so much. That place is too expensive for her now. And when she does sell, who knows how long the money will last? I'm thinking we may need to take care of her the rest of her life."

"God, I hope not, but you might be right about it taking all of us, even if I don't live there anymore. I have an idea. I'm supposed to be in New York next month for a cooking segment on *The Today Show*..."

"No way! You're going to meet Katie Couric? I *love* her. That show is my inspiration for everything. If Matt and Katie don't talk about it, then I don't know about it," Tricia interrupted.

"Yeah...so, let's all meet in New York with Mom. Then we can talk to her and come up with a plan," Suze said.

"Count me in," ML said.

"Girls' trip? I'm there, just say when," Tricia added.

❧

From what she had seen on TV over the years, Mary Ann was well aware that New York had changed since her last visit decades ago. But being here? She couldn't believe her eyes. The midnight blue night sky was a stark contrast to the brilliant dazzle of the enormous LED billboards. More than fifty years earlier, she and her mother had walked the streets of New York many times, but they never went near Times Square. Back then it was the seedy party of town, home to corruption, prostitution, gangs, and crime. It was known worldwide as a red-light district. When ML first told her they were staying at a hotel in Times Square, Mary Ann thought she was joking. When she realized ML was serious, she told her daughters she wasn't going on the trip if that's where they were staying. Not until Suze told her that NBC was paying for their rooms at the Hilton did Mary Ann believe that they were actually staying in Times Square. She told herself that if a hotel in Times Square was good enough for the guests of *The Today Show*, it must be safe. To be sure, she put something comforting in her handbag—her rosary. Not that she was still worried; it was just for extra protection and peace of mind.

It was nearly ten at night, and the traffic was worse than rush hour anywhere in Cleveland and maybe the world. Mary Ann, Tricia, and ML sat patiently in a cab while the driver accelerated, stopped, accelerated, stopped, jerking them around the back seat. Hundreds of pedestrians were standing on the median, heads tilted up to the sky, as if they were watching a UFO.

"What's everyone looking at?" Mary Ann asked.

"Over there is where the New Year's ball drops; they are reading about Princess Diana dying in a car crash," said the Indian taxi driver. "She and that businessman Dodi Fayed," he continued.

Mary Ann craned her neck to look out the windows at the news ticker that was scrolling the tragic story of Princess Diana's death. A wave of silence passed through Times Square as pedestrians and cars slowed and stopped, silently reading that the paparazzi had caused the fatal accident. Even taxi drivers stopped beeping their horns.

"She was so beautiful but so troubled. I feel badly for her sons having to grow up without her," Mary Ann said. She was wondering which was worse: losing a child or losing a parent as a young child.

"Prince Charles is such a jerk. I can't believe he chose that horsewoman, Camilla Parker, over her. She even has the teeth of a horse. Getting divorced was the best thing that happened to Princess Diana. She could have done much better than him," Tricia said.

"I knew when I woke up at four in the morning to watch her wedding that it would never last. There wasn't a hint of emotion in either one of their faces. And it was their wedding day, for God's sake," ML said. "And with a mother-in-law like that? Diana didn't stand a chance."

The bar at the hotel was exactly as Mary Ann had envisioned. Standing there, she realized that over the years when she thought about New York this was the image that came to her mind first. Dark, smoky, crowded rooms with professionals dressed to the nines and sipping martinis. A tuxedoed piano player was filling the air with Cole Porter-style music, helping patrons forget their worries. At the end of the bar in those visions, a flashy, well-dressed ingénue sat, her long stocking-clad legs crossed, an unfiltered cigarette dangling from her red-tipped fingers. At the end of *this* polished mahogany bar sat one of Mary Ann's daughters, chatting with the bartender.

"Over here!" Suze gracefully waved her arm in the air so her mother and sisters would see her. She sat sideways on the bar stool with her toned, tan legs crossed at the knee, twirling her right ankle and showing off her black Prada pumps. A gentleman at the bar offered his seat to Mary Ann, ML, and Tricia after they hugged Suze hello.

"Three Cosmopolitans for my sisters and mother, please," Suze called to the bartender.

"Don't make mine too sweet," Tricia added.

"Girls, it's so nice being here with you. I'm the luckiest mother in the world to have such wonderful daughters. A toast to my beautiful daughters, and let's not forget Mary Margaret: we wish you were here," Mary Ann said. They clinked their pink drinks and took small sips.

"I'm not so sure we're all that wonderful, Mother. But today we'll accept the compliment," ML said.

"Mom, if you could change anything about each of us, what would it be?" Tricia asked.

"Nothing, you're all perfect in my eyes."

"There must be something that you wish we did, didn't do, or did differently," ML said.

"Hmm, I'll have to think about this for a moment," Mary Ann said. She took a sip of her Cosmo and peered at Tricia over the rim.

"See, I knew there was something. You're looking at me like you have something to say. Go ahead. I can take it," Tricia said.

Mary Ann held her breath, and her conscience told her to keep her mouth shut. The alcohol told her inner voice to speak up.

"Well, I probably shouldn't say anything, but I really wish you would have married a nice Catholic boy."

"Why? Don't you like Scott? I thought you loved him," Tricia said.

"Yes, I love Scott. It's just that he's not, well, he's not Catholic."

"Why is that so important to you?"

"How can you ask that? You were raised Catholic, our family business is supported by the Church and your uncle is a bishop. I wish you would have continued to go to Mass."

"What do you mean by a 'nice Catholic boy'?"

"You know exactly what I mean, Tricia."

"No, I'm not sure I do. Like a nice Catholic boy from a large family who went to St. Xavier Prep School for boys? Or like the nice Catholic boy who married Mary Margaret and beat the crap out of her? Or like the nice Catholic boy who was the coach of the girls' high school tennis team and slept with the freshmen? Oh, I know, maybe like the nice Catholic boy from St. Theresa's who worked for the family jewelry store and went to jail for replacing diamonds with cut glass in rings brought in for repair?"

"Cubic Zirconium," Suze said.

"That's not the point. The point is what kind of 'nice Catholic boy' is Mom talking about? Mom, I can't believe you still feel that way, especially after what's been going on. Don't you read the papers? One of the priests charged with sexually molesting a boy is Fr. Gellin. He was Mark's coach, and you've had him to the house for dinner dozens of times. Doesn't that make you sick?" Tricia asked.

"Yes, and I'm glad that Mark's name was never in the paper when they were covering the impropriety of the priests," Mary Ann said.

"Mom, what are you talking about?" asked ML.

"Never mind, I'm not making any sense. I think I've had a few too many drinks," Mary Ann said.

"Wait a minute, Mother. Don't be so quick to blame it on the alcohol. Are you implying that something happened between Mark and Gellin?" Tricia asked.

"No, no, no, let me explain it this way. The devil is a powerful entity that wishes us to be sinful, and it's most sought after conquests are God messengers. Priests are not infallible and are as susceptible to temptation as all mankind," Mary Ann said. She read the papers and watched the news, and at first she refused to believe that a priest could do such a thing. She talked with Don about it at length, and although he defended the church he never said it didn't happen. After reading about how the victims were affected by the alleged impropriety, Mary Ann kept a close eye on Mark.

"Mom, please don't try to defend those priests. They have 'guilty' written all over their faces," Suze said.

"You might be right. Back to what you were asking me about nice Catholic boys, I'm sorry I brought it up. I love Scott. You've made a good point—the character of a man is much more important than his religion. We've all made mistakes with men, or at least I have. Sometimes we need to follow our hearts and hope they lead us down the right road. Enough of this, I don't want to spoil this weekend with my girls." Mary Ann raised her glass to her girls and took another sip. Her daughters saluted back.

"It's a shame that your brothers can't get together like this," Mary Ann continued to babble as her daughters sipped their drinks and listened. Mary Ann usually didn't have much to say, but tonight she was on a roll. "They can't stand to be in the same room. It seems like they actually *hate* each other, and I don't know what to do. Do you know that they asked me to choose one of them to be president of Divine? How can I choose one over the other? Fortunately Mark isn't interested in running the company, but Trip and Patrick are fighting constantly about who's going to be the boss. I'm not a businesswoman, I'm their mother, and I resent being put in this position by them. No matter whom I choose, I will lose. One of them will hate me, and I can't bear the thought of that happening."

"Mom, it doesn't matter what you say or do, they are going to fight until one of them wins," Suze said. "That's how boys are. It's the fight that's important to them, even more so than the prize."

"You've got that right," ML agreed, finishing her Cosmo and signaling the bartender for another round. "Angela says her husband can carry a grudge for years. That he's not interested in resolving things between him and other guys unless it involves getting even. Thank God Trip and Patrick aren't vindictive, or you'd have a real problem no matter who becomes president."

"Mom, you may not know anything about business or about running a company, but Suze does. Suze, you can help Mom," ML said.

"I don't have that kind of business sense. I wish I could help, but I only know about food, and I don't have time to help. Give the boys time, and they'll figure it out," Suze said.

"That's okay, dear. I understand. I wouldn't ask you to get involved. I want to see you make your own dreams come true. I'd feel guilty if I made you lose that chance."

"Mom, I'll be fine. It's not that I don't want to get involved, so don't feel that way...you've lived your whole life feeling guilty."

"You have no idea." Mary Ann pulled a handkerchief from her purse and wiped her nose, as if trying to prevent tears from spilling.

"I'm no good at business. I have trouble even balancing my checkbook, but if you want me to say something to the boys, let me know," ML said.

"Thanks, but I don't want them to be mad at you too. I'm the mom, so I'll handle it. It's just that it's so, so, distasteful. Those two are so uncooperative. I can't stand it."

"You're right, Mom. It's your job to take care of the boys. I'll take care of Divine," Tricia said.

"You, Tricia?" ML said. "You don't know anything about business either, do you? Oh, that's right. I forgot about your Internet business. I'm still waiting for you to give me some of those six-hundred-thread-count sheets, or are you waiting for me to place an order online?"

"You'll get your sheets. I'm just saying I want to help," Tricia said, pulling her cherry off at the stem and chewing it thoughtfully.

"I know you do, dear. All of you, I appreciate your concern. But I think Suze's right. The boys will work it out," Mary Ann said.

Mary Ann was tired and began pondering excuses to go up to her room when the bartender, a wannabe actress from twenty years ago, set their second round of Cosmopolitans in front of them. When she left, Suze resumed the family-focused conversation.

"Mom, what about Mark? Did you ever hear if that baby was his?"

Mary Ann pretended not to hear Suze's question and focused on her Cosmo. But she had, and she wasn't anxious to talk about it. However, the liberating affects of her second drink were starting to take hold, and she decided that this was going to be a night for truth and honesty. Unless, of course, they started asking *her* truth or dare questions, then she'd plead being the mom excuse. What they didn't know was good for them.

"I decided I wasn't going to get involved. I can't lead Mark's life for him. So, if he *says* that baby's his, then as far as I'm concerned it is."

"Mom, that addict is taking him for a ride, and you know it."

"Tricia, I won't hear that kind of talk. I told you what I think, and that's it."

"That's not it, Mom," ML chimed in. "Tricia's right. Mark needs our help to see things like they really are. If he's not careful, who knows what kind of trouble that woman will make for him? Kevin tells Angela stories all the time about those kind of people, and how they'll do and say anything to get high or take your money."

"Who knows how things are really going to turn out? Did I? Did I know when your father died that I'd be broke? Penniless? Left with a giant old house that sucks money like a black hole? And that's not all that sucks. Life sucks."

The girls jerked in unison at their mother's unusually aggressive language.

"Sorry, but it's true. Sometimes life just sucks; there's no other way to say it. And there's nothing you can do about it, except go on and follow your dreams, which is exactly what I'm going to do. Now enough of this...this... crap. Tell us Suze, what's going to happen on *The Today Show* tomorrow? That's why we're all here, after all. To see you become the star you were destined to be."

"I don't know about that...the star part, anyway. But you're right about the dream. This is what I want to do, and if I'm going to be my best tomorrow, I have to get some beauty sleep. I don't know who else is going to be on the show. We'll find out when we get there."

Suze stood to kiss and hug her sisters and mother good night. Soon after she headed for the elevator, ML said, "When she ran away, I never thought I'd see her again. And I certainly never thought I'd see her as a world-famous chef and a TV star. But look at her now."

"Yes, it's remarkable," Mary Ann said. "I thought we lost her for good. It's no secret I thought about her every day she was away from us. But in the long run everything turned out well, and I'm glad for her. She deserves this. Now, I think it's time for my beauty sleep too. Lord knows I need a lot of it these days."

As they had planned the night before, Mary Ann was waiting in the lobby for ML and Tricia to go meet Suze at One Rockefeller Center. She was in a fog. Was it the drinks last night or the emotionally arduous conversations about priest impropriety, a Jewish son-in-law, feuding sons, and a failing business that made her head feel heavy and cloudy? Whatever the cause, she needed coffee before she could have her picture taken with Katie, Matt, Al, and Ann. ML and Tricia rounded the corner of the lobby, each holding two cups of coffee as the elevator door opened. Suze walked out with her handbag hanging from the crook of her arm.

"Suze, what are you doing here? I thought you had to be at the studio at five-thirty?" Tricia asked.

"I've been bumped. Princess Di has taken over the whole show."

"Oh, that's terrible," Mary Ann said. "I'm so sorry for you." She put her arm around her daughter in the same motherly, consoling way she'd done for all her children for as long as anyone could remember.

"But there's an upside."

"What's that?" ML asked.

"I've been rescheduled for tomorrow, and NBC has extended our rooms another night, so we have all day to play. I thought we could go to the Statue of Liberty. Anyone up for a boat ride?"

"Row, row, row your boat," ML sang as they took the elevator up to their rooms to put on their sightseeing clothes.

Dear Diary,

Here I am in a plane, miles above the earth and closer to God than I was before we took off. Although I'm not as close as Princess Di. Certainly there is a lesson in her death—at least for me. And that lesson is: Life is short, so don't wait. Don't put off love when it's there to be yours.

All I have to do is pick up the phone. As I sit here thinking about my future, I am as nervous as a young girl. As nervous as I was that first time with Joseph. Maybe I should have been the gambler. Well, I don't think this will be a losing bet. And as silly as this is making me feel, I will be strong.

Life is short.

Don't wait.

Mary Ann

chapter

FIFTEEN

2003

Blood is thicker than water, and when one's in trouble, best to seek out a relative's open arms.
Author unknown

It was a classic case of the sardonic "No good deed goes unpunished." Mark ran into Tina and Louisa at McDonald's. Tina's hands were shaking and her eyes were red and watery. He tried to have a conversation with her, but she gave him a blank stare like she didn't know who he was. When he asked her if she was okay, she told him to go fuck himself. Appalled that Tina would talk like that in front of Louisa, Mark told her she was in no condition to raise a child, especially since she was high.

When he asked her why she wasn't at school, Louisa said, "My mommy forgot to sign me up."

Mark knew there was no chance for a rational discussion. Tina was using.

He left McDonalds and went to St. Theresa's to pray for guidance to do the right thing. On his knees, he realized he had no choice but to file for custody. He couldn't bear the thought of Louisa living in pitiful conditions with a strung-out mother who couldn't take care of herself, let alone his child.

He wanted Louisa to grow up safe and self-confident. He wanted her to go to St. Theresa's and get the same education he had. As her father, the least he could do was give her a safe home, an education, and a good life. A better life than she was headed for now.

Her mother was uneducated, a drug abuser, and lived in a run-down house in a rough neighborhood with two unemployed uncles, two sisters, and their seven children, all of whom had no idea who the fathers were. For Louisa to receive all that Mark wanted for her, she needed a strong home and a strong parent. She needed Mark in her life on a daily basis.

Ever since the blood test confirmed he was the father, Mark had tried to help Tina and Louisa. For some reason, Tina was suddenly threatened by Mark's presence. He was certain her sisters were the main cause. They must have convinced Tina that Mark was nothing more than an evil white man who would corrupt Louisa and take her away from them.

But there was more to it than that. He knew it was about money. As a single unemployed parent, Tina received seven hundred dollars a month from the government. If Mark got custody of Louisa, then Tina would lose that money and have nothing to live on. And her sisters and the others in the house would see that monthly income disappear forever, or at least until she had another illegitimate child. Mark was also convinced that Tina's sisters coerced her into pressing charges against him to prevent them from losing Louisa and her monthly check.

From his social work clinical with the county Department of Child and Family Services, Mark was all too familiar with the practice of mothers accusing fathers of molesting their children in order to win custody battles. Even though Tina had trusted and relied on Mark for years to help her get sober, finish her GED, get a job, and move away from her controlling sisters, he knew Tina wasn't smart enough to think of accusing him herself. Her sisters were the architects behind these false accusations.

One day Mark was filled with hope and plans for his daughter's future and was filing for custody. The next day he was accused of rape by digital penetration. These women were smarter than he originally thought. Digital penetration was rape without DNA and without signs of abuse, making it a much more difficult charge for the accused to defend against.

For the hundredth time, he dialed Tina's number. There was still no answer. By now he was convinced that Mooney wasn't lying when he said Tina had testified to the grand jury, all because Mark had tried to do the right thing.

His nails were chewed to the quick, and he was starting to gnaw at his cuticles. His life was spinning out of control.

On one hand, he had been on the road to recovery for six years following decades of alcohol abuse. He was back at school and about to earn a degree as a social worker, and he hoped to go on and get his masters in rehabilitation counseling. Ever since he had gotten sober, he wanted to help others change their ways and fight the triggers that lead to abuse—step twelve—the final step to recovery. For the past two years, he hid the fact that he was taking college courses from his family to avoid ridicule in case he failed. He was known for never sticking with something for more than three months, a fact that his brothers and sisters constantly reminded him of. He finally had his life on track and he didn't want to jinx himself by telling anyone until he was holding the degree.

On the other hand, the charges Tina's had aimed against him had put him in a tailspin without the tools to help himself. He was going down fast with no apparent hope for recovery. No possibility of landing and no parachute. He was beside himself. He didn't know what to do. He needed to talk to someone and get a trusted opinion. He picked up the phone and called Tricia.

"If you didn't do it, there won't be any evidence," Tricia said. "Even if she was raped by someone else and they took her to the hospital, the DNA won't match yours so they won't have a case. How could the grand jury indict you without evidence?"

"In Ohio, digital penetration—inserting a finger—even an eighth of an inch, is considered rape. And that's what they're saying I did. Tricia, I didn't touch her, I swear. I could never hurt her."

"Mark, I believe you. Don't worry, we'll figure something out. Are you sure they've indicted you?"

"That fucking asshole Kevin Mooney called to brag about it. He's hated me since high school. He said Tina made a statement that the *'alleged incident'* happened six months ago when I had her and Louisa over to my apartment. She set me up. *And* he said that Louisa told a social worker I touched her private parts."

"Jesus Christ, Mark, how the hell did you get yourself in this position to begin with? This is a nightmare!"

"No shit! Mooney said I'd be arrested within the next twenty-four hours. I don't know what to do."

"First, we have to get you a lawyer, but I suppose you don't have enough money to pay for one, do you?"

"No, I don't. Plus, someone will have to post bond. Please don't let me go to jail, Tricia. Please, I didn't do anything. I swear. Please help me. I could get life in prison if they believe her." Mark doodled voraciously on the cover of an old *Time* magazine as he waited for her to respond.

"Where are you?"

"I'm at my apartment, and I'm not going anywhere, don't worry. I'm not running from something I didn't do." He tore the cover off the magazine, bunched it into a ball and threw it against the wall.

"Do me a favor and don't say anything to Mom about this. She'll freak out, and she has enough to worry about. Let me deal with this, and we'll tell her only if we need to," Tricia said.

"I won't say anything to her. Just promise that you'll help me," he begged.

"I will, I'll figure something out. But how will I know if you've been arrested?"

"I don't know. I guess I'll try to call you. They have to let me call someone, don't they?"

"I think so. In the meantime, I'll call ML and ask her if she can get any information from Angela. Maybe she can talk Kevin out of arresting you. Hang in there. I love you."

"Thanks, Pooh. I love you, too."

Mark hadn't called her Pooh in eons, maybe twenty-five years. When Tricia was a baby, he couldn't pronounce Patricia—all he could manage was Pooh. Reflexively calling Tricia by her childhood nickname tugged at his heartstrings and took him back to his childhood. Suddenly he was back in the fantasyland of the Hundred Acre Woods, where they spent countless hours pretending to be their favorite Winnie the Pooh characters. Tricia had deemed Mark as Christopher Robin, and Patrick had become Piglet. *God I wish I could go back to Pooh-time... back to the House at Pooh Corner, back to the days of Christopher Robin and Pooh.*

❧

Tricia held the Egyptian cotton, zero-looped, plush towel to her face and slowly inhaled the chemically created dryer-sheet fragrance of spring rain as she stepped out of the shower. She held it to her face longer than usual, wishing she could just climb back into bed. She woke that morning angry and resentful. In her dream, her father was talking to her on the phone. Then abruptly Mickey Mouse interrupted the conversation by telling her to '*rise and shine.*' She was using her son Chris's alarm clock because hers was broken. *Note to self: get new alarm clock.* A psychologist was on *The Today Show* telling Katie Couric that the parents of the students who committed the Columbine and other recent school shootings are to blame for their children's actions.

"Screw you, doc," Tricia said before turning off the TV in her bathroom.

The recurring dreams of her father exhausted her so much that she dreaded going to bed. Most mornings she woke more tired than when she went to sleep. Night after night in her dreams, her father told her to '*Take care of it.*' In last night's dream, she screamed at her father, '*what the hell is it, Dad? Tell me.*' He never answered her, but she knew what he meant. A realist and a skeptic, Tricia didn't put much faith in dreams. But her father's words began to nag at her throughout her days.

Scott stood in the doorway to the bathroom and watched as her lips quivered and tears welled in her eyes. She pinched her lips together and attempted to smile, but within seconds of seeing him, she began to tremble.

He wrapped her in the towel and took her into his arms.

"What is it? What's bothering you?" Scott asked.

Tricia tried to compose herself and stand tall. When she told her husband about the dreams, he said she was burdening herself with Mark's problems.

"Tricia, you can't solve everyone's problems, nor does anyone expect you to," Scott said.

"But he's my brother. I can't walk away from him and not help. If I do, he'll end up with a public defender who won't give a damn, and he could end up in jail for life. I couldn't live with myself if that happened."

"When you sleep with dogs, you get fleas. I'm not saying he did this—I believe he's innocent. But at some point he has to pay the consequences for his actions. What the fuck was he thinking sleeping with that sleazy girl?"

"That's the problem, he wasn't thinking. He was using and drinking, which led to all of this. Yes, he's made some terrible decisions in his life, and for years he's struggled to find his way, but he's been sober for six years. He doesn't deserve to be accused of raping his own daughter. This is so far out of control; I can't believe this is happening. It's like an episode of *Law and Order,*" Tricia said.

"Trip called while you were in the shower. Mark was arrested last night, and there's a hearing this morning to set his bail. Trip is going to the hearing, and he'll write a check for the bond. If all goes well, Mark will be home by the end of the day," Scott said.

"I should go with Trip."

"No, look at yourself. You're an emotional wreck just thinking about this. I know you, and you can't handle seeing Mark in an orange jumpsuit and handcuffs. Let your brothers go to the courthouse and take care of this. Get dressed and focus on your business. Your office phone rang at eight-thirty, and I saw on caller ID that it was Werners. Call them back before they withdraw their offer to buy TLC."

Tricia's new online catalogue of fine linens, TLC (named after Tricia, her daughter Lauren, and her son Chris), was an overnight success and recently discovered by Werners, a purveyor of home accessories. In its second year, TLC's gross sales were over seven hundred thousand dollars and Werners was interested in a buyout.

"Mark needs to get a decent lawyer, but he can't afford one," Tricia said.

"That's Mark's problem. When he gets out of jail today, he can worry about getting a lawyer."

Scott started to walk out of the bathroom, then stopped and turned around.

"By the way, the new bath towels are awesome. If you price them right, you won't be able to keep them in stock," he said. "And one more thing, your mother called. She wants you to help her decide whom she should choose to run Divine. I told her you'd call her back."

chapter

SIXTEEN

Look in the mirror. The face that pins you with its double gaze reveals a chastening secret.
Diane Ackerman

Mary Ann was a nervous wreck. For days, she had been thinking about calling and rehearsing the conversation over and over in her head.

Her hands shook when she dialed his number. Her breath was uneven. Adrenaline rushed to her head, making her thirsty. As soon as he answered, her fears subsided. The sound of his voice released a wave of calm throughout her body. She could hear classical music in the background. She pictured him sitting in his living room, drinking sherry, reading the latest issue of *Bon Appetite* or *Wine Spectator*, none of which Joseph would have been caught dead doing. If it didn't include hard liquor or cheap beer, or watching something on TV that involved teams fighting over some sort of ball, Joseph wasn't interested. Unlike most men Mary

Ann knew, Jack was a gourmet cook, loved music, art, and theater, and enjoyed fine wine—not the kind that came in a box.

"Hello?" Jack said.

"Jack? Hello," Mary Ann paused and took a deep breath. "It's me. How are you?"

"I'm fine, but more importantly how are *you?* I've been worried."

"You don't need to worry about me. I have six kids who have made it their full-time job. There's enough worry around my house to last a lifetime."

There was a pause, as both of them tried to put their thoughts in order so they wouldn't leave their mouths all jumbled. Jack was quickest.

"I've been waiting for this call for years, decades. Now I'm nervous about what you might to say."

"I know this phone call is long overdue. Believe me, I know. Thank you for being so patient. I've wanted to do this for years, but I had to push thoughts of you into the back of my mind. I know you understand, but still I have to say it. It wouldn't have been right. It wasn't right when I was married."

"Mary Ann, you don't owe me an explanation. You don't owe me anything. If you don't want to do this, I understand."

"No, that's not why I'm calling. I do. I *do* want to give us a chance, I'm just scared. I know we're both single, consenting adults, and there should be no reason why we can't be together. Yet I feel guilty, probably because we started this the wrong way thirty-some years ago."

"Mary Ann, we need to forgive ourselves for our mistakes. Guilt will eat away at your heart and soul. It's as toxic as hatred and stress."

"I know you're right. It's just easier said than done," Mary Ann said.

"Let's not get into this over the phone. I need to see you. May I come over?"

"That's not a good idea. I never know when one of the kids is going to walk in the door. They show up unannounced all the time. Not that I mind, but if they showed up while you were here, I *would* mind. I know they think of you as an uncle and wouldn't think anything of it, but can we meet somewhere else, at least this time?"

"Yes, of course. Come over to my house, unless you're not comfortable doing that."

"No, that's fine. I'd be more comfortable there than in public—at least for now."

"Then come over for dinner. I'll cook us something special. Just give me a couple of hours to go to the store and get organized. How's seven o'clock?"

"Fine, I'll see you then. Can I bring anything?"

"Are you kidding? *You're* the greatest gift you can bring."

Mary Ann had less than two hours to find something to wear, and she knew it wouldn't be in her closet. The last time she shopped for a dress was for Tricia's wedding. She'd occasionally pick up tops or slacks to keep her wardrobe fresh, but it had been a while since she considered buying something fashionable. Jones & Co. boutique was only six blocks away. Plenty of time to find an outfit, get home, and change before dinner.

"Hello, Mrs. Von Guten. Can I help you find something today?" the sales clerk asked.

"I'm sorry, I'm sure I know you from somewhere, but I can't remember your name," Mary Ann said.

"I'm Leeza Moreice, Patrick's friend."

"Oh, yes, of course. I'm sorry I didn't recognize you, Leeza. I think the last time I saw you, you had braces. You've turned into a beautiful young woman. How is your mother?"

"She's fine. I'm so sorry about Mr. Von Guten. I was at the funeral. I still keep in touch with Patrick."

"Thank you. As you can tell by the way I'm dressed, it's been a while since I've been shopping, and I don't even know what's in style. So if you can help an old lady like me find something to wear to a casual dinner party, I'd appreciate your help."

"What size are you? Six?"

"I think so, but I wouldn't be surprised if I were an eight or a ten."

"Mrs. Von Guten, you have a great figure, don't fool yourself. You're no bigger than a six, and you may even be a four."

"I don't have much time, so if you can pull a few things for me, I'll trust your judgment. By the way you're dressed I can see you have good taste."

Mary Ann surprised herself when she looked in the mirror after slipping on the first dress. The size four silk jersey wrap dress looked like it was made for her.

"How does the Diane Von Furstenberg dress fit?" Leeza asked through the dressing room door.

"It's perfect. I'm not crazy about patterns, but I like this one. And it doesn't need to be hemmed."

Mary Ann opened the dressing room door and Leeza and Margaret Jones, the owner, were gaping at her.

"What? What's wrong? It's not good on me?" Mary Ann asked.

"No, quite the opposite. You look fabulous. You have the figure of a thirty-year-old, and your legs look great. Were you a dancer?" Margaret asked.

"No, I guess it's from years of chasing seven kids around, and these days my daughter Tricia makes me go to yoga with her three times a week."

"Mrs. Von Guten, I would love for you to model for us. We do a lot of fashion shows around town, and you are exactly the kind of woman we are targeting. With your looks, you must have modeled before," Margaret said.

"No, no, never. Are you kidding? I haven't worked in years. And I've never modeled."

"Here's my card. Call me next week and we'll have lunch to talk about our next fashion show. Leeza, put this dress on a house charge for Mrs. Von Guten, and I'll settle up with her over lunch. Ciao!"

Mary Ann left the store wearing the dress and glowing. Leeza told her to wear sling-back black pumps with it. She had the perfect pair of Fendi's that Tricia had brought her from Italy. She never thought she'd wear them, but now she was grateful for Tricia's impeccable taste, not to mention foresight. She put the shoes on and stood in front of the full-length mirror on the back of her closet door. For the first time, she understood why women love designer Italian shoes. The heels were higher than she was used to—about two-and-a-half-inches higher—but she liked what they did for her legs. At seventy-two, her legs were as sexy as ever.

Margaret was right; she had the legs of a dancer. *Ginger Rogers, eat your heart out. These shoes are worth every dollar Tricia spent.* She spritzed her neck with the Chanel #5 ML gave her for her last birthday. For the past twenty-five years, she had only ever worn Estee Lauder's Youth-Dew, Joseph's annual Christmas gift to her. She never liked it, but she wore it for him.

She didn't want to look overdressed, so she kept her jewelry simple. She fastened on pearl stud earrings and the Cartier watch Joseph gave her for their fiftieth. She took a deep breath and held it while she slipped off her wedding rings and put them in her jewelry box. As she exhaled and closed the box, she felt the weight of the world soar off her shoulders. For the first time in fifty years, she was leaving the house without wearing a wedding band.

Jack lived a mere four blocks away. Mary Ann preferred walking to Carol's house unless she had too much to carry. When she and Joseph had been invited over for dinner, they always preferred to walk, especially home. It enabled them to walk off the wine or martinis they'd consumed during the course of the night. They drove when the weather was bad, and although the weather was perfect Mary Ann wasn't sure she'd be able to walk the four blocks in three-inch heels. She thought about calling Jack and asking him to pick her up. But if one of her kids came by and saw that her car was there and she wasn't, they'd panic and expect the worst.

When she pulled into his driveway, Mary Ann was relieved to see that Jack had widened the turn-around in his backyard, allowing her to pull over to the side and conceal her car behind the house. *This is ridiculous. I feel like I'm sneaking around.*

In one continuous motion, Mary Ann knocked lightly on the back door, opened it slowly and walked in. She had never waited for someone to open the door at Jack and Carol's before. No reason to start now.

Johnny Mathis was crooning from the living room stereo, and the sweetness of gardenias permeated the air. Jack was well aware she was infatuated with Mathis and that gardenias were here favorite flower. He was at the butcher-block island trimming fresh basil the way he had once taught her, stacking several leaves on top of each other, rolling them lengthwise like a cigar, and then quickly slicing narrow strips with a sharp chef's knife.

"I didn't hear you come in. Wow! Don't you look...absolutely beautiful," Jack said. He put down the knife and walked over to her. She prepared for the kiss on the cheek they had always exchanged as friends, but instead he paused, put his hands on her upper arms, and slid them down to her waist. He slowly tilted his head and moved close. He kissed the side of her mouth where it met her cheek. Then he put his lips on hers and she felt herself go limp in his arms. Now her arms wrapped around him almost involuntarily, and she was kissing him back. Their lips parted slightly then met again. They kissed deeper, longer, and more passionately. Fearing she was rushing into this too quickly, Mary Ann pulled away from him slightly, still holding his hands. Their breathing was heavy. Mary Ann was doing her best to stay composed. She wanted to act as if this were the same as any other visit they had during the past thirty years, but she couldn't kid herself.

"Would you like a glass of wine? I pulled a bottle of Opus One out of the cellar. I know it's your favorite," Jack said.

"Please don't waste an expensive bottle of wine on me. I'll drink anything. I've only had Opus once, but I remember loving it. Joseph called it O-piss. He couldn't understand how wine could be so expensive, or why anyone would spend that much money on wine."

"It's not a waste, and I'll drink some with you. I feel like celebrating. This is a special occasion that deserves a special bottle of wine. Don't you think?"

"Yes, I agree."

"Can we make a pact tonight?" Jack asked, pouring the deep burgundy wine into a dainty crystal glass.

"It depends. A pact on what?" Mary Ann took the glass from him with both hands to ensure that she didn't drop it in her nervousness.

"Let's not talk about Joseph or Carol. Tonight is about us."

"Deal."

They lifted their wine glasses and touched them together, almost missing because they were looking into each other's eyes so intently.

"Hmmm. This has a nice underbelly, but it's a little young. It's a 1991, and in a few more years it will be sublime. I'd rate this a ninety-three," Jack said with an English accent.

"Sublime? You sound like one of those wine snobs on PBS."

"I'm joking. I was imitating the obnoxious sommeliers at fancy restaurants. Half the time they make things up to intimidate the customer into buying something expensive."

"Can I help you with the basil? A good friend taught me the proper way to cut it without damaging the leaves," Mary Ann asked.

She could feel Jack's eyes glued on her as she gracefully moved around the island collecting the basil, cutting board, and chef's knife. She couldn't wipe the sophomoric smile off her face. Like young lovers on a first date, they flirted, trying not to make a wrong move or say the wrong thing. Mary Ann focused keenly on the basil and barely recognized her own manicured hands, which were soft, smooth, and unwrinkled like those of a young movie star who had never worked them too hard.

Without looking up, she said, "I can tell you're staring at me. You're making me nervous. Are you watching my technique to make sure I do this right?"

"You're doing fine. But you're right, I *am* staring at you. I can't keep my eyes off you. You're as beautiful as you were thirty-five years ago." Jack put his hand on top of hers. She stopped cutting and lifted her head. His face was inches from hers and slowly moving closer.

"I can't believe you're here. I can't believe we're finally together and alone. This was worth the wait," Jack whispered.

"You smell good," she replied. He was wearing Chrome aftershave, a gift she had sent him last year for Christmas.

He took her face into his hands, stroked her cheek with his thumb, tenderly moving his fingers down her neck to her breast bone where he traced her sternum until it met the deep V in her dress. With a deep inhalation, Mary Ann closed her eyes and slightly tilted her head back as he kissed her neck.

"Take me," she quietly exhaled. "Take me to bed."

His eyes locked with hers.

"Are you sure?"

"I've never been more sure of anything in my life."

Jack's favorite blues singer, Etta James, was playing on the stereo. He held Mary Ann's hand tight in his and led her up the stairs as Etta sang "At Last."

Nancy Kaufman

At last, my love has come along
My lonely days are over and life is like a song
At last, the skies above are blue
My heart was wrapped in clover the night I looked at you
I found a dream that I can speak to
A dream that I can call my own
I found a thrill to press my cheek to
A thrill I've never known
You smiled and then the spell was cast
And here we are in Heaven
For you are mine, at last

Dear Diary,

One more time, I damn you Joseph Von Guten. There is no doubt that I will have to sell 2822 Devonshire. There is simply not enough money to keep it going. And really, if I'm honest with myself, there's no reason to hang on to it.

It has served us well. We watched our family grow up here. I really have no regrets about having to sell it. I never liked it from the beginning. Maybe if you had shown it to me before you bought it I'd feel differently,

Tricia will be the one most upset, I think. She has some sort of connection to this house the others do not. They all love it, but Tricia adores it. But it must be done.

Oh, Joseph, you were such a scoundrel, my dear...such a damn scoundrel. But for some reason, for many reasons, I still loved you.

Mary Ann

chapter

SEVENTEEN

Cruel is the strife of brother.
Aristotle

The Smythe Cramer Realty contract with its bright red house logo sat on top of Mary Ann's 'to do' pile. For days she had been shuffling it to the bottom. Now, here it was again at the top, glowing and calling to her.

When the realtor said her house was worth one hundred and seventy-five thousand dollars, Mary Ann was shocked. The estimation of value was a hundred thousand more than they'd paid for it, sure, but nowhere near what the comps showed. Several houses in the neighborhood had recently sold for more than twice that. The Von Guten home, though, hadn't been updated in years. From the street it looked like any other Colonial or Tudor in the neighborhood. "On the inside," the realtor had said, "it's a little dated."

Many homeowners in the area—her friends and neighbors, members of St. Theresa's—had put in custom kitchens with high-end commercial appliances, swimming pools, and elaborate outdoor grills and patios. They had updated bathrooms and hired interior designers to help them decorate their homes. Mary Ann and Joseph had been content to live with the warm familiarity of their old furniture and their perfectly functional appliances. The realtor rolled her eyes when she saw that they still used an electric stove and that there was commercial-grade carpet in the kitchen. The fact that the garage wasn't attached, had no doors, and looked like the leaning Tower of Pisa brought the value down as well.

Tricia convinced her mother not to use the first realtor they had talked to after the woman had told them, "Mrs. Von Guten. I hate to be so blunt, but the black walnut tree in your back yard is worth more than your house."

Mary Ann had replied, "Well, then exclude it from the contract. I'll take it with me."

&

"Knock, knock, anyone home?" Tricia called from the back hall.

"I'm in here," Mary Ann said.

Tricia kissed her mother on the cheek before sitting down. "Mmmmm, what smells so good?"

"That bouquet of gardenias."

"Where did you get them?"

"They were a favor at a dinner party. Aren't they beautiful? And they do smell so nice. But, never mind that. Tricia, I need your advice."

"About what?"

"About the house. Should I sell it? Or stay and fix it up?

"It depends."

"Depends? On what, dear?"

"On things like how much money you have to live on and the future of Divine. Isn't that why you wanted me to come over? To help you decide what to do with Patrick and Trip?"

"Yes, it is. I'm so frustrated. You may not want to hear this, but I am so angry at your father for leaving me with this mess. I don't understand why he didn't have a plan for the future of the company after his death. It's like he thought he was immortal, like he'd be here forever, playing cards and running Divine. But, now he's gone and he left me with nothing. Nothing but this mess he created."

"Mom, being angry at Dad isn't going to help solve the problem. So let it go. Let's move on. Update me on what's going on at Divine," Tricia said.

"Well, in spite of everything, the company is holding ground, at least as far as I can tell. Trip and Patrick are keeping things going but without talking to each other. Trip handles sales and accounting, and Patrick oversees production and shipping, but both want to be in charge, to be president. So, they continue to refuse to work together. Patrick doesn't like the way Trip treats him and the employees, and Trip thinks Patrick isn't doing his job well enough."

"Mom, I've been thinking about this for days. I've consulted with my lawyer and an investment banker who handles mergers and acquisitions. I've also talked to some friends who are involved in running family businesses. They all gave me the same advice: sell the company. If you choose one son over the other, you'll split the family in two. And chances are the one you *don't* choose will never talk to you again. But, if you sell it to an investor, then Patrick and Trip would *have* to report to the new owner. That is, if they choose to stay on."

"Who would buy it? I can't imagine there are a lot of people interested in buying a candle company."

"Don't worry about that. The investment banker will find a buyer. But I need to know that this is what you for sure want to do before I tell him it's for sale. Mom, *I* think it's the best thing to do, both for everyone involved and for the future of Divine. Unless things are clearly mapped out and planned, family businesses almost always create animosity and greed within families. And the way things look now? It's a disaster waiting to happen."

"Tricia, I don't know. I don't have a good feeling about this, and I'm certain Trip and Patrick won't want to sell."

"Mom, if you sell, chances are you'll all walk away with enough money to carry you through the next decade. Patrick and Trip can use their share of the money to start their own businesses, or most likely the new owner will want them to work for them for a few years."

"I can't. Your grandfather, father, and uncles worked very hard to build this business. I don't feel I have the right to sell it. There's a lot of history with Divine, a lot you don't know about."

"I know more than you think I know. Everyone has secrets, or at least they like to think they do," Tricia said.

"Oh, really? Do you know something I don't know?"

"Maybe, or maybe I know something that you *do* know, but you don't know I know."

"And maybe I know something that you don't know I know," Mary Ann replied.

"Mom, sell the company and your secrets will be safe with me, and I'll make sure you are financially secure. You won't even have to sell the house. If you don't sell Divine, well, who knows what will happen?"

"Mary Patricia, are you threatening me? Because if you are, I can do the same to you."

What was she doing? Using emotional blackmail to manipulate her mother just as her father used to? She knew her mother was vulnerable, *and* she knew her most intimate secret. What else could she do? Tricia was desperate to put out the fire at Divine. She couldn't stand how her brothers and sisters were taking sides with Trip or Patrick and barely speaking to one another. Ever since their father died, the fabric of the family was unraveling at the seams—seams that she had once thought were made of steel. But the irony was that Joseph wasn't the glue in the family. He had little to do with their family being a united front. It was only the perception that the head of the family, the patriarch, was the commander in chief and that without him everyone would falter. But Joseph was far from being the leader of this family; they only let him think he was.

Tricia didn't want to gerrymander her mother, but she was impetuous. She wanted and needed to get this deal done. A major transformation had to take place in the family, mostly because her brothers' egos had ruined the once stable family dynamics. She couldn't bear to see them run the company into the ground after her father, grandfather, and great grandfather had put their blood, sweat, and tears into it. If Divine failed, not only would Mary

Ann suffer financially, but also Trip and Patrick would have no income and wouldn't be able to help with Mark's legal bills. She would give Mark all the support he needed, and she could afford the hefty legal fees, but she didn't go to college and work her ass off to pay for his bad judgment and mistakes while her brothers and sisters' wallets stayed in their pockets. Her mother held the key to the solution but was dangling it in front of Tricia.

Mary Ann was more worried about Jack and what to do with the house, when she should be concerned about Divine. Tricia's anger toward Mary Ann had been escalating for years. She resented that her mother acted like she was a saint, a holy roller who went to church every Sunday and made them feel guilty if they missed Mass or ate meat on Fridays during Lent. Her mother was living a lie. And it was a lie that Tricia had carried with her in the pit of her stomach, wreaking havoc on her insides for years. But who was Tricia to judge her mother? Like mother, like daughter. The apple didn't fall far from the tree, and Tricia harbored a grudge for inheriting her licentiousness. Tricia didn't have a choice. If she had to, she would reveal her mother's secret if she didn't agree to sell. If Mary Ann knew that Tricia was Ashley's mother, she wouldn't expose the truth for fear of hurting her granddaughter. Tricia was confident that *her* secret was safe.

"I'm just saying. Telling you like it is."

"I respect your business advice, and I appreciate your *offer* to make sure I'm set financially. But I'm very irritated by the way you're speaking to me. What has gotten into you? Don't try to push me around or intimidate me into selling Divine. I've made a decision about the house. I'm selling it. I'll make a decision about the business later after you calm down and can talk to me with more respect and less bullying."

"What? Five minutes ago you were staying in the house and fixing it up."

"I was until just now. I'm selling it and moving in with Jack after we're married. I won't *need* your financial support."

The guilt attacked Tricia with a vengeance, starting in her gut and surging up through her chest, pushing against her sternum. How could she resort to such tactics with her mother? Now Mary Ann was going to suddenly marry Jack so she wouldn't have to depend on Tricia for financial support. Tricia stopped cold. She hated herself for treating her mother with such disrespect.

"Mom, I'm sorry. Please forgive me for acting this way. If you truly love Jack, I'm happy for you. I'm not surprised. It makes complete sense for the two of you to end up together. Are you already married? Secretly? Are those gardenias your wedding bouquet?"

"No, Tricia, I wouldn't get married without telling all of you. I have *nothing* to hide. But now that you've mentioned it, maybe we should elope so I don't have to listen to everyone's two-cents. Can we get back to talking about Divine?"

"Will you sell it?"

"Bring me an offer and I'll call a stock holders meeting," Mary Ann said.

Before Tricia could call her banker to tell him to proceed, she had to get Trip and Patrick on the same page. They would be contentious, just as they've always been. They fought now as much as they did twenty-five years ago. Growing up, they had argued over everything from who should trim the hedges and cut the grass to who got to split the Thanksgiving turkey wishbone. No sense in calling her bank advisor if her brothers were going to be stubborn roadblocks. That evening, she began talking to each of them, separately at first, then all three of them in the same room at the same time.

The result was several weeks of angst, pain, and animosity. As difficult as it was for Trip and Patrick, Tricia was developing an ulcer.

Tricia was about to concede that the current situation between the boys was untenable and unlikely to change when the boys reluctantly agreed that things couldn't go on as they were. It took the rest of three straight days of Tricia mediating with the patience of a saint for them to agree that selling was the only reasonable option.

The boys gave in with the understanding that the sale would be contingent on them continuing to hold their current positions for at least two years. Tricia also got them to agree in writing that they would work respectfully and supportively under whoever was going to be installed as the new president. She was relieved when they finally realized that any angling to be installed as president would undermine the future of Divine, regardless of who purchased it. She had the new owner's interest at heart, and she wanted to ensure her brothers employment.

"What's Ashley doing here?" Patrick asked Tricia. The two were getting coffee in the lunchroom before Tricia's investment banker presented the offer he had prepared.

"She works for Divine and should be here. Besides, Mom didn't want to be here and asked Ashley to represent her. Do you have a problem with that?"

"I guess not. It's just a little weird."

"What's weird about it?"

"I don't know. I wasn't expecting her to be here, that's all."

"Well, get used to it. Ashley's been doing the books for years, and now that she has a degree in accounting, she'll be taking on a more important role. Besides, she's family. I'll see you in the conference room."

Divine's facilities were unpretentious. The aging brick of the buildings made it look like it was part of GE's Nela Park Lighting Division across the street. Inside, the office space resembled interconnected cubes sitting on the floor of an open, twenty-foot high warehouse filled with boxes and boxes of candles waiting to be shipped. The other two buildings contained the materials needed to make the candles. Rows of wick-spinning machines that looked like band saws were churning out spools of string; hot vats were melting wax, and shelves of vials and bottles of aroma stood among pallets of raw beeswax.

The conference room was last updated in the early '80s. The light green walls were scuffed from decades of chairs being dragged against them, and they desperately needed repainting. Photos of Divine dating back to its first days hung on the wall. In the center of the room was a twelve-foot mahogany table with matching chairs, the only evident aspect of a standard business environment. Tricia made a note to herself to call her decorator to update the décor. A new owner should have a new look.

Trip sat at the head of the table. He was the first to arrive and took his coffee to what he considered his rightful place. Next to him on his right and facing the door was Ashley. Tricia sat down next to her, coffee in hand. Across from them was a chair for Patrick. When he was seated, all eyes turned to the far end of the table. Patrick Rockefeller O'Neill was Tricia's investment banker. She chose him as her business advisor because of his lineage to John D. His family's generations of experience in the financial industry made him one of the most trusted investment bankers in Ohio. When Patrick Rockefeller O'Neill spoke, Tricia listened.

She expected Trip's reaction to be one of surprise, but she didn't expect this.

"You scheming, conniving bitch! This whole thing has been nothing more than you trying to con Patrick and me out of our birthright. I can't believe you'd do this to us. Does mother know what you're doing?"

Tricia's stomach curled into a knot. She took a breath, placed her hand on Ashley's arm, then stood and began to walk around the table.

"Yes, she does. Mom isn't a businesswoman; she just wants this family to get along again. And this was the best option to keep Divine in the family. Trip, there wasn't any other way. If I had talked to you and Patrick directly about buying the business, you would have treated me like a girl, like your little sister, and blown me off. I never would have been able to buy Divine, and the two of you would have run it into bankruptcy."

"What do you mean? We're doing fine."

"That's not what the books show, do they?"

Trip glared at Tricia and then turned to Patrick, who looked down at his folded hands. Trip looked at Ashley, who met his gaze steadily, and then he turned back to Tricia. "Okay, so that's what they show right now. But I can assure you, it's only temporary."

"PR, what do you have to say about that?" Tricia asked.

The investment banker, known by his first two initials, pulled out a spreadsheet and read a series of numbers out loud. "Trip, the numbers don't lie. Divine has been trending down for years. It seems your father was taking money out; on the books it shows up as loans. A few years ago, several companies from Singapore began to go after the America candle market, as you know, and Divine slipped further. Today it appears that Divine will not make the end of the year without an infusion of cash," PR said.

"So why don't you find some?" Patrick asked.

"I did, from your sister."

Tricia returned to her seat at the table and looked at her brother, feeling a little better with PR speaking on her behalf.

"Are you saying that Tricia was the only person you could find who wanted to buy Divine? I don't believe this. I think you two were in this together." By this point, Trip was out of his chair and pointing accusingly at his sister.

"Mr. Von Guten, I don't appreciate being painted as a scalawag. I do appreciate that you feel blindsided. Believe me; I researched all legitimate sources of funding. There were no takers. I did have an offer from a company in Russia, but they are believed to be Russian Mafia, and I couldn't live with myself if I connected you with the likes of them.

"So when it appeared that there was no other way to save Divine, I decided to ask Tricia if she'd consider investing the money she'd made from the sale of her online linen company. She declined saying, and I quote, 'I couldn't do that. Their sister buying the company would embarrass my brothers. They'd think people would say they were incompetent.'

"I told Tricia I understood, but that if she didn't buy Divine it would fail within a year, and then people would really think her brothers were incompetent. Eventually, I was able to convince her that buying Divine would solve two problems: Divine would be saved and her money would be safely invested."

PR continued, "I'm passing around a document for each of you to read and sign, plus one for your mother. What it says is this: Mary Ann has agreed to sell forty shares of her Divine stock for two million dollars—one million in cash, and one million as a line of credit. Twenty of her current shares will be assigned to Ashley and twenty to Tricia. In the spirit of reengineering the company for the next century, the shareholders agree to elect Tricia as president, Ashley as treasurer, Trip as vice-president of sales, and Patrick as vice-president of manufacturing. Mary Ann will assume the position of chairman of the board. You will also find a detailed and specific course of action and protocol covering the future of shares with regard to the death of shareholders and any future decisions to sell stock. Also included is a provision to create an ongoing fund to support Mark's appeals and provide for him and his daughter based on various possible results.

"I ask you to read this document carefully, and then each of you will need to sign all five copies. Please return them to me tomorrow. Any questions?"

A bell went off throughout the complex. It was three o'clock and time to go home. No more candles would be made today at Divine. Trip picked up his copy of the agreement and walked out of the room. Tricia wasn't sure if it was out of habit from years of listening to the bell or because he was furious—it was probably a combination of both. *Note to self: Get rid of the bell.*

With any luck, however, production would resume tomorrow and every day thereafter for many years to come.

With any luck at all.

chapter

EIGHTEEN

An ounce of blood is worth more than a pound of friendship.
Spanish proverb

"Come to my office," Reynolds, the court appointed attorney, said to Mark and his siblings. The Von Gutens were all there to support Mark—everyone except Mary Ann. It was a unanimous family decision not to have her attend the trial. They followed Reynolds like ducklings waddling behind their mother duck down the hall of the twenty-third floor of the Justice Center. Reynolds didn't have an office in the building but used the concrete stairwell to talk to his clients privately while sneaking a cigarette in the non-smoking federal building.

He flicked his Bic and lit up, took a deep breath of tar and nicotine, and exhaled gray smoke through his yellow teeth. Reynolds was explaining an offer the DA had put on the table, but Tricia didn't hear a word he said. She tuned everything out and was staring at Mark, her fifty-year-old brother whose life was now in the hands of twelve morons – the only ones who were not smart enough to get out of jury duty by calling a lawyer friend with a lame excuse about not being able to afford to miss work or having previously bought a plane ticket out of town. Mark was wearing one of Joseph's sport coats. Mark called it his "lucky jacket" because it was his father's. Tricia couldn't understand why he called it that, because Joseph was never lucky, especially when it came to odds.

Tricia didn't see a grown man who was up against a life sentence when she looked at Mark; all she saw was his unruly hair as he taught her how to dribble and do lay-ups in the backyard. She saw the brother who used to spray her with the kitchen faucet nozzle as they did dishes together after dinner, and the brother who played hoops with balled-up paper napkins, shooting at the chandelier above the dining room table during dinner. When one would get stuck, he'd yell, *"and the crowd went crazy as he made the winning basket at the sound of the buzzer!"* Even Mary Ann laughed when milk came out of his nose as he laughed at his own jokes.

"Tricia, don't you agree?"

She blinked her eyes several times as she re-entered the conversation.

"What? I'm sorry. I was just thinking about..."

Mark interrupted, "There's no way I'm spending one day in prison for something I didn't do. I'm not admitting guilt because I didn't do anything! And I'd be labeled a sex offender for the rest of my life!" Mark exploded. "The jury has to see that Louisa's lying because she's scared that if she doesn't, her aunts will punish her. She's been intimidated and coached into saying those things!"

"I agree, but it's a huge risk. We know the facts, but the jury might see it differently. They want to protect Louisa and all the other kids in the world. They might not want to second-guess what she said on the stand," Tricia replied. "But, if you lose ..."She stopped herself. She couldn't say what she was thinking. *Life in prison without parole.*

"No way! I'm not accepting their offer. God will prevail, and I will be free. Freedom comes to those who believe. We have to believe. We must have faith," Mark said as he walked out of the stairwell and back down the hall toward the courtroom. The DA had offered a plea. Three months shock probation in jail, and they might let him out after a few weeks. But he'd have to report in with the sheriff every ninety days, and he'd be registered as a sex offender for the rest of his life.

Scott opened a bottle a Far Niente Chardonnay on the screened porch as Tricia plopped down on the couch with an arm flung over her forehead. It was her favorite wine and was always served at their house on special occasions. There was nothing to celebrate this night, but it was the only cold bottle in the refrigerator.

"Where is this God I've been praying to my entire life?" Tricia said. "Okay, I admit not my entire life. I took a break for a few years in college, but I prayed continuously over the past week during the trial. How many rosaries do I need to say? I'm sure God doesn't have a file on me where he keeps track of how many times I've prayed or gone to church. Who knows, maybe he does?"

Scott handed her an extra-large glass of wine. She needed something to calm her nerves. Ever since Mark's verdict, Tricia had been jumpy and twitchy. At one point she had begun hyperventilating. Tricia stared at Scott waiting for a reply.

"What? You want me to answer that question? I was hoping it was rhetorical. You're asking the wrong person about God. You know that."

"I know. I'm just rambling, but thanks for listening," Tricia took a large sip of her wine followed quickly by another. "I even promised God I'd start going to church again and take the kids with me. I've never asked God for anything besides a good grade on a test. But now I've lost all faith. Forget about me and *my* prayers, Mark has devoted his life to prayer and spreading the 'good word of the Lord,' and this is the hand he is dealt? He's been holding unlucky cards his entire life. He was always the kid who got blamed for things he didn't do, and he humbly took the blame for others, even me. But this? This is outrageous! Life in prison for something he didn't do? Isn't God almighty and all-powerful? How could he let this happen? I give up. Mark says there is a God, but like the jury, I don't believe him."

"Tricia, we'll file an appeal and turn this around," Scott said.

"I wish you were there with me, you should have seen the look on his face. His fear was palpable. Once the verdict was read, they immediately handcuffed him, and he couldn't bear to turn around and look at us before they led him away. It was horrible." Tricia tucked her feet under Scott's legs on the couch and wrapped her cardigan around herself more tightly.

Scott poured more wine into her glass.

"I can't handle knowing he's in prison with a bunch of lunatics. Scott, how the fuck did this happen?" The wine was influencing her choice of words.

"It just goes to show you where a life of alcoholism and drugs gets you. I know he's not guilty, nor does he deserve this, but he made some bad choices in his life. Unfortunately, he's paying the consequences for associating himself with the wrong people."

"I agree, but just because he was an alcoholic who made bad choices doesn't mean he should go to prison."

"I know."

"He's been clean and sober for the past six years, and now look where he is. I can't imagine how I'd feel if he were our son. I didn't go into the house with Trip, ML, and Patrick when they told Mom because I couldn't handle seeing her reaction."

"It's a good thing she and Mark have their faith," Scott said, leaning over to rub her shoulder in sympathy. "More wine?"

"Yes, I feel like getting drunk."

"Maybe you should plan on staying home tomorrow. You know, sleep in?"

"I can't, I've got other brother troubles at work. Even though they signed the agreement to cooperate, Trip and Patrick are still going at it."

"Can't you do something?"

"Not really. They know I won't fire them, and other than that, what power do I really have? I just have to see to it that their being pissy at each other doesn't cost us money."

"Well, good luck. Take it easy on the wine. I'll be in bed reading if you need me." Scott got up from the couch and kissed the top of Tricia's head.

"I'll be there in minute." She held her second, half-filled glass up for him to see. "And then you better be ready to be needed."

"I'll be there."

"Thanks. You always are." Tricia set down the unfinished glass and stood up. "Enough wine for me. Let's go to bed."

"Now there's something I can get into."

Nancy Kaufman

Dear Diary,

My children don't understand why I wouldn't go with them to see Mark. They must think I no longer love him, or that I can't stand to be with him. Neither is true. I love Mark, perhaps more than all of them. And he loved me unlike any of the others. He was the one who needed my love the most. Like the time he was accused of peeing on the radiators at St. Theresa's. I always knew he was innocent, and that the real villain was Francis Mooney. Of course I knew that. I knew his mother.

It's amazing how we are not what we seem—myself included.

But, that is how it is in life. I only hope my children learn that before their trust destroys them. And isn't that exactly what's happening to Mark? What's happened to him all his life?

Perhaps the thing about him that makes me love him the most is the way he trusts the rest of the world to do the right thing. As if they even know what the right thing is.

It was best for me and for Mark that I went to see him by myself without the other children knowing.

And as for ML, Tricia, Trip, and Patrick, I only hope that one day they see that I was neither heartless nor heart-stricken. In the end, I was only trying to be the best mother for them I could be.

Mary Ann

chapter

NINETEEN

"Whenever God closes one door He always opens another, even though sometimes it's hell in the hallway"
Unknown

It was like an out-of-body experience. Tricia watched herself pull into the chuckhole-filled parking lot of the state prison as if she were on the outside looking in. *My God, they really have barbed wire fences and barren buildings with tiny, nondescript windows. There's no landscaping, nothing green. Every thing's drab, cold, and grey.*

Tricia had a lump in her throat, she shook with nerves and was extremely dehydrated—symptoms that always precipitated an anxiety attack.

"Can I have a sip of your water?"

Sitting in the passenger seat of Tricia's Lexus, ML passed over her bottle of water. Tricia took a sip and a deep breath. She was thankful she practiced yoga. Yogic breathing helped her nip anxiety attacks in the bud. And today was no day to have an attack in front of her brother. Not one of the brothers she was with, the ones looking absently out the back seat windows so they wouldn't have to talk, but the one she was about to visit. Patrick and Trip couldn't bear being in the same car with her. They hadn't talked to each other, outside of what was required at work, since Mary Ann sold her shares of Divine and Tricia took over. They reluctantly agreed to ride to the prison together as a family for Mark's benefit and for no other reason.

"I shouldn't have shared my water with you. I woke up with a terrible cold. I hope I don't have a coughing fit while we're here," ML said.

"Now you tell me," Tricia said, annoyed.

As ML retrieved her water bottle, Tricia intensified her Pranayama breathing. They'd both taken the same yoga class, but this was the first time she'd practiced it outside the yoga studio. ML began to breathe in sync with Tricia. Slowly, they inhaled... abdomen then chest...three seconds in…exhale...chest then abdomen…three seconds out. Silently, they repeated the calming breathing technique several times while Tricia drove, searching for a parking spot amongst the cars and pickup trucks that were better suited for a junkyard. Tricia's heart rate dropped as the Pranayama released some of her emotional anxiety.

"Trip, tell me again what we're allowed to bring with us."

"No more than twenty bucks, change for the vending machines, and your driver's license and birth certificate. Other than that, you can't bring in anything. Take your keys off your key ring and leave the car lock remote. They won't let you bring that in either. Something about remotes being used to detonate bombs?" Trip was the one who called the prison to find out about visitation times and rules.

From her experience during the trial, Tricia knew not to wear anything flashy and to leave her diamonds and good watch at home. She and ML wore little makeup, punishment for Tricia who never left the house without being completely put together. Her blonde hair was in a ponytail. She wore small fake pearl earrings, an old Timex watch, her gold wedding band, jeans, a turtleneck, and her daughter's down jacket. For once in her life, she didn't want to be noticed. She wanted to blend in and be a plain Jane. But when they walked into the prison entrance and saw the other visitors waiting to be processed, it was clear that no matter how much they tried to keep their appearance run-of-the-mill, they would never fit in.

Trip had been to see Mark the first day he could have visitors, so he knew the drill. Get a number, sit in one of the cold steel chairs, and wait for your number to be called. Tricia was grateful no one could read her mind. *We don't belong here. How the fuck did this happen? We're good people, well educated, and we come from a good family. Someone please tell me this is just a dream, a nightmare. Mark can't really be in prison and not for life.*

"First-timers?" The toothless, old woman sitting in the row behind Tricia asked. "Is this your first time here?"

Tricia turned around and looked at the woman. "Are you talking to me?"

"I ain't seen you here before. It's usually the same folks the beginin' of the month, after we git our checks."

"Um, yeah, it is," Tricia answered and turned away.

Tricia, Trip, ML and Patrick exchanged looks without saying a word. ML rolled her eyes. "She needs to buy some shampoo with her check," Patrick whispered. Tricia and ML quietly chuckled. Discreetly Tricia and ML looked around. The place was filthy. The people were gross, with clothes that were not only old, but also dirty and ragged. Because Mark's brothers and sisters were wearing clean, ironed clothes and their hair was shampooed and combed, they stood out as the unusual ones in the room. They were *them* to the other's *us.*

"Twenty-eight," the man behind the glass window called.

Tricia nudged Trip, "That's us,"

After proving that they were Mark's siblings using their birth certificates, the foursome was instructed to go through the metal detectors. It was not much different than going through airport security, but surprisingly the prison guards were much nicer and friendlier than airport TSA screeners. At first it appeared they were being nice to them because of the way they looked, but it quickly became clear that they were nice to all the visitors. After all, the guards weren't the ones who had committed the crimes. They could smile and go home at night.

Three electronically opened doors and two hallways later, Trip, Patrick, Tricia and ML found themselves in a large room that resembled a school cafeteria. One wall was filled with old-fashioned vending machines like the ones Trisha remembered from her days of hanging out at the bowling alley in the '60s while her mother played in the Thursday morning league. The wall across from the vending machines was filled with windows that looked out on a concrete yard surrounded by concrete buildings.

The room was filled with groupings of chairs and tables—three or four plastic chairs on one side of a small plastic table that was only big enough for a dinner-size plate and two cans of soda, and one chair on the other side of the table—the prisoner's seat. Unlike in the movies, there were no glass walls separating the inmates from the visitors. They wouldn't have to talk to Mark over an old black phone with glass between them. It was a small blessing, perhaps, but a blessing nonetheless.

Once Trip identified themselves as visitors of prisoner #A514683, the guard at the desk assigned them all seats at a table in a corner, away from the other visitors. Above their seats was a hand-written sign that read "ISOLATION." Tricia wondered about the sign, but she didn't ask and sat down to wait for Mark. As they waited, they watched the other prisoners as they walked in and took seats across from their families. Tricia wondered why they were the only group that had to wait for their loved one, their prisoner, to arrive. Concerned and nervous, she stared out the window across from her seat nervously picking the clear polish off her nails.

That can't be him. In the distance, through the window, she saw a prisoner walking with two guards, one behind and one in front leading the way. *Can it be him?* The prisoner wore a blue jumpsuit and shackles on his ankles and wrists. Slowly and awkwardly he shuffled his way across the courtyard toward the visitor building. *Please, don't let it be him.* A lump grew in her throat. *Breathe. Breathe.*

As the prisoner got closer to the windows, Trip said, "Oh, shit."

The lump in Tricia's throat was too big to swallow. Her eyes filled with tears. She wanted to cry, she wanted to run fast and far away from there and from the situation. *Hold yourself together for Mark's sake. This isn't about me. It's about him. What I'm feeling is diddlysquat compared to what Mark has to go through every day. I'm just visiting. Stay calm. Don't cry. Look him in the eye. Don't mention the shackles and handcuffs. Hold it together.*

The guards led Mark to the seat under the "ISOLATION" sign.

He *looked* okay. He didn't have any bruises or cuts on his face, something Tricia had feared. She'd had nightmares about him being beaten up in prison. She knew that convicted child molesters are often brutally beaten and even raped by other prisoners once they find out their reason for incarceration. The female guard working the desk in the visitation room approached them.

"Just because he's restrained, doesn't mean he did anything wrong," the guard said. "He's in isolation for his own protection, because we're concerned for his safety. It's standard procedure for all prisoners in isolation to be put in cuffs when we move them. He's not like this all the time." She cleared her throat and continued as if reading from a script. "You are allowed to hug him at the beginning and end of the visit, but don't touch him any other time. And stay in your chairs unless you're going to the vending machines or bathroom."

Trip was first to put his arms around Mark to give him a big hug that lasted nearly a minute. Tricia and ML could tell their brothers were crying. Tricia was afraid they weren't going to let go of each other and that the guard would come separate them and kick them out.

Finally Trip let go. Patrick gave him a quick hug and manly pat on the back, and then it was the sisters' turn. Tricia and ML hugged Mark simultaneously and kissed him on his sweaty cheeks.

"Thanks for coming," Mark said as he sat down, his chains clanking so noisily that other visitors turned their heads to watch.

"Are you okay?" Trip said.

"Yeah, can you get me something to drink? A Sprite or Coke?"

"Do you want anything to eat?" Tricia asked.

"Not right now."

Trip volunteered to go to the vending machine. As he rose to leave, Tricia spoke to Mark.

"We interviewed two new lawyers and met the one Reynolds recommended."

Once the trial was over, Reynolds had told them he was unqualified to represent Mark on appeal. As far as Tricia's was concerned, unqualified was an understatement. She thought Reynolds was the worst lawyer in the world. How he had become an attorney in the first place and how he slept at night were two questions Tricia constantly asked herself. Her brothers and sisters felt the same way. They were all certain Reynolds must have been in cahoots with Judge Gallagher, the living definition of a political animal. Mark's trial took place the week before the election. To improve his chances of winning, Gallagher needed to convict anyone that week, guilty or not. Of course, convicting someone who was charged with sexually molesting a child would be even better. It was a conviction that would ensure his return to the bench. Wrap it up and tie a ribbon around it. Done deal. On the other hand, if Mark got off or even if there were a mistrial, the press would have destroyed the judge. He would never be re-elected and would no longer be a judge feared by all who stood before him. Besides, rumor had it that he needed the job.

"What about that private investigator? Did he find anything? Was he able to prove those two convicted rapists lived in the same house as Louisa?" Mark asked.

"Mark, we've been over this," Tricia said, uncomfortable with the prospect of having to answer this and God-only-knew the hundreds of other questions Mark would ask. Patrick, as usual, sat there listening silently. "The trial's over so it no longer matters what he finds out. Even if it turns out to be true, there's no way to get the evidence into court."

"What about at the appeal?"

"You know that answer. You're not allowed to introduce new evidence into an appeal. An appeal is not a new trial. It's exactly what it says it is—an appeal for another judge to look at *the same* evidence and determine if the right judgment was reached in a fair and equitable manner; basically to see if your lawyer represented you to the best of his abilities. Frankly, that's the only hope we have—that another judge will see how incompetent Reynolds is and what a political hack Gallagher is."

"It doesn't seem fair that if we find out the truth we can't use it to get me free."

"No, it isn't fair. It's the law. If that wasn't the law, trials would never end."

"And innocent people wouldn't wind up in jail."

ML interjected, "And guilty people would go free."

"So, I'm a sop to the wheels of justice? What kind of God let's that happen?"

"God doesn't give a shit about the law," Patrick said. "At least not about man's law. You have two hopes left in your life—a reversal on appeal and your reward in the hereafter. I'm going to help Trip find you something to drink."

"That's a first," Tricia said.

Patrick slid his chair back and walked toward his brother who was still working the vending machines. Mark sat watching his two brothers battle the machines. Tricia also looked across the room, hoping that by doing so she could speed up Trip's return. It seemed to work.

"They didn't have Coke. I hope Pepsi is okay." Trip popped open the can and set it on the table in front of his brother. Tricia was unsure how Mark would be able to drink a pop with his wrists cuffed together and attached to a chain wrapped around his chest. He couldn't move his arms away from his chest, and it didn't look like his hands could reach his mouth.

As he sat down again, Patrick reached for the can, in an effort to help.

"Leave it alone," Mark said.

With great effort, he bent over and grabbed the can with his cuffed hands, brought it as close to his mouth as he could, then tilted his head forward until his lips reached the can. He then leaned back a little, took a sip, and returned the can to the table.

"Are you still friends with that asshole detective's wife, Angela?" Mark asked ML.

"I'm not sure what that has to do with what we've been talking about. Angela has nothing to do with this, trust me," ML said. "Angela is sick about this. She told me Kevin never talks to her about you or the case. Mark, I can't stop talking to her because of who her husband is. Angela will always be my friend, no matter what."

"Is there anything we can do for you? I mean, I know you aren't allowed to have much in here, but you know we'll do anything for you," Patrick said.

"I don't want any *things*," Mark said. "But there is something I want. You might say it's my third hope left in life."

"I'm sorry, Mark. I deserved that. What's your hope? If I can make it happen, I will," Patrick said.

"I was hoping you'd say that." Mark took another difficult swig of Pepsi, his chains clanking noisily, as if underscoring the importance of what he was about to say.

"I want you two assholes to stop being such pricks."

"What do you mean?" Trip said.

"You know exactly what I mean. You and Patrick are acting like spoiled brats, making it hard for Tricia and Ashley at Divine."

"Hey, they bought the business," Patrick said. "If they don't think we're doing a good job, why don't they fire us?"

"You know Tricia can't do that. You're family. But you have to get it through your heads that Tricia loves you so much she put her hard-earned money into a business that could turn into a total loser. And with the way she tells me you're acting, it just might."

"How'd you tell him about us?" Trip said to Tricia.

"I sent him a letter and explained how the two of you have been jerks. Now listen to him."

"You'd use a man who could be spending the rest of his life in jail to blackmail us into doing what you want? What kind of person are you anyway?" Trip crossed his arms and leaned back in his chair, causing it to rock off its front legs.

Before Tricia could respond, Mark did. "Listen to me, Trip, and you too, Patrick. I'm not doing anyone's bidding, and I can't blackmail anyone who's not guilty. The point is I'm in here, maybe for life. The only chance I have— the ONLY chance I have—is for my family to get me out. And to do that, you're going to have to work together, and Divine is going to have to stay solvent. You know that's the only source of money this family has. So, if you want to be pissed at anyone, be pissed at me. I caused this problem, and my selfishness continues—I need my brothers and sisters to keep our father's company making money so I have at least one chance of getting out of here. Do you understand?"

From their silence, Tricia knew Mark had gotten his point across. Patrick and Trip sat with their arms crossed as though they had put up walls around themselves. The muscles in their faces and necks were tightening, and it was obvious that they were gritting their teeth. Tricia also knew that even though her brothers might agree with Mark, it would take a while for them to say so out loud.

Mark continued, "You don't have to say anything about this to me or to each other. Just do the right thing, okay? If not for you and your sisters and your mother and your family, then do it for me. Now, thank you all for coming. I've got important things to do this afternoon so I've got to go. Please feel free to stop by anytime," Mark said with a bitter and sarcastic tongue.

ML and Tricia both burst into tears and started to stand up to hug Mark.

"Stay seated! There's five minutes left before good-byes." The female guard's voice sounded stern, her eyes, however, showed that had she been Mark's sister she would have tried to hug him herself.

Five minutes of small talk, tears, promises, and messages to deliver to Mark's friends, and visiting time was over. They hugged and cried and shook hands.

Trip pulled Tricia's chair back to let her out from under the table. She smiled. She knew things would be right between them, and that Divine would get its legs back under it and begin to prosper.

What she didn't know was what would happen to Mark.

Nancy Kaufman

Dear Diary,

Of all the aches I have, the biggest one, the one that has never been filled, is the loss of my best friend. There is a love for a man, but there is also love for a fellow woman—my best friend. Carol, I truly miss you. Every day I think of you and what you would say or do in every situation in which I find myself.

And now....

How strange life is.

Here I am, missing you, my best friend, and planning to spend the rest of my life with your husband. My new best friend. My new lover. But the ache I have for you will always be there.

You are the void I could never refill.

Mary Ann

chapter

TWENTY

2004

"There is no glory in honesty if it is destructive. And no shame in dishonesty if its goal is to offer grace."
M. J. Rose

A day she knew was coming. A day she had absolutely no interest in trying to avoid. Oh, she could have avoided it. She could have simply stopped, but her gnawing lasciviousness got the best of her. The love she experienced was like no other. The gentle touch of her lover's hand triggered a rush of euphoria that flowed from her sternum to the void in her soul…a feeling she never experienced with Stan.

Rather than ending the affair years ago, she chose to just think about what she would do if she were caught. And after seven years, she was caught.

It was the first Friday of the month, and Stan was supposed to be playing poker with his friends. But this month, this first Friday, for some reason, he decided to surprise ML and come home early.

But it was Stan who was surprised.

Shocked. Stunned. Stupefied. Speechless.

For all these years, how could he have not known when it was right before his eyes? He and his friends had always fantasized about watching two women together in bed and kidded about being asked to join in.

The music was playing on the iHome so loudly that she didn't hear him come upstairs. ML didn't invite him to join them when he walked into the bedroom. Instead she gasped and sat up in bed, the sheets falling to her waist, exposing her reddened breasts.

"Oh shit," Angela said, a dead giveaway that this wasn't about to be a fantasy come to life for Stan. ML and Stan stared at each other, her heart racing as though it were going to leap from of her chest.

Angela got out of bed, grabbed her clothes from the chair and held them close to her body, covering herself. With her head hanging low in embarrassment and her long wavy red hair partially covering her face, she grabbed her iPod, cutting off the music, and whisked past Stan. He and ML were left staring at each other, thunderstruck by the unexpected moment. ML was unable to talk, to offer an explanation of any sort.

Seconds passed. Then minutes.

ML wrapped the sheets around herself up to the neck, concealing herself from her husband of twenty-six years. The silence was broken only by the sound of Angela's high heels on the wooden stairs, followed by the creek and clank of the front door closing behind her.

"Where's she going so quickly?" Stan asked.

"Stan, I can explain." ML started to answer.

"I thought maybe she'd stay, and you could put on a show for me?"

Stan's tone of voice warned that there was no possible way ML could have a reasonable conversation with him at the moment. There was nothing she could say that would make the situation better. If anything she'd only make it worse. She was caught, and there was no way she could convince him that what he saw wasn't real—because it was.

ML began to shake. The look of contempt on Stan's face was scorching.

"Call her back here. After you humiliate and ridicule me by sleeping with a woman, that's the least you can do for me. Call her now."

"Stan, stop! You're making this worse than it is."

"I'm sure you're going to tell me this was the first and only time you were with her. I should have known. No wonder you never want to have sex with me. You were having sex with a woman. A fucking lesbian. My wife's a fucking lesbian. So tell me, do you fuck her? Do you have a double dildo hidden in this room? Under the mattress maybe?"

Stan lifted the mattress, knocking ML out of bed and onto the floor. He flipped the mattress over on top of her. She was crying but knew he didn't give a damn. He was the one who should be crying, but in his family men weren't allowed to be weak. Stan stomped down the stairs, leaving ML to find her own way out from under the mattress. Before leaving the house, he yelled a final message to his wife.

"What will your mother and uncle think when they hear that you're a fucking lesbian? You'll tarnish the family name and disgrace your uncle's position in the church. Wait till the media finds out and knocks on his door for a statement!"

The sound of his Volvo starting up and pulling out of the driveway cued her that it was safe to come out from under the mattress. She made her way to the bathroom and turned on the shower. Stan's words hit her hard. She was trembling and shivering, as she stood naked in front of the sink waiting for the shower to heat up. He was right. She would be an embarrassment to her mother and family. She hadn't intended to hurt anyone, but her mother would be humiliated, mortified, and would suffer the most. ML didn't care how Stan felt. She never had feelings for him, not even in the beginning. Ever since high school, ML had been attracted to Angela, but she had ignored her feelings. She was certain it was wrong for a good Catholic girl to feel that way. To hide her thoughts, she went along with the boyfriend-thing and married Stan. A few years later, Angela did the same with Kevin Mooney.

After a ten-minute shower, ML stepped onto the bathmat and placed a towel around her shoulders. She couldn't see her reflection in the mirror because the bathroom was so filled with steam. It reached into her lungs like a hungry beast and loosened the mucous in her chest from the cold she'd been battling. She coughed violently and swallowed some of the phlegm she was bringing up, which made her sick to her stomach. She dropped to her knees and held onto the toilet for support, throwing up until there was nothing left but dry heaves and sore abdominal muscles.

She put the mattress back and lay on her disheveled bed, naked and wet from steam and sweat. She could smell Angela's perfume on the sheets as she faded in and out of sleep, drowsy from the Hycodan cough suppressant she'd been taking. She tried to rally herself to get up, dress, and face the problem she had created with Stan and her family, but she was weak and delirious. While she was lying there, she imagined Stan trying to find Kevin Mooney to let him know that his wife was a lesbian. And because he had no shame, Mooney would tell Mary Ann. Stan was hurt and humiliated, and she was sure he would want company. Especially after the way he yelled from the bottom of the stairs about her uncle the bishop. Yes, Stan would want company at his pity party.

Her cell phone chimed once. It was a text from Angela. Angela was the only one who ever sent her text messages. She mustered the energy to open her eyes and read it: *OMG! Stan's car's in my drive. He's telling Kev... he will kill both of us! What should we do?*

This was the beginning of the end of her life. Stan was known for blowing things out of proportion and making sure everything is about him. But this time? This time, for the first time, he had every right to turn the situation into a major storm. What she had done was more than a slap in the face. She had belittled his masculinity and sexuality completely. This was a heterosexual man's worst nightmare: being kicked out by and replaced with a woman. It was one thing to be outperformed by another male, to lose a head-butting contest to another ram, but to lose a wife to another woman? She couldn't have done anything more degrading to her husband.

ML closed her eyes and thought about how she should respond to Angela. But she couldn't come up with an answer. She wanted to ask her the same thing: *What should I do?* She wished she had an answer, an inkling about what to do. No matter how much she tried to explain herself or come up with a solution, she couldn't see any way to repair the damage. Maybe if she were caught in bed with another man, they could have worked things out. That was a sin he might forgive and move on but not this.

There's no way out. No way to fix this. My fucking life is over. I'm an embarrassment to my family and to myself. Ashley will hate me when she finds out. I can't bear to think about how I've disgraced myself to her. I can handle what the others will think of me. But my daughter? I'll die. She won't have any respect for me. Why should she?

She took another big swig of the Hycodan, dragged herself out of bed to her desk, and began to type on her laptop.

Dear Friends and Family ~

Please don't feel sorry for me, because I am not sad, just broken. Broken from the onset. I was born wrong and defective. I denied my true identity and went on with my life, pretending that everything was normal, that I was normal. I hid the pain deep down inside me because to reveal the true me would have been a disaster for all. Especially for Mom and Dad, Ashley, and Angela, all of whom I love deeply, as I hope they have loved me.

I can't turn back the clock. I can't right what is wrong. Although I'm not sorry for what I have done or for whom I have loved, I am sorry if I've hurt you. You don't deserve to be disgraced and humiliated. There is enough pain in our family. The last thing I wanted was to be the cause of more pain.

It's time for me to go. Time for me to join Nana, Mary Margaret, and Dad.

See you all on the other side.

She paused before she typed her signature. Instead, she opened Safari and Googled *suicide prevention hotline, Cleveland.* She dialed the toll-free number. A woman's voice asked if she could help her. ML said, "I only have one question for you: Will my life be worth living from this point on?"

After nearly thirty minutes of talking and listening, ML was depleted both emotionally and physically. Her new friend, the suicide prevention counselor, convinced her not to harm herself and told her what she needed to do in the next few days, starting with a good night's sleep. This step was made almost too easy by the cough syrup she'd taken. A few more mouthfuls and the sleep she'd experience might be eternal. As it was, the Hycodan began to soothe her, to smother her exhaustion, to make her breathe deeper, to make her dream.

Her life was dissolving into a jumble of pictures from the past, melting and sliding not so much in front of her eyes as directly through the middle of her brain. There she was confessing at church, crying at her father's grave, drifting on a boat with Ashley, and begging for forgiveness, all while trying to wake herself up. She heard the creek and clank of the front door opening and closing and footsteps. She saw him grab a pillow, take a deep breath and hold it. Her own breath caught. Between them there was no air. Nothing to breathe. What she had done had sucked the air out of the room, out of her life. She was crying and gasping and praying and most of all, she was sorry.

She was slipping away. Her mouth tasted like Margaritas and the air turned into cotton as it trudged up her nose. She couldn't breathe nor did she want to. Angela's face appeared in the middle of her mind, and she heard a creek and a clank. Then there was silence and everything went black.

chapter

TWENTY-ONE

Relations are simply a tedious pack of people, who haven't got the remotest knowledge of how to live, nor the smallest instinct about when to die.
Oscar Wilde

Just one day without feeling sad, one day without being depressed. That's all she wanted. Was that too much to ask? Too much to hope for?

Instead, she had spent the last ten hours watching it snow and thinking about Mark. These days, her constant thoughts about him made her sad and depressed. Damn him. Damn that bitch and Mooney for putting him in jail.

As if life weren't bad enough, now she had to worry about living through a fucking blizzard.

Holly, the Channel Three weather girl, warned that the worst storm of the year was heading toward Cleveland. She'd promised her viewers that it would be far worse than the storm of '78, for those who could recall the weather twenty-five plus years ago. Jim Cantori on the Weather Channel agreed with Holly's assessment or vice a versa, whatever.

Tricia remembered the '78 storm, so like her mother had done back then, Tricia went shopping. And like her mother, Tricia loaded up on her family's favorites—Oreos, Ben & Jerry's, Cool Whip light, light lemonade, cream for Scott's coffee, Chardonnay, a chicken to roast, ingredients for turkey meat loaf, osso bucco, banana bread, and of course biscuits for the dogs. Tricia usually didn't shop for more than a day's worth of food at a time, but she knew that living in the Snowbelt they were likely to be snowbound for days if the storm even farted snow. Her mother would be proud.

The blizzard never materialized. Not like Holly had predicted, anyway. Oh, there was plenty of snow, but no wind to speak of and no blinding whiteouts. However, by nine that night the storm had deposited more than sixteen inches of heavy, bright-white, glistening snow on everything in Tricia's yard and for thirty miles around.

During the storm, there wasn't much to do except sit in the dark, watch the snowfall, and drink. Tricia had consumed at least three glasses of wine since cocktail hour—five o'clock by most Irish-Catholic standards. She claimed to be one of them since her mother was Irish. Scott had cooked the chicken for dinner. She had to admit, it was pretty damn good. After dinner, Tricia poured one more glass of vino and went back to the den while Chris and Lauren finished doing the dishes. Scott, being the night's chef, was freed from further duties and was busy on the Internet doing God-only-knows what.

Tricia was both happy and sad that Mary Ann and Jack were in St. Croix getting married without family. She took a sip of her Chardonnay and had regretful thoughts about giving her mother the idea to elope. Not surprisingly, Tricia felt left out not being there. Mary Ann and Jack thought it was inappropriate to have a big wedding celebration while Mark was in prison, but Tricia planned on having a party for them anyway when they got home.

So, Mary Ann was in St. Croix while she was in the Snowbelt with her family. If the roles had been reversed, she knew her mother wouldn't be sitting in the dark drinking wine. That would have been her father's job. No, Mary Ann would have been keeping the kids from going crazy, getting bored, or fighting with one another. Was she less of a woman than her mother?

Hell no!

Tricia quaffed the remains of her wine and called out. "Let's go out in the snow and make angels."

Scott looked up from his laptop and declined her invitation. He had no interest in going outside. She wasn't surprised as he wasn't the spontaneous type, and putting on a jacket, boots, hat, and gloves to play in the freezing snow would never be his idea of a good time.

Her children were another matter.

"Great idea! I'll get my camera." Lauren ran up the back stairs.

"Wait for me," Chris said. "I'm looking for the video camera and snow pants. I'll be right there."

"You don't know what you're missing." Tricia sashayed behind Scott and tickled his ear.

"Stop that. And I know what I'm missing, that's why I'm staying inside."

"Party pooper!"

Dressed in mismatched snow gear, Tricia and her children headed past their three SUVs in the heated garage, opened the overhead door, and trudged into snow that was above their knees. Chris and Lauren handed their cameras to Tricia and buried themselves in the snow. As she watched, Tricia's thoughts returned to Mark. Did the boots she ordered for him three times ever arrive? Was he warm? Did he have a blanket? Was he hungry? What was he doing? What was he thinking about tonight while she had the pleasure of playing with her teenage kids in the snow? Even before he went to prison, she had hoped that someday Mark would be able to experience the joys of having his own children. He loved hanging out at her house with her kids, playing basketball in the back yard, and making whale waves in the pool. He even liked to help them with their homework while Tricia cooked dinner. But as much as he enjoyed them, Chris and Lauren weren't his. She wouldn't let her depressing thoughts ruin this moment.

At fifteen and seventeen, her children were beyond putting on snowsuits and going outside with Mom. It had been years since they had done anything like this, but the roads were closed and they were stuck at home with their parents on a Saturday night—any teenager's nightmare.

Tricia was determined to make this one of those moments they would remember for the rest of their lives. They might not remember what they got for their fourteenth birthdays or what was in their Christmas stockings that year, but by God, this was going to be one of those memorable times filled with goofiness and laughter that they would tell *their* kids about.

Like the time they all laughed so hard during dinner at the country club for Scott's forty-fifth birthday, that root beer squirted out of both the kids' noses at the same time. Or the boat trip that they took to the British Virgin Islands when everyone got seasick. It was still the greatest family vacation ever.

Tricia put Lauren's camera in her pocket, turned on Chris' video camera, and started recording moments to remember.

"Hey, Mark! Stop throwing snow in your sister's face. Look here."

"Mom! I'm Chris not Mark. Get with it." He shook his head and went back to pummeling his sister with handfuls of wet snow.

Maybe she'd had a bit too much to drink. Either that or she was deep into déjà vu. Growing up, Tricia and Mark had a love-hate relationship. One minute he would tease and torment her, the next he was the amazing brother who taught her how to dribble and shoot a layup. She watched Chris and Lauren in the snow and felt like she was back on Devonshire Road in 1978.

But she wasn't.

She was in Chagrin Falls in three feet of snow, and Mark was in jail for life. She did her best to keep the lump in her throat at bay.

To not think about Mark.

To live in the moment.

At first she didn't hear it. When she did, she jumped and turned toward the house. Scott was knocking on the living room window, motioning for her to come inside.

"Don't be an old fuddy-duddy. Get out here with your family!" Tricia turned the camera on Scott inside, knocking.

Why does he have to take the fun out of everything? If he'd come out and join us he'd realize how much he was missing.

Scott knocked harder and waved her in more urgently.

She shook her head *no,* put the video camera in her other pocket, and motioned him to come outside. She put her hands on her hips, tilted her head to the side and mouthed *please?*

Scott walked out of sight. She could see he was angry as he opened the front door a crack.

"Tricia, come inside, right now! I need to talk to you!" Scott shouted.

"Can't you wait a minute? I won't be out here much longer. I can already feel my toes going numb."

"No! It's important. Ashley just called." Scott shut the door. Hard.

Chris and Lauren continued to bombard each other with snowballs. They had either chosen to ignore their parents or they were having so much fun by themselves that they didn't hear them.

But Tricia had heard the hard, terrible edge to Scott's voice. Wild thoughts began to run through her head. Maybe Ashley went out in the bad weather and was in an accident. Maybe...

But why wonder? Why not go inside now and find out for sure?

Tricia hurried inside and ripped off her hat, gloves, coat, and boots and left them on the mudroom floor. Scott was pacing in the living room, the phone in his hand.

"Jesus, Scott, what's so important?"

"Ashley called and . . ." Scott looked at her for a moment with liquid eyes.

"What? Tell me! Is she okay?"

"Ashley's okay. It's ML. She . . . Stan found her in bed. She wasn't breathing and he couldn't revive her. It took a long time for the paramedics to arrive because of the weather."

"Is she okay? Did they bring her back? Oh, God. Please tell me she's okay. No, not ML. Scott, please tell me she's alright."

Scott tried, but he couldn't make a sound. Instead, he wrapped his arms around his wife as waves of grief collapsed down the length of her spine.

Outside, visible behind them in the picture window, Chris and Lauren continued to laugh and play in the snow.

It would be ten minutes before they found out their Aunt ML was dead.

chapter

TWENTY-TWO

"An eye for an eye would make the whole world blind."
Mahatma Gandhi

A hundred days in prison. A hundred days out of the rest of his life. Mark knew the number for certain. He was counting. He was counting every second, every minute, every hour, every day, and every meal. There wasn't much else to do with his time. Except pray. This was his two hundred and eighty-first meal, and the thirtieth time he had tomato soup and grilled cheese for lunch. The first two days he'd been a prisoner, he hadn't eaten at all. This was partly because he didn't have an appetite, and partly because he'd missed a few meals for a random strip search, a visit from his siblings, and a visit to the doctor for a broken finger. It seems a guard *accidentally* slammed his hand in a metal door. And because it was an accident, they wouldn't let him see a doctor for more than a week.

When he did eat, he was often sorry he had. Prison soup tasted metallic, like it was cooked in a pot of old pennies. And the grilled cheese sandwiches—two about the size of a three-year-old child's hand—were soggy, obviously not grilled, and filled with cheese that resembled melted plastic mixed with something distantly related to Velveeta. Early on he figured out that if he dipped the sandwiches into the soup, it made eating both more tolerable. Not necessarily better, just not quite as bad.

He had just sat down at the long brown sticky table with his beige tray when a guard yelled, "A514683, Von Guten, you have a visitor."

Since visitors weren't allowed on Mondays, Mark hoped it was the lawyer his brothers and sisters had hired to represent him on appeal. Without a second thought, he left his food on the table to be eaten in seconds by the dining hall vultures and walked through the sickly governmental-green room to the guard's desk by the door. He knew the routine. He was to be escorted down the hall to be stripped-searched, then handcuffed, shackled, and put in the so-called conference room to meet with his lawyer. There, he would sit waiting, staring blankly at the cold metal table, while his stomach growled from hunger. As soon as the door opened, Mark lost his appetite.

"How's the basketball team here?" Detective Mooney pulled out the chair on the other side of the table and sat down. "What kind of balls do they play with? Or do they just dribble yours?"

"Fuck you, Mooney. Is that why you're here? You looking for some balls since you don't have any?"

"I'm certainly not interested in yours. But I'm sure the bangers in here are waiting for the day they can suck your sweaty little white ones and shriveled cock. Me? I don't need to swing that way. I have a beautiful wife at home who can't get enough of what I have to offer."

"Oh, really? That's funny." Mark gave a horselaugh. "Talk around the Heights is what you got to offer, she don't want. They say pussy is her thing. I guess your balls just didn't do it for her. You must be a lousy fuck if you made her go lesbo. You always thought you were God's gift to women, but apparently *He* didn't give you a gift."

"Watch your damn mouth, Von Guten. I know plenty of assholes in here who will do a favor for me with a broomstick in a heartbeat. All I have to do is ask."

"You don't have that kind of power, except maybe in your own demented mind."

"A lot you know. Who do you think sprung your girlfriend's rapist uncles from jail?"

"You son of a bitch! You put those scumbags in the same house as my daughter? I ought to beat you to a pulp."

"You're still a dreamer, Von Guten. That could never happen. And if that brother lawman on the other side of the one-way mirror wasn't there watching out for your sorry ass? I'd kick it right now. But I already beat you good, didn't I? Look at you, you pathetic piece of shit child molester. I kicked your ass all right—right into prison for life."

"Get to the point. What the fuck do you want? To torment me some more? Or are you here for a reason?"

"Yeah, I'm here for a reason. Since family can't visit Mondays, and I know yours would want you to hear this in person, I thought I'd do you all a favor and deliver the news myself in person."

"What are you talking about?"

"Apparently, ML had a wicked cold recently," Mooney said, feigning sincerity.

"What about it? Is she okay?"

"Okay? Yeah, I guess she's okay. She's resting…in peace. She took matters into her own hands. Took too much cough syrup and washed the taste down with a few too many Margaritas. Seems once her pussy preference was no longer a secret, she couldn't bear humiliating your mother and family."

"You're full of shit, Mooney, get out of here! Now! Guard! Guard! I'm done in here."

"Yell all you want, but I told my *partner* out there not to open the door until *I* told him to. So, you don't believe me? About ML? Here's the police report from when they found her dead."

With a smile on his face, he slid a paper across the table in front of Mark.

Mark read the report in silence as Mooney smugly looked on. Then Mark spoke, still looking down at the paper in front of him.

"I don't believe ML would commit suicide for any reason. It's a sin. You went to school with us. You know that, I know that, and ML knew it too."

"A sin? You stupid motherfucker. Your sister was fucking the hell out of my wife, a woman, for god's sake. Short of killing someone, there isn't much more of a sin than that. And with your mother being all holier-than-thou, and your uncle hoping to be a cardinal, don't you think ML would rather take her chances in the next world than live in this one with all the embarrassment and pain she caused? Of course she offed herself. Who wouldn't?"

Mooney stood and leaned down, the knuckles of both hands planted firmly on the table in front of Mark.

"Maybe you should take a lesson from your sister. Swallow a shiv. Catch a fatal disease up your ass. Make a break for it and commit suicide-by-cop. The world would be better off with one less child molester hanging around, living on the public dole. Then you could ask her yourself if she thought she'd committed any sins in this life."

"You're a sick mother-fucker, Mooney. I hope you rot in hell. You know damn well that I didn't touch Louisa."

"I don't know that at all. For all I know, you were teaching her to do things to you like your basketball coach made you do to him."

Mark made a move to get up. Mooney quickly shoved him back down with both hands. "Don't even try it. You'd be bled out before Amos back there could find his keys." Mooney pointed over his shoulder with the thumb of his left hand at the mirror behind him and reached into his sport coat pocket to pull out a switchblade with his right, making sure to keep it hidden by his considerable bulk. Then he returned it to his pocket and sat down.

"How the hell did you get that in here, you prick?"

"Mark, Mark, Mark, you forget. I'm the law, and I have God on my side."

"You're crazy!"

"Don't be saying shit like that. Me and Jesus will make you pay."

"You really are whacked. You get off on making life miserable for others, don't you?"

"Life is a series of plusses and minuses keeping things in balance. When someone takes advantage of someone else, why then, someone else has to make things right. That's what I do, make things right."

"Are you still trying to make things right for Francis? Is that what this is all about?"

"If you hadn't been Fr. Gellin's boy toy, Francis would have been a starter. And he would have played for Ohio State and then maybe the NBA. But you stole that from him. You were the minus, I'm the plus. I'm the one who has to make things right. That's my job."

"Get over it, Mooney. Francis didn't make the basketball team because he sucked, he wouldn't practice, and he was a drunk all the time. You've spent your life trying to get revenge, for what? Francis not making the team? How pathetic. Now it's about Angela loving my sister more than she loved you? For letting your wife screw another woman for years? Right under your nose? Are you happy now? I'm in prison and ML's dead. Now what are you going to do with your life?"

"Don't you worry. I have plenty to do. It's a big world out there and there are plenty of minuses that have to be turned into zeros. Balance must be restored. Wrongs must be avenged. Now that I've taken care of you and ML, Angela's next."

"What do you mean you took care of ML? I thought she killed herself?"

"Geez, that's sure what it looks like. Don't it? A little Hycodan cough syrup? A lot, actually. And wash it down with some margaritas? Why, that's enough to kill a horse. Even a lesbian. I didn't really need help from the pillow."

"What are you telling me? You killed ML?"

"Patience, little one. You'll get to ask ML herself any day now. But now, this day, we have this situation with Angela. As you can imagine, the bitch is sick with grief. Not only because ML killed herself and she's stuck with me, but it seems that with all that kissing? She caught ML's cold. As soon as I leave here, I'm on my way to comfort her. Nothing more comforting to a lesbo than some cherry-flavored Hycodan mixed with her favorite strawberry daiquiri. After three or four, she'll actually be quite peaceful—for quite a long time."

"You'll never get away with it," said Mark.

"You don't think so, Mr. Righteous? Your sister left a note. A heart-wrenching sob story about how life isn't fair. Besides, what are you going to do about it? Tell on me?" Mooney chuckled. "Now that's really funny. Who would believe a felon convicted for raping his daughter? Think again, Von Guten. They don't listen to child rapists in here. They deal with them once and for all. Guard! Open up, I'm done in here!"

chapter TWENTY-THREE

Call it a clan, call it a network, call it a tribe, call it a family: Whatever you call it, whoever you are, you need one.
Jane Howard

"When I thought about my mother dying, I always pictured her old and gray. But here I am, picking out something for her to be buried in, and she was far from old."

Ashley pulled clothes from her mother's closet, roughly throwing them in a heap on the bed.

"This sucks."

"Yes, dear, it does. It really sucks," Tricia said.

Ashley watched her aunt pick up each garment as it landed and stack them neatly in a pile of clothes deemed not worthy of spending an eternity with her mother.

"Aunt Tricia, what's wrong with us? Is our family cursed?"

"No, Ash, we're not cursed. Try not to look at life that way. Focus on the good things," Tricia answered.

"Bullshit, I know that death is a *normal* part of life, but you can't tell me that Aunt Mary Margaret's death was normal. Or that Mark going to prison for something he didn't do is normal. And now my mom? A closet lesbian who committed suicide? This doesn't happen to other families. If you ask me, I'd say we're cursed."

She was annoyed that her aunt ignored her rant and continued folding the clothes as Ashley threw them on the bed. Tricia held up a dark maroon A-line dress with a scoop neckline in front of her at arm's length.

"What about this one? Didn't she wear this to your graduation?"

"No. I mean, yes she did, but I don't want her buried in it. Angela gave it to her. I'd rather burn it along with everything else that woman gave her or even touched. I get sick just thinking about it."

"I'm sorry," Tricia looked at her with a mixture of concern and understanding. "Ash, don't hate Angela."

"You've got to be kidding me! How can I not? If it weren't for her, my mother—*your* sister—would still be alive. I can't believe I never knew. I can't imagine what other secrets Mom kept from me."

"I didn't know either, I swear. I have to believe she kept her real life secret from us because she wasn't proud of it."

"Don't say that. Angela wasn't her *real* life. We were."

"We may never know what your mother thought was more real, but in any case, I believe with all my heart that she kept her secret to protect you. She loved you more than you'll ever know, and she didn't want to hurt you. I'd do the same."

"Well, *obviously* she wasn't thinking about me or Dad. She was only thinking about herself and about how *she* felt about Angela. God, it makes me sick to my stomach. Suicide, infidelity, lies, deceit, and secrets, am I missing anything? Oh, I can't forget mortal sin. She can't even have a proper funeral."

"Thankfully, that part's not true. The church doesn't consider suicide a mortal sin any more so we can have a *proper* funeral. But Uncle Don isn't comfortable delivering her funeral because homosexuality *is* a mortal sin. Personally? I think the church is still in the Dark Ages. Every Catholic I know has committed a mortal sin. And the Church is still having funerals. But, maybe it's better if we keep ML's funeral private, just family and a few close friends. You do want Uncle Don to be there to bless her grave, don't you?"

"At this point, I don't know what to think. I can't think. Whatever you all decide is fine with me. I just want this to be over with. But that bitch better not show up."

Tricia picked up a pair of ML's jeans. "When you picture your mom happy, what do you see her wearing?"

"Those, her Seven jeans—ironed of course—with a white t-shirt and her J. Crew flats."

"Then that's what she'll wear. We'll send her off in style. Her style."

In the face of the mystery of death, there is comfort in the familiarity of tradition. Catholic funerals are rituals, ceremonies that have a prescribed order, a predictability that provides consolation for the survivors. Visiting hours are held at the funeral home two days after the death, a Mass and burial performed on the third day, and a reception following for friends and family at home.

But her mother's funeral was different. Three days after Stan discovered her body, the family met the undertaker and the casket at All Souls Catholic Cemetery, the site where Joseph and Mary Margaret were buried. There was no Mass or visitation. The event was private and short, and no one was dressed up. Even Don and Burns didn't wear their funeral vestments. Don started the memorial with a prayer, and Ashley read a poem she wrote about her mother being her best friend.

It was wintry, quiet, lonely, and somber at the gravesite. Everyone stood frigid in the cold, their hands in their pockets. Ashley held onto the arm of Mary Ann's fur coat to keep warm. Unlike many funerals where the deceased's life is celebrated, none of that was happening. Ashley was uncomfortable with the unconventional funeral. She felt that her family was sweeping ML's funeral under the rug, as though they were embarrassed, and she resented them for it. But they were her family and her support system, so she went along.

Patrick changed the mood.

"Let's tell funny stories about ML, like we used to on birthdays."

"That's a great idea," Jack said.

"That will take forever, and it's freezing out here," Suze complained.

"Since you moved away, you're not used to this weather," Mary Ann said. "I think that's a wonderful idea, Patrick. Let's gather close together and do this for ML. She suffered more than we know, so we can suffer in the cold for her."

Tricia started, "One time at band camp...." Ashley laughed. She knew her mother's life would now be celebrated properly with Von Guten tradition.

Tricia continued telling her story about the time ML taught her how to do dishes. "One night there was a show we wanted to watch on TV, and we were out of dishwasher soap, and we didn't want to do the dishes by hand. ML said we could put a small amount of Palmolive into the soap dispenser. She showed me how to turn it on and we went into the den to watch the Flip Wilson Show. About fifteen minutes later, we looked down and saw soap bubbles around our feet. The dish soap had bubbled up, oozed out of the dishwasher, crept across the kitchen floor, down the hall, and into the den."

"I don't remember that," Mary Ann said, cocking her head and looking over her sunglasses at her daughter.

"That's because we cleaned it up with the bathroom towels."

"Why didn't I see that the towels were missing?"

"You did. But we told you we decided to wash them."

"And I believed you?"

"You always did, Mother."

"At least that's what you like to think."

For the next thirty minutes, the others took turns telling stories, laughing, and crying until there was nothing left to say. Burns recited a few more prayers, followed by a moment of silence. Stan broke down and was on his knees hugging the casket, crying, "I'm sorry, I'm so sorry," over and over again. After each family member placed an individual rose on the casket, Ashley put her arms around her father to comfort him and led him away from the grave. The rest of the family followed.

As they drove away, Ashley gave one last private look at the casket being lowered in the grave.

❧

There were no deli trays or Swedish meatballs waiting at 2822 Devonshire. After the service, the family went to dinner at the Hillbrook Club in Chagrin Falls where ML and Stan had been married. When Mr. Coughlin, the club owner, heard of ML's death, he had called Mary Ann and offered to provide dinner at the club after the service.

Hillbrook wasn't far from the Catholic cemetery. For Ashley, it was the perfect place to commemorate her mother. She'd only ever seen the club in the photos from her parent's wedding album. During dinner, her father reminisced about their wedding. When Stan reminded them about the wedding crasher, everyone laughed. When he and ML returned from their honeymoon and looked at the photo proofs, neither recognized the man in the purple shirt who kept popping up in the pictures. On the day of the wedding, ML thought he was a relative of Stan's, while Stan thought the man looked crazy enough to be a Von Guten. The man was in the photos, smiling, drinking, eating, and dancing with guests. They never figured out who he was.

After dinner they had coffee and dessert by the fireplace in the club living room. Suze held her hands out in front of the fire, still trying to get warm after standing in the cold for what seemed like hours.

"Can someone drive me to the airport Friday?" she asked.

"You're leaving that soon?" Tricia was surprised.

"Unless you have a good reason for me to stay, I have to get back to work."

"Well, it just so happens I *do* have a good reason," Tricia said. "Mom and Jack, you need a proper wedding reception. So let's have a party before Suze leaves."

"That's sweet, dear, but I don't feel like celebrating, especially this week. What would people say if we had a party so soon after ML's death? I'm sure Stan and Ashley aren't up for it either."

"Grandma, Aunt Tricia's right. We can't let your wedding go unnoticed. Don't you agree, Dad?" Ashley asked.

"I think it's a great idea. I know your mother would approve," Stan said.

"Mom, you wouldn't let Mary Margaret get away with not having a proper wedding and reception after she eloped. So why should we let you? Uncle Don, don't you think your sister should practice what she preaches?'

"Tricia has a point, Mary Ann. Maybe you should let her throw you a reception," Don said. "I think a party might do our souls some good."

"Is that your priestly opinion?" Ashley asked.

"Let's just say I strongly recommend it along with a few Hail Marys."

"Mom, you won't have to do a thing," Suze said. "I'll do the catering. I'll even make you a wedding cake. Maybe Mr. Coughlin will let us use some of his servers to help me in the kitchen."

Mary Ann and Jack looked at each other. Jack shrugged his shoulders. "Don't look at me. I'm not going to be the one to make this decision. I'm just the groom. It's too early for me to get involved in decisions like this. You're the bride and whatever makes you happy makes me happy."

"I don't know. It just doesn't seem right to have a party."

"Mary Ann I know what you thinking. You're worried about what people will say but don't. Anyone who knows you well, who knows us well, won't judge. And if people talk, who cares? You have to do what's right for your family. And I think you should take advantage of the fact that Suze is home," Don said.

"Alright, I give in. You can throw it, but we'll do it at my house. I was thinking of having one last party before I move," Mary Ann conceded. "I just didn't think it would be a wedding reception."

&

Just as her daughters had done for their wedding receptions, Mary Ann was dressing and primping in her blue and white bedroom. Suze, Tricia, and Ashley did their part, offering advice on hair, jewelry, shoes, and makeup.

"My mom should be here," Ashley said, tears in her eyes.

"Ash, there are going to be hundreds of special moments when we will wish she were with us. We all miss her, and we will never forget her. Just like Mary Margaret and your grandfather," Tricia said.

"ML's here with us. I can feel her presence. She's sending me a message that Mom needs more rouge," Suze said and they all laughed.

"Enough makeup. How do I look?" Mary Ann turned around in her heels like a model.

"You look *mahvelous, darlin'*," Tricia said.

"Suze and Tricia, would you mind leaving me and Ashley alone for a moment? I'd like to talk with her in private," Mary Ann said.

"Sure, come on Tricia, you can help me in the kitchen," Suze said.

"Grandma, is something wrong? Did I do something?"

"No, dear, I have something I want to talk to you about and I don't want you to get upset, so listen to me for a minute. For years, I never stood up for what I believed was right. I went along with whatever Grandpa wanted. But today and from now on, I am going to stand up for my beliefs. I realize it may be difficult for you to hear this, but your mother loved Angela, and Angela is not responsible for her death. Angela has been a part of our family celebrations since she was in middle school, and I want her here tonight. I extended an invitation to her, but I'm not sure if she's coming."

"Grandma..." Ashley started to talk.

"Don't interrupt, please listen to me until I'm finished. We all choose people to be in our lives. And so did your mother. She chose you and she chose Angela, because she loved both of you."

"Grandma, please stop talking about Angela."

"No! Listen to me, Ashley. This is *my* daughter who died, not just your mother. You were chosen to be her daughter, and you're lucky she chose you. And you're lucky that Tricia was her sister. So don't hate those your mother loved. Don't hate Angela for loving her."

"What do you mean *I was chosen*?" Ashley laughed nervously. "And what does Aunt Tricia have to do with this? I'm not following you."

There was a knock on the door, and Tricia's voice came through from the other side.

"Mom, the peppermill is empty and Suze is freaking 'cause she can't find the peppercorns."

"I'll be right there," Mary Ann said.

"She doesn't want you in the kitchen. Just tell me where they are."

"I'll be down in a minute," Mary Ann replied without opening the door.

"Ashley, we'll finish this conversation some other time. Just promise me that if Angela comes, you will be hospitable. I'm not asking you to go out of your way to talk to her, just don't be rude. Do this for me? This is my day with Jack." Ashley nodded silently and followed her grandmother out the door and down to the party below.

Like every Von Guten affair, the party was populated with the usual cast of characters. Joseph's brothers and their wives; Don, Burns, and other priests from St. Theresa's; neighbors; friends from bowling, golf, bridge, and the parish; ML and Tricia's in-laws; and Mary Ann's new modeling boss, Margaret Jones, from the boutique.

The guests arrived without gifts. "Your presence is our present," Mary Ann had told her friends and relatives when she had invited them over the phone. "The last thing Jack and I need is more stuff." As it was there was no room in Jack's house for their combined things. They decided to turn the tables and wrapped items from their homes—Waterford ashtrays, Hummel figurines, vases, and candlesticks—to give as party favors to their invited guests.

In Mark's absence, Patrick and Trip were in charge of the bar on the screened porch. Since it wasn't a year-round room, they used a space heater to keep it warm. Mary Ann insisted that the bar be stocked with top-shelf offerings only, unlike Joseph who had loaded it with cheap wine, sale beer, and well liquor.

On the left side of a large table, bottles were lined up like soldiers. On the right side, rows of Waterford crystal glasses in every size—Jack and Mary Ann's combined collection—were neatly arranged behind a fanned-out pile of cocktail napkins that read 'Mary Ann and Jack.' Hidden under the tablecloth were bottles of Macallan and Louis XIII Remy Martin, reserved exclusively for the bishop and other discriminating priests. Club soda, tonic, and an assortment of juices were on a smaller table behind the fill-in bartenders. Cans of soda and bottles of non-alcoholic beer were in a cooler on the floor at the opposite end of the room; it was self-service for those who wanted soft drinks, were in AA or not old enough to drink.

Suze buzzed around the kitchen with her hired help from the Hillbrook Club, shouting out orders like a stereotypical restaurant chef. Typically, people would gather in Mary Ann's kitchen during her parties. But today, Suze kept the swinging door shut and politely ordered anyone who walked in to *stay out.*

Tricia's assigned tasks of having her housekeeper clean the house, encouraging her son Christopher to shovel and salt the walk, ordering monogrammed cocktail napkins, and arranging flowers were all completed. Now all she had to do was to make sure that her mother and stepfather had a good time.

Despite the recent calamities in the family, Mary Ann and Jack were on top of the world. Mary Ann wore a black and white St. John knit sheath dress with a cropped trapeze jacket embellished with a diamond and sapphire floral pin Jack had given her for their wedding. Jack wore a black Armani suit with a geometric woven silk tie by Zegna and Gucci loafers.

Dinner was close to being served when Don took a sterling knife off the buffet table and tapped his wine glass.

"May I have everyone's attention, please? I'd like to make a toast to the bride and groom. Mary Ann and Jack? Please, come stand by me. Let us raise our glasses," he said. "To Mary Ann and Jack." Don continued with the familiar Irish blessing.

"May the road rise to meet you.
May the wind be always at your back.
The sun shine warm upon your face.
The rains fall softly in your fields.
May the light of friendship guide your paths together.
The laughter of children grace your home.
When eternity calls you,
At the end of a life filled with love.
May the good Lord embrace you

With the arms that have nurtured you
The whole length of your joy-filled days.
May God hold you both
In the palm of His hands."

"Hear, hear!" shouted Burns.

"Cheers!" the guests responded and sipped their cocktails.

As the talk began to die down, Don gently clinked his glass again. When quiet returned, he continued.

"And now, I'd like Mary Ann and Jack's children to stand by me as well. I have an announcement to make. The Holy Father, known better to most of you as JP2, has blessed me. In four weeks, I will be appointed as a Cardinal by the Holy Father at the Vatican."

Mary Ann put her hands over her mouth in amazement as her eyes filled with tears and the guests gasped with joy.

"Mary Ann and Jack, you and your children and their spouses will be guests of the Vatican."

From behind his back, Burns handed each of them a large white envelope embossed with the cardinal coat of arms, a red wide-brimmed hat with fifteen tassels and *Donatus Cardinal Maloney* imprinted in gold. "These are your plane tickets, hotel reservations, and invitations to the ceremony," Burns said.

Mary Ann wrapped her arms around her brother and hugged him tightly. Through her tears, she whispered, "Mother would be so proud of you. I know I am."

Everyone applauded and cheered.

Don put a forefinger and thumb together in his mouth and whistled like he was hailing a cab. "Please, please, stop. I needed to tell you before I leave tomorrow, but today? Today is about Mary Ann and Jack. Let's give a *really* big hand for Mary Ann and Jack," he said in his best Ed Sullivan voice.

⁂

"Oh, shit," Suze whispered to Burns. "I have to get back to the kitchen before dinner is ruined." Burns followed her into the kitchen.

"Fr. Burns, I'm not trying to be rude, but I rarely let anyone in the kitchen when I'm cooking so if you don't mind..."

"Is that Maytag? Don won't eat blue cheese unless it's Maytag." Burns asked. "And is that French endive? And Carpaccio? My favorites. Do you have capers?"

"Burns, I'm impressed. How do you know so much about food?"

"It's one of our many priestly secrets. Unlike the old days when we had cooks, today we cook for ourselves. We often have cooking parties at the rectory and watch Emeril and the other celebrity chefs on the food channel."

"Don't you watch EWTN?"

"Mother Angelica? She drives us crazy. She's so annoying, and her voice...it's torture to listen to her. If she weren't a nun, I'd hope she'd have a facelift. She has more chins than a Chinese phone book."

"Burns, you crack me up. Here, chop this parsley for me. But don't tell Mom I let you in here."

"Knock, knock," Jack said as he tentatively opened the swinging door to the kitchen. "May I come into your sanctuary for a moment?"

"If I let the two of you in here, then everyone will end up in here. What is it you want?"

"I have one request. Can we use the orange serving bowl tonight? You know the one your mother always uses for potato salad?'

"You've got to be kidding me. No way! That thing is so ugly. I can't believe she still has it. Why in the world do you want to use it? Please don't tell me you're the one who gave it to my parents," Suze said.

"No, but there's a story behind that bowl," Jack said. "Never mind. I don't want to ruin the presentation of your food. Someday ask Trip to tell you about the orange bowl."

"Good-bye, Jack. Let me be or dinner will never be served."

❧

Trip walked toward the kitchen with an empty water pitcher as Jack walked out.

"I just asked Suze if we could use the orange bowl tonight, for old-time's sake," Jack said.

"You're never going to let me forget about that ugly thing, are you?" Trip asked.

"You have to admit there's a great story behind it."

Trip laughed at himself as he recalled the story. When he was ten years old, he emptied his piggy bank of the change he had collected for a year from underneath the cushions on the couch, the floor of the car, his dad's pants pockets, the bottom of his mother's purses, and from random pay phones he would dig his fingers into to find forgotten dimes. For Mother's Day, he rode his bike to Seitz-Agin, the hardware store on Lee Road, and walked back and forth in the aisle of kitchen utensils until he spotted it—the perfect gift for his mother: a large orange melamine bowl with black and yellow flowers. It looked like a dish you might win at a carnival penny toss and then use to pass out Halloween candy. But to Trip it was the most beautiful bowl in the store.

The bowl was perched on the top shelf of a metal display case, which Trip couldn't reach. Determined to get it down himself, he moved the Pyrex measuring cups with red markings to the side of the bottom shelf, removed the aluminum stove burner liners and a stack of potholders from the second shelf, and carefully placed them on the linoleum floor behind him. With a clear path to climb up and reach the bowl, Trip stepped onto the bottom shelf with his new Keds, grabbed the third shelf with both hands, lifted his left foot to the second shelf, and pulled himself up. With his arm stretched out fully, he was able to get the fingertips of his right hand over the edge of the bowl to grab it. The weight of his body shifted backward tipping the entire case over on top of him as everything it held crashed to the floor.

The store shook as though an earthquake trembled and customers shrieked. The owner and clerks rushed over to pull the display case off of Trip, who was lying on his back with the bowl upside down over his face. As he moved the bowl from his face, an embarrassed and red-faced Trip said, "Sorry, I didn't mean to knock it down." It was amazing he wasn't hurt. If it weren't for the potholders that cushioned his head as it hit the floor, he might have cracked open his skull.

As fate would have it, Jack was in the store that day and insisted on giving Trip a ride home. The owner, fully aware that his cases were unstable and rickety, worried about a lawsuit from

Trip's family so he didn't ask Trip to pay for the Pyrex measuring cups that shattered. Instead, he helped put his bike into the trunk of Jack's brown Mercury Marquis and gave Trip the bowl free of charge. On the way home, Trip, sitting in the front seat with the bowl in his lap, begged Jack not to tell his parents what had happened. Jack said he had to so they could keep an eye on him and make sure he didn't have a concussion. Jack agreed not to tell Mary Ann why Trip was at the hardware store. Jack spit in his hand and stuck it out to shake on it with Trip. Surprised by this but happy to seal the deal with his cool 'uncle', Trip spit in his hand and shook with Jack. "Deal," they said in unison.

From the bar, Mary Ann heard the doorbell and hoped that Angela had decided to come after all. When she stepped into the living room, she saw Don talking with Angela's husband in the front hall. They were laughing and patting each other on the back like old friends.

"Congratulations. Will you still be able to play cards when you're in town? Or don't cardinals play?" Mooney joked with Don.

"I don't see why not. Being a cardinal isn't going to put me under house arrest," Don said. "In my heart, I'm still a member of the same parish as you are."

"We're much more alike than you might think, the flip side of the same coin, both raised Catholic. You're ordained to save souls. I'm ordained to save the community from thieves and lawbreakers," Mooney said. "It's my personal task in life to level the playing field. It's my way of saving souls, you know?"

"Hello, Detective Mooney. Is Angela with you?" Mary Ann asked as she joined their conversation.

"She's not feeling well. She hasn't left the house in three days, and she's acting like she's on her deathbed. She must have caught ML's cold."

Mary Ann was dismayed by his choice of words.

"I have to refresh my drink. Would either of you like one?" Don asked.

"Not I," Mary Ann said.

"Not right now," Mooney said. "I have to leave soon to check on Angela and make sure she gets all the rest she needs."

"Well then, I'll see you at cards Wednesday," Don said.

"Let me walk you out," Mary Ann said, putting her hand on Mooney's arm, turning him toward the door.

"I said I couldn't stay long, but I didn't think I'd be leaving quite this soon."

"Angela was welcome at my party, not you." Mary Ann reached around the much larger man, opened the door, and with her body language, encouraged him to walk out.

"I came to let you know that Angela sends her best," Mooney said, glancing over his shoulder toward Mary Ann, "and to tell you that some cars are parked on the wrong side of the street."

"How thoughtful you are to keep such a close eye on things."

"It's my job, Mrs. Von Guten. I was just telling your brother that. He was ordained a priest, and I was ordained to keep the playing field level; to watch out for folks like you and your family."

"I'm quite capable of watching out for my own family, thank you. And I have my own way of leveling the playing field."

"Oh, you do? Interesting. Why haven't I seen that in action, hmm?"

"When one is good at one's job, the only thing apparent is the result. No one sees you coming, and no one sees you leave. So if I were you, Detective Mooney, I'd watch my back. You had your chances. You could have righted the wrong with Mark but you didn't. You chose to make it worse and to punish him over some unimportant, self-perceived slight. Hardly the sort of behavior I think would be *ordained* by anyone, let alone by God. You could have been more Christian with Angela and ML. But I don't believe you were. I'll have you know that I was proud of ML. She was true to her feelings like I nurtured her to be, and I'm sure that now that you know, you'll add me to your vendetta list. If I'm not already there for god-knows-what reason that lives in your sick brain."

"Are you telling me that you *knew* about ML and Angela?"

"I didn't need to know. I encouraged my children to follow their hearts, and I told them not to deny their feelings. I never asked, and I didn't care. And I don't care about you, but I do care about Angela and your mother's reputation, God rest her soul."

"My mother was a saint. Leave her out of this."

Mary Ann took two steps forward, encroaching into Mooney's personal space, and looked up at him, her face devoid of emotion.

Mooney did not move his body, but his head moved backwards on his neck several inches, as if to keep it out of striking distance from Mary Ann's tongue.

"If you want this town to go on thinking that your mother was a saint, if *you* want to continue thinking your mother was a saint, leave my family alone. And watch your step with Angela. I'll expect to hear from her this evening, just to see how she's feeling. If not? Well, we may have to have another conversation about your mother. About some of the choices she made in her life and with whom she spent her time. Now go on your way. I'll ask my guests to move their cars."

Mary Ann turned her back on Mooney and walked into the house. It was the last party she would have at 2822 Devonshire, and she was going to be damn sure it was a good one.

"Mary Ann, I've been looking for you. You should have seen Patrick and Trip bartending," Jack said. "They were laughing with each other like they're best friends. It's nice to see them getting along so well after not talking to each other for months. Do you think we'll be like that? Hot and cold? Good days and bad days?"

"I'm too old for that. Maybe if we were married forty years ago we could play those games, but from here on out it's going to be all good," Mary Ann kissed him long and hard. "The party's almost over, and you haven't played. How about a little music for your new bride?"

The sound of Jack's piano drew the few remaining guests, mostly family, into the living room. Patrick arrived with a white Russian for his mother. It was her favorite drink, and her first and only of the night. She sat on the couch next to Ashley while Patrick took a seat next to Jack at the piano.

"Any requests?" Jack asked. After no one responded he said, "Then I get to choose." He played the first few chords of an old familiar tune.

"No, not "Heart and Soul!" You can play much better than that!" Mary Ann shouted from the sofa.

"Then suggest something," Patrick said over his shoulder.

"Something from *The Phantom of the Opera*," Suze called out.

Without hesitation, Jack began playing the richly melodic tune. Moments later, Patrick joined him on the bench, playing a soaring, jazz-based countermelody that took the familiar musical favorite to an intricate, near-spiritual level.

"Patrick always seems to know what Jack is thinking. Look at them," Ashley said quietly to Mary Ann. "They could be father and son."

"Now that you mention it, I noticed today that you and Tricia look a lot alike," Mary Ann replied.

"That's not surprising, she *is* my aunt."

Mary Ann gave Ashley one of her famous read-between-the-lines-because–I-can't-say-it-out-loud looks.

"Some people just complement each other well," Mary Ann said. "When you're the only pea in the pod, it's easy to finish your parent's sentence."

"What do you mean by that?"

"I mean that's a story for another day. I'm exhausted, and we've had enough talk. Let's enjoy the music."

Jack and Patrick finished playing and everyone applauded.

"I'd like to dedicate the next song to my bride." Jack started to play a sweet melody that brought Mary Ann to her feet. She walked to the piano and Patrick relinquished his seat.

Together, Mary Ann and Jack sang "At Last."

Dear Diary,

Although it's been a rough road, I can easily say that at this point in my life, I am the happiest I've ever been, and my heart is in the hands of the love of my life. All my life I have tried to raise my children to be good; to be the best they could be. I tried to make Joseph into the man I always thought he could be. And for my efforts? I got death, anger, and separation. Two of my daughters are dead, along with their father. I have one son in jail and another daughter with a child born out of wedlock and being raised as her niece. But I can't look back at what could have been. I can only look forward.

Tonight I stood up for what was right. My mother would have been proud. I hope ML is also looking down, proud of her mother for doing the right thing… for saving Angela's life. Lord, forgive me for my evil thoughts, but I am as certain about this as I am about heaven. Kevin Mooney killed ML—his own blood—and he was about to kill Angela, too. And I'm not going to let him get away with it. He certainly fell from his mother's tree as my children fell from mine.

But I will not allow that sapling of a man to continue to kill.

If I have to, I will chop down that tree myself.

Lord, keep me strong, give Kevin Mooney the sense his mother never could, and above all bless and watch over my children and grandchildren.

This is the finale of my diary. It's the end of my life at 2822 Devonshire and the beginning of my new life. It's been a tumultuous journey, but that's what life is—a journey, not a destination.

Mary Ann

Epilogue

Tricia
2006

Dear Diary,

Whenever I find myself back in the Heights, I take a drive through the old neighborhood. I know we aren't physically capable of going back in time or of reliving memories, much less changing what happened way back when. But I like to try. Not to change things but to relive them. And sometimes I'm happy not to relive the curses that Ashley is convinced have been bestowed upon us.

For me, simply being on the streets of St. Theresa's parish is as close as I can come to booking passage on that impossible journey. Traveling these streets is my own personal time machine. These streets of my childhood are the arteries leading straight to my heart.

In some ways, not much has changed here. Kids still play kick ball in the streets and catch fireflies in their yards. The mansions are still west of Bell Street. Devonshire is still lined with oaks that are now close to a century old, and it is still one of the most beautiful streets in Cleveland. And 2822 is still on the south side of Devonshire, and my name is still carved into the bark of our old dogwood tree.

Uncle Peter continues to live across from our old house. From the looks of his yard, he'll win the yearly prize for the best-looking yard. But now he lives alone. Aunt Judy died four weeks ago, one year after Mother passed away. And his children, like my siblings, are spread all over the country—at least those of my siblings who are alive or not in jail.

After Mother moved in with Jack, it took her more than a year to put the house on the market. Mostly because they were busy traveling and enjoying life together. Once the house was listed—at an unreasonably high asking price—it sat empty for another six months. At that price, no one was willing to fix it up, and God knows it needed major renovation. Mother wouldn't lower the price. Deep down, I think she didn't want to sell. Maybe she was afraid the walls could talk. After she died, Jack lowered the price and it sold in a week. God bless him. He lost two good wives when most men would have settled for one.

Last Saturday, Ashley and I drove down Devonshire just for kicks and stopped in front of our house. It will always be our house. The azaleas Nana planted are still there and doing well. But now they share space with the most bizarre display—an empty claw foot bathtub, standing on end and half buried. The inside of it is painted robin's-egg blue, and it is sheltering a hand-painted statue of the Virgin Mary. Mother would be appalled. Religious statues were certainly fine with her; God knows we had enough growing up, but they were never to be displayed in the front yard. Some things are not for tacky display.

Shivers ran down my spine, in a good way, when I looked at the old oak tree on the lawn. It still has a large lesion on its trunk from where Kevin Mooney's car was slammed into it by a drunk driver. From what the police could decipher, he was parked in front of the empty house in the middle of the night, for no known reason, when a speeding drunk killed him on impact. My mother was determined to bring justice to ML's death, and I have to believe that after her death she had more power to get the job done.

Ashley and I sat in the car silent, watching two children play with hand-held video games of some sort while their father was busy removing our old brass address plaque from above the front door and replacing it with a brightly colored ceramic tile version, complete with palm trees and coconuts. Then Ashley broke the silence and our conversation went something like this:

"Grandma would have a heart attack if she could see this," Ashley said.

"I think she knows. She always seemed to know everything that went on, even if there was no way you thought she could."

"Yeah, it was hard keeping secrets from her. It was like she could read your mind."

"Reading minds isn't so hard, especially if you share the same blood."

Ashley then went on to say that she didn't believe in mind reading and all that gobbledygook.

Trying to get a point across, I replied, "It's not gobbledygook. It's true. For instance, right now I can read your mind. You want to go up there and ask that man if you can have the old plaque, right?"

"How do you do that? You always seem to know what I'm thinking. Even my mother couldn't do that," she said.

"I told you, it's blood. Now, are you going to go get that or am I?" I asked her.

I watched Ashley walk up to the house and talk to the owner. I had no doubt she'd be able to convince him to give her the plaque. I know I could have.

And so could my mother.

It was a matter of blood.

Watching Ashley pick up the plaque and shake the man's hand, I wondered if I would ever be able to tell her about her blood—about our shared blood.

Was that a secret or a lie of omission? Was I too ashamed of what I'd done to be able to tell her the truth? Or would I be as strong as my mother, able to keep secrets all my life, sharing them only after death with anyone who read her diary?

Of all the gifts my mother gave me, both directly and indirectly, her diary may have been the greatest. Certainly it was the most surprising.

It was at that moment, with Ashley opening the car door proudly displaying her trophy that I knew what I had to do, and how I would tell her what she deserves to know.

I will write her a story. "My name is Mary…"

Tricia

Acknowledgements

If it weren't for the encouragement and support of my husband Jim, *Hail Mary Full of Secrets* would still be living inside my head or suspended in the catacombs of my MacBook Air. Thank you for having faith in me, supporting me, and for keeping me on task. Brittany, Michael, and Kylie: thank you for believing in me, reading my blog, and for always asking about the book. I'm blessed to be your mother.

A special thank you to Randy Martin for challenging me to do better and helping my creative juices flow whenever I thought they were dried up. His feedback, insight, literary experience, editorial input, and sage comments helped me create characters with strong voices, improve the story line, and propelled me over the finish line. I already miss my weekly coffee dates with my book savant.

Thank you to my dear friends who read early drafts and offered constructive criticism: Missy, Patty, Bethany, Kimberly, Kelly, and Erin.

Last but not least, I would be remiss if I didn't thank my functioning dysfunctional family members who unknowingly provided me with the skeleton for my story. We may not always like each other, but deep down we love each other.